Dream Catcher

Amanda Sheridan

Preface

The *dreamcatcher* is a talisman used to protect people from nightmares and bad dreams.

Contents

Prologue

Syria. After the IDF attack on Qahtani's compound.

He didn't know how long he'd been unconscious. In the first few minutes after he woke, he had no awareness of anything other than the terrible pain encompassing his body—it went deep, from his skin, into his bones, and right down to his soul. His face contorted into a rictus of agony as he tried to breathe through the worst of it. For a while, all he could do was lie still.

The pain didn't ease or improve. If anything, it was worse as his consciousness returned, and he was aware of his surroundings. He tried to stand. He rolled onto his stomach and gritted his teeth as waves of burning agony washed over him, but he managed to get his hands flat on the ground—even if it was hot to the touch—and he lifted himself until he was on his hands and knees.

That was enough for now. The pain was too much, and he lowered his head and closed his eyes as he rested.

His breath came in sobs as he sucked in the burning air. But he forced himself to continue. He was a holy warrior, and it was his duty. And if need be, he would die trying.

He stood up, testing his balance, but his legs trembled and almost failed him. He stood unsteady in the burning night air.

His arm hung limp and useless by his side. The flesh, muscle and tendons had been burned away by the force of the blast, leaving some bone exposed. The wound was cauterised on-site—by the fire. It wasn't just his arm. His left side was ravaged by the blast. His thigh had been cooked by the heat, and the smell of burning flesh—his burning flesh—made him dry swallow to keep the vomit at bay. It was futile. He retched and spewed out a thin, watery mess of liquid bile that burned his throat and mouth. It splashed on the ground and sizzled in the hot dust.

He wiped the vomit from his lips and opened his eyes. Staring at the night and the landscape surrounding him, he saw the devastation through pain-filled eyes.

Like high-powered floodlights, the scene was lit by all the fires, including the one that had burned him and caused his skin to blacken and blister, searing his body with agony.

He didn't know Israeli missiles had caused this. He was surrounded by death, and he was in hell. The stench of roasted flesh, mixed with the acrid tang of burning, made him want to vomit again. He could taste it in his mouth, and he spat to get rid of it, but his mouth was dry as if every drop of moisture in his body had evaporated in the fire.

He gathered his wits and forced clear thinking. Surveying his surroundings, a comprehension of what happened crippled him and his heart pulsed with hatred and anger that burned as bright as the fires enveloping the compound. He forced it away. His rage couldn't help him, and he'd save it for later. He needed to get away and find somewhere safe. Food, shelter, and water are the three basic needs of mankind and, therefore, his immediate priority.

His anger would come later, and with it, he'd take his revenge.

Chapter 1

Tel Aviv

It was the same house. Nothing had changed in the eight months, three weeks, and two days he'd been away from home and working in Syria. And yet Ilan explained to Jennifer that it was different, and he couldn't put his finger on how. It didn't seem to be there. It had lost the feeling of homeliness and the sensation of going in and being met by the things that made up his normal life. He said it lacked the feeling you get from the comfort of familiar surroundings, the warmth, images and scents that go unnoticed but make up the picture of a home. She wondered how he felt about the love of the person he shared his house with. She didn't dare ask, and his words already spoken broke her heart.

He said he detected a chill in the air, but they heard the hum of the central heating and knew it'd be warm and comfortable soon enough. But would that be enough to make it feel like home? She didn't know.

Jennifer went straight into the kitchen when they got home, and she stood in the doorway watching him. She had taken her coat off and was wearing a warm sweater and a pair of jeans. Her face was pale, and she looked exhausted. They faced each other for a moment and were strangers.

'It seems weird to see you here again.' Jennifer spoke first, and her voice sounded unnatural to her.

'It seems weird being here.'

'Do you want a shower first or something to eat?'

Ilan said he didn't know what he wanted—everything probably. A shower, food and sleep, all at once. He couldn't decide and was helpless. He looked at his wife and sounded pathetic when he asked for her guidance.

Who is this person standing in front of me? Where is Ilan?

'Take a shower, and when you're ready, I'll fix you something. Is that okay?'

'Yes. Todah. I mean, thank you.'

'Okay then,' Jennifer realised she had to take charge. But she wasn't comfortable with the situation. It wasn't what she expected. It was natural for him to be strange and silent for a while when he came home from a mission. He always had a phase of re-adapting—she had learned that over the years. But this was different. He was guilty and knew it. It was his fault for getting her involved with Saul Mueller and his operation.

And you bloody well should feel guilty, Ilan. The pair of you concocted this scheme, knowing I would leap into it to save your life. I'm in it up to my neck and can't get out of it. You didn't think about that consequence, did you?

But she didn't voice her thoughts. This wasn't the time, and besides, he didn't know about the promise she made to Saul.

And there was the other matter. She couldn't put it into words, but fear and anger gripped her every time she thought about it—his hands on her throat, choking her life away. It would have to be dealt with, dragged, kicking and screaming, into the open. They'd put it on the table to dissect, analyse, and argue over. But that was for another time and probably another place. It would keep.

Jennifer watched as her husband walked to the bathroom. A minute later, she heard the sound of the water running in the shower.

While Ilan was showering, she busied herself in the kitchen, finding a carton of fresh eggs and some mushrooms among the food Reuben had left in the fridge. There was spinach there, too. She would use these ingredients to make an omelette. It was his favourite. She lifted what she needed out of the refrigerator, ready to cook when he was finished in the bathroom. In automaton mode, she put on a pot of coffee, enough for both of them, although she'd had gallons of it through the night.

6

Ilan leaned his palms against the tiles and lowered his head as the hot water flowed over him, and the rising steam filled the stall. It clouded his vision and gave him temporary relief from the terrible things he had done and seen. He felt the dirt of the last eight months rinsing from his skin, but he knew it would take a lot more than a hot shower to rinse it out of his soul. He closed his eyes, and he was back in the village.

No, don't go there. You're home and safe. Don't think about that place.

The journey home seemed longer than it was. Maybe it was the noise or the bumpy ride on the plane, but, despite the whiskey, sleep escaped him as they soared through the night sky. Aboard the plane, he was congratulated and told that the mission was successful. The live feed from the aerial reconnaissance drones confirmed the camp had been destroyed, and it was unlikely anybody had survived. Qahtani's body hadn't been identified, but Ilan knew he couldn't have survived the village's destruction. Qahtani was classified as a successful kill. His name was added to the intelligence agencies' list of deceased terrorists—the agencies friendly to Israel. Others, the not-so-friendly ones, would say he survived the attack, and he'd be hailed a hero. But it was ninety-nine per cent certain he was dead. Ilan would prefer a hundred per cent confirmation, but this was the best he was going to get.

Besides the congratulations and the celebratory words of praise from the few who knew him, he was left alone on the journey home. He didn't look like someone who'd want to engage in casual conversation to pass the time. In the middle of the night, he was the ragged stranger they'd picked up in the wilderness.

Another hip flask would have been welcome, but no one produced one, and he sat with his thoughts, a distance from the others. His nightmares belonged to him alone as the plane flew through the night.

Stop thinking about it. You're home now. It's over.

He unscrewed the cap on the shampoo bottle and poured a generous amount onto the palm of his hand. It was coconut scented, and he inhaled its richness. When she showered, washed her hair and slipped into bed beside him, he could smell her coconut shampoo as he wrapped his arms around her. He'd spent so many nights dreaming about this smell—about her.

Ilan washed his hair and used Jennifer's shower gel—coconut again. It was her favourite. He soaped his body from head to toe and luxuriated in the hot water and the soft soap as he scrubbed away the past eight months. He glanced at the bathroom door, hoping she would come in, slip out of her clothes and join him as she had done many times before. But the door didn't open, and he finished showering, turned off the water and stepped out. He lifted the towel Jennifer had left for him and dried himself. Wrapping himself with the soft towel around his waist, he went into the bedroom and opened the wardrobe door. He stared at the clothes hanging there. There were shirts and sweaters, jeans and trousers, with a couple of suits for formal occasions.

He was undecided—it felt as though he'd lost the ability to make the simplest decisions. He found a comfortable old sweatshirt, pulled it over his head and stepped into a pair of jeans. They were baggy—where before they had fit well—they hung at the waist from the weight he'd lost, but he put them on anyway.

Jennifer smiled as he went into the kitchen. She was feeding the cats, and they ignored him, concentrating on the food in their bowls.

'Sit yourself down. This will be ready in a few minutes,' Jennifer said, pouring his coffee into a large mug and then turning her attention to making the omelette.

He sat down at her request, and his eyes took in the familiar sights of home—the post-it note stuck to the fridge with a list of groceries written in Jennifer's scrawling, lopsided handwriting. He read the list, eggs, bread, cat food, chicken, coffee, tea bags, and wine. The basics. She had underlined wine to emphasise, not forgetting to buy several bottles. His eyes glanced over the toaster, the kitchen roll and a towel hanging on a hook. There was a jar of mixed herbs, his e-cigarette and a charger. All the normal, everyday things that were alien to him. Even the coffee mug was an artefact from another world. His gaze dropped to the tabletop, and he pressed his fingertip against some crumbs. He stared at them as they transferred from wood to him as if it was a spectacular magic trick. This was real. He was home. He was safe, and the other place where he'd almost died was a bad memory. He wanted so much to free himself of that memory.

'You need to get rid of that beard and cut your hair.' Jennifer's voice cut into his thoughts as she commented over her shoulder.

He looked up, and her back was to him as she poured the egg mixture into a pan.

'I will.'

Jennifer put the omelette piled with spinach and mushrooms in front of him. Ilan inhaled the scent of home-cooked food before lifting his fork to eat.

Jennifer pulled out the chair and sat down opposite him as he took a small, hesitant mouthful. It had been so long since he'd eaten a decent, home-cooked meal, and she knew the taste was unfamiliar to him. After a few hesitant mouthfuls, he regained his appetite and ate like the deprived man he was.

Jennifer watched him devour the eggs and toast, and he drank the coffee like a man dying of thirst. He looked better, but his eyes were haunted, and he couldn't meet her gaze as he concentrated on his food.

'I'll cut your hair when you've finished eating.'

'I would appreciate that, neshama. Todah.'

Why so polite and formal? Speak to me, Ilan. Please. Tell me you're glad to be home and how much you missed me. It'll be Christmas Eve in a couple of days. Ask me what I want to do this year. Tell me you have a gift for me or haven't had the chance to buy one, but you will tomorrow. Tell me anything. But most of all, let me know you're okay. Please.

Ilan put his knife and fork on the empty plate and drained his coffee. Looking at his wife, he was withdrawn and silent. She could tell he had drifted away somewhere and was lost in his own thoughts—they didn't include her.

'Give me some time,' he asked.

'Of course. Just tell me you'll be okay. We need to be okay.'

'Why wouldn't we be?'

Taken aback by his question, Jennifer fumbled with her empty coffee mug. 'I don't know. You seem different this time.'

'It's been eight months. I need time to adjust. You know that.'

'Yeah. And who's fault is that?'

'It's mine. I had a job to do, and I did it. It took eight months to complete, but I'm back now.'

'You're only back because of me,' Jennifer said, and the anger rose inside her. She glared at him. 'Because of what I had to do.'

'I never thought it would come to that. Neither of us did.'

'Well, it did. And I think you and Saul planned it that way.'

'No,' he shook his head and reached for her hand.

Jennifer moved back in her seat and folded her hands under the table.

Her hand reached to touch her throat as the memories, the real reason for her anger, came back. She needed to be out of reach. But, even on opposite sides of the table, she was still too close. She had to put some distance between them. Pushing her chair away from the table, she stood up, gathered the empty plates, and dropped them into soapy water.

I need to get over this. It didn't happen. It was only a dream.

But the memory of his hands around her neck—strangling her—refused to go away.

'You need to get rid of that beard and all that hair. It's horrible, and I hate it,' she told him, her back still to him.

'Fine. I'll do it now, seeing as it bothers you so much and you feel the need to keep going on about it.' Ilan muttered a curse under his breath. His chair scraped across the tiled floor as he got up.

Hot, angry tears filled Jennifer's eyes, but she refused to turn around. Instead, she inflicted physical abuse on the washing-up. She heard the bathroom door slam as she washed the plates and set them on the drainer. Her hands gripped the edge of the sink, and she watched the soapy water swirl down the drain.

'Screw it.' She dried her hands, got a pair of scissors from the drawer and went to the bathroom.

Ilan was in front of the mirror, with a pair of nail scissors, hacking at his beard. Tufts of hair fell into the washbasin and onto the floor. He stopped as she came in and looked at her helplessly.

'I can't cut it evenly.'

'I'm not surprised with those little scissors. Sit on the edge of the bath, and I'll do it for you.'

He saw the size of the scissors in her hand. 'Are you planning to rip out my jugular with those things?'

'I'll try not to.'

Ilan sat on the bath rim, and Jennifer draped a towel across his shoulders. She cut slowly, and her face was a mask of concentration as she tilted his head and trimmed the hair on that side of his face.

'Do you hate me?' he asked.

'No, Ilan. I don't hate you. I'm angry with you, but I don't hate you.'

'Do you still love me?'

It took her a few moments to reply. 'Yes. I've already said so.'

'But you had to think about your answer?'

'It was a stupid question. You know I love you. I just need time, Ilan. Tilt your head to the left some more. You've been away for so long, and it was hard. I missed you, and I worried about you all the time. So, yeah. I still love you, but I'm still angry with you.'

'And you're holding a pair of scissors to my throat.'

'Chose what you say very carefully then,' Jennifer said and caught his eye as she glanced at him in the mirror. There was no humour in her words or in her eyes. 'Seriously, though. It's not that you went away after you promised you wouldn't, although I am pissed about that. But this thing with Saul and how I got caught up in your work has messed with my head.'

'I am sorry.'

'Not half as sorry as I am.' She stopped cutting the hair on his face and stepped back to look at her work. 'I think it's short enough for you to shave what's left. Now, about your hair. I can style it, or I can cut it short. I can be Delilah to your Sampson.'

'What?'

'Saul explained the Delilah missiles you lot use. He thought I'd be interested in his fancy high-tech weaponry. I wasn't. I only needed to know if they would work.

But, like Delilah, who the missiles are named after, if I cut off your hair, you can be Sampson and stay at home with me instead of running off, risking your life for the greater good.'

'You want to neuter me?'

'Your words, not mine. Now, do you want me to cut your hair or not?'

Ilan nodded, and Jennifer picked up the scissors again. He was silent as she tilted his head with a frown of concentration on her face, as she combed and clipped around his ears and the back of his neck. He watched the clumps falling onto the floor and saw it as another part of the exorcism of his Jamal persona. He would be rid of it completely soon.

'That's the best I can do.' Her voice was cold and matter of fact. 'You'll need to get it cut properly, and getting some colour put in would be a good idea. You look like a ninety-year-old with all that grey.'

'I appreciate it, neshama. And I'm sorry for everything I put you through.'

The two people in the mirror didn't look happy, and their images reflected her unhappiness. She didn't know those sad people.

I should count my blessings. He's home and safe, and that's all I ever wanted. I hate feeling this anger and fear. But I don't know how to not feel this way or if I'll ever feel different. I might never forgive him.

'Oh, you don't know the bloody half of it, Ilan,' Jennifer stormed out of the bathroom, leaving him to finish shaving his beard and clean up the floor.

14

Chapter 2

Jennifer was certain she was unique because, in today's world, most spies are found through the normal channels, usually through a recruitment campaign. People with exemplary records and recognition for bravery are headhunted from organisations like the police and the military. Government agencies run advertisements on websites and in the newspapers. They host open days at universities and colleges. And sometimes, spies are hired because their career has flagged them to be of interest. It puts them in a position where valuable intelligence can be gathered.

In Jennifer's case, two men knocked on her front door one afternoon in early December. She remembered how terrified she was when they invited her to go with them—it wasn't a request—not really—though it was couched in pleasant terms. They'd taken her to a large building that she thought was a hospital. She thought she was going to be asked to identify Ilan's remains. But when she got there, she was introduced to a man called Saul

Mueller. He interviewed her, although it seemed more like an interrogation at the time.

She found out later that he was a senior ranking Mossad officer.

He wanted to know how she met Ilan. He was suspicious of her and asked if Ilan was a target. Was meeting him something she had been tasked with? And if so, by whom? And he questioned her for two hours on subjects about her life in the UK before coming to Cyprus.

His questions got Jennifer's temper up, and she glared at the man sitting opposite. She told him that she met Ilan by chance, and if he didn't believe her, he could go fuck himself.

There were a few heated exchanges, although the heat and anger came from Jennifer—Saul always maintained a cool, professional demeanour throughout the interview. But it set the basis, and tone, of their volatile future relationship.

She was with Ilan when he crashed into a logging truck on a back road in Cyprus while they were being chased. During the interviews, Saul questioned her about her experiences in the medically-induced coma after the accident. He insisted she knew the woman whose life she'd experienced and lived through in her comatose dreams. Jennifer told him she didn't know Lucy Wilson before she dreamed about her. She had never met her or had even heard of her.

Saul told her what they wanted her to do for them. After repeating the same questions, phrased differently but on a repetitive loop, her answers must have convinced him she was telling the truth. He was satisfied, and she was given a security pass to their headquarters.

In her recent past life, Jennifer was a successful interior designer. She'd made her career by interpreting what people wanted in their homes. With the influx of EU money, tourism in Cyprus had stepped into the twenty-first century. Hotels and apartment complexes sprung up overnight, and the bulk of her clients were the developers. But it was the private clients—those wishing to move, or retire, to the beautiful, sun-kissed island—that were her favourites. When they'd been forced to relocate to Israel, things changed, and over time the joy she derived from textile and fabric had waned. She put that chapter of her life behind her and got a job as an assistant helper at an animal rescue centre, where she was paid a meagre wage to look after the dogs.

She didn't need a session with her therapist to explain why her former career no longer appealed to her and why she cut all aspects of it out of her life. It was blatantly obvious, even to her, that she was afraid to put down roots again. She had made a happy home with Ilan in a house she adored. She had built up her business only to have the carpet ripped out from underneath her when they had to flee, and, deep down, she was terrified of it happening again.

That fear would never leave her. It remained there, under the surface of her seemingly normal, happy life.

Jennifer wasn't someone who met the criteria necessary to be a potential spy with her history. At least not on the surface.

But she had a singular and remarkable talent, which she didn't even know she had. It was this ability that Mossad wanted.

She agreed to join them and do what they asked. They told her it was her only chance to find her missing husband and bring him back safely.

In truth, they wanted to pinpoint Ilan's location so they could blow him and the terrorist group he had infiltrated to kingdom come. They preferred not to take such an extreme route, but if it meant preventing a major terrorist attack, one man's life was expendable. It meant blackmailing the Israeli government, and Jennifer had no choice. She just wanted her husband home with her.

Blackmail was a strong word, but it's what it amounted to. They asked her to help them, and Jennifer offered her services, but only in exchange for her demands being met. She made it clear that rescuing her husband came as part of the deal. She refused to work with them until she had a cast-iron guarantee that Ilan wouldn't be harmed. He was given time to make it to a pick-up location before the attack on the terrorist compound was launched.

And because of her, here they were. Ilan was rescued, the terrorists' plans were stopped, and Jennifer was Mossad's new secret weapon.

It was an easy job. When she was called in, all she had to do was show up with her overnight bag containing her favourite, comfy pyjamas and her toiletries slung over her shoulder. She was given a twenty-minute briefing with details of the subject and what they required of her. Jennifer would get into bed, wait for them to hook her up to the monitors and fall asleep.

She was being paid to fall asleep. The wage wasn't much, just a bog-standard civil service salary, although it did include medical and sickness benefits. But there was no holiday pay, and her name wouldn't appear on any public records. If Jennifer decided she wanted to visit Australia or Canada or take an excursion up the Amazon, she would have to do it on her own time and at her own expense, which seemed unfair. The same applied if she wanted to re-decorate the spare room or if she had friends visiting from the UK and wanted to spend time with them. The computer that calculated her wages and sent them to her bank account would pause and not move again until she was back at work.

The meagre pay didn't bother her. As well as the pensions he received from Mossad and his earlier service in the army, Ilan had various business interests, all legitimate and successful. It kept them more than comfortable. Jennifer had asked him what he did for a living years ago when she met him in Cyprus. He was evasive and told her he was in the import and export business, and for a time, she was concerned that he was a drug dealer or a people trafficker. The knowledge that he was a spy came as a relief. When he wasn't off spying, she discovered that Ilan had a legitimate small but successful import-export business. It answered any questions that people felt they needed to ask. As a cover, it was a useful one.

Jennifer's family and friends didn't visit often. Her relationship with Ilan was strained to the point that a holiday or weekend break somewhere would end up a disaster. It made her despondent to realise that she didn't need much time off—paid or otherwise.

Her friends thought she was weird. She went from being a well-known interior designer with a cool website and lots of clients to a person who mumbled something about being in the civil service. And when she was pressed about what exactly she did, she'd say, 'Filing,' and change the subject—usually to cats. They had two, so it was a topic she was well-versed in.

The work Jennifer did was interesting and exciting. She travelled the world—without ever leaving her bed, and she was highly respected in her field. That wasn't too hard, considering she was the only one in her field. She was unique, and Jennifer was the talk of the espionage community. Her existence was known, but they didn't know who she was or how she had learned the secrets she did.

This chapter in Jennifer's life happened three years before when they were in the car crash. Her subsequent serious head injury was the catalyst for everything that had happened to her since.

Ilan had sustained a broken arm due to the impact, and Jennifer had what she insisted was only a bump to her head. They were taken to a hospital in Nicosia for a checkup and to set Ilan's arm. Jennifer seemed to be okay. She had no headache, dizziness or nausea and insisted she was fine and didn't need further medical attention. Although advised not to, she was allowed to fly to Israel with Ilan. After their arrival, she became confused and disorientated. Then she collapsed and was taken to a hospital in Tel Aviv. She was rushed into surgery and operated on to remove a subdural haematoma on her brain. Jennifer was in a medically-induced coma for nine days.

While she was in a coma, her life changed forever. She was a normal woman with a better than average life, and extraordinary things didn't happen to her. Something strange occurred in Jennifer's brain. It could have been the impact. Nobody knew how it happened, but her consciousness connected with another woman in a similar condition in a hospital in Yorkshire, England. Jennifer and the woman spent those nine days experiencing one another's lives through the dreams they exchanged.

She was called Lucy Wilson, and on the ninth day—the day—at the exact moment Jennifer had woken up, Lucy died. One lived, one died, and Jennifer was left feeling guilty about her death.

When she was fit to be discharged from the hospital, Jennifer rebuilt her life with Ilan in their new home in Israel. He hadn't suffered any after-effects from his broken arm, but Jennifer was left with more than her fair share of physical and psychological problems for months afterwards. It took time, but between Ilan, good doctors and excellent whiskey, she made a complete recovery and put that episode in her life in the past where it belonged.

Or so she thought.

Ilan was taken off operational duty. He grumbled about how much he hated being behind a desk, and he complained that the office wasn't as comfortable as it should be. Jennifer insisted he stay safe behind a good quality, sturdy bomb-proof desk in a comfortable, well-furnished bomb-proof office. She said they'd buy some nice prints for the wall and a cactus or two, and she kept her fingers crossed that he'd stay behind it forever instead of running off to risk his life saving the world.

He did well and stayed behind that desk for three years. Then one day, he got bored and off he went on another mission. Because of that episode, Jennifer's life took a surprising turn when she had to rescue him in her dreams.

Chapter 3

Jennifer walked through the doors and then woke up. She didn't know where she was. She sat up on the bed and looked around. The room she was in was like a hospital suite—it was a comfortable room with a kitchen, living area and a small en-suite bathroom. The bed was similar to a hospital bed but more comfortable, and she was hooked up to monitors that beeped and flashed at a computer terminal on the nearby desk.

This sense of confusion regarding her whereabouts and the disorientation that came with it happened every time she woke up from one of her dreams. Within a minute, it went away, and she knew she wasn't in a hospital bed. She was in a secure building in Tel Aviv, and the staff were made up of Mossad and military personnel.

No one was in the room at present, but it was clear that someone had popped in recently because there was a pot of coffee and a plate of croissants on the table in the living room. Jennifer breathed in the smell, and her stomach rumbled. She was always hungry when she woke up after a night of dreaming.

She swung her legs over the bed and switched off the monitors. She unhooked herself from them as she'd been taught to do. It played havoc with the computers if she pulled the sensors off her skin before switching them off.

Jennifer yawned and went to the table wearing her normal uniform of pyjama shorts, vest top, and dressing gown. She wanted coffee first and poured the steaming black liquid into a mug, shuffled into the small kitchen and got a carton of milk from the fridge. She added a small amount to the coffee and sat down.

Although there wasn't much to see, Jennifer gazed out of the window as she drank her coffee. It was early, and dawn was breaking. The sky was clear, and it looked like it was shaping up to be a lovely day. She ripped a croissant in two and nibbled it.

Coffee and croissants first. Then a shower, and she was ready to face the day. There had been a few complaints from Saul. This was her working routine and one Jennifer insisted on. He tried to explain that her intel was vital and urgent. It was always wanted immediately, but Jennifer told him that she needed to collect her thoughts to recall all the details of her dream before she could put it together and relay it to him. Or, if he wasn't available, write it up in a report and email it to his office via a secure server. Saul considered it before agreeing that her suggestion made sense, and he allowed her to do it her way.

It shouldn't have worked, but it did. Jennifer found she could remember every detail if left to her own devices for an hour before she was debriefed.

While she didn't play the diva too much, she enjoyed keeping them waiting. She was their star, so Saul had no choice but to give in to her demand. It wasn't much, but Jennifer chalked it up as a victory in keeping some control over her life.

They gave her an hour. More than enough time, they said, to have breakfast, take a shower and get dressed. This morning she had bad news to relay. Bad news came in the form of no news. So, she lingered over the coffee and decided to forsake the shower until she got home. But she still made them wait until she had finished eating.

'I'm sorry. I saw nothing,' Jennifer said as, dressed in jeans and a warm sweater, she opened the door and walked into the small room they used for the debrief. She didn't bother sitting down. There was no need to this morning. She sensed their disappointment blow through the room.

'Okay,' Saul said. He rubbed his eyes and switched off the recording device. 'Are you prepared to give it another try tonight?'

'I'll do one more night, but that's all. And make it tomorrow night because I need a night at home in my own bed. We've been at this for a week now, and it isn't working. Maybe we should rethink this idea,' Jennifer suggested. She'd try anything for a way out, even if it was only a temporary reprieve.

'It is possible he isn't sleeping. Or perhaps he's sleeping too heavily,' Nathan suggested.

'We'll try once more, and if it fails, we'll move onto another target,' Saul told them.

'Tomorrow night?' Jennifer asked.

'Yes. Okay. Tomorrow night is fine. But you'll be going solo. Nathan has other plans tomorrow and for the next two weeks.'

'Ah, yes. The wedding,' Jennifer smiled at Nathan. 'How are the nerves?'

'Much the same.' Nathan closed his laptop and packed it into his old leather briefcase.

'Oh, you'll be fine. Have a stiff whiskey ten minutes before the ceremony, and it'll be a piece of cake.'

'Says the woman who told me she had to be dragged kicking and screaming to her own wedding.' Nathan grinned as he headed out the door.

When Jennifer first tried out the process of finding Ilan in her dreams, she'd needed Nathan beside her. He taught her the prompts that allowed her to open the door and go through. This was his hypnosis technique, and since then, they'd worked on perfecting the process. Count down from ten, then go to sleep. Open a dream by walking through the door. Find the bad guy so he can be arrested.

Find the good guy so he can be rescued. Or the secret file. Or someone who is telling secrets they shouldn't be telling. And who they are telling them to. Or whatever. Just get the intel. Go back through the door. Wake up. Tell your handler what you saw. Job's a good 'un.

It sounded easy in theory. It was more hit and miss in practice because, while she could slip into her dream state easily, there was no guarantee her subject was dreaming. Or if he was even asleep at the same time. It was a two-way system, so it didn't always work. However, failure was unusual because, even if the subject was dreaming of something else, Jennifer could poke around in his subconscious and find what she was looking for. Sometimes, she interacted with her subject inside the dream and found what she needed through a conversation.

'Isn't that too risky? I can't just ask them. What if the person I'm interacting with passes my description on to somebody else, and they come looking for me?' she had asked Saul.

'It comes with a risk. But most people don't remember their dreams. They'll assume you're a manifestation of their guilty conscience on the off-chance that they do remember the details.'

'That is either very cool or very creepy. I can't decide which. But are you sure my identity is secure?'

'As sure as we can be,' Saul told her.

Nathan Cohen was still on the team with Doctor Miriam Melandri. Neither of them was present every time Jennifer went to sleep, but Nathan was usually nearby and ready should Jennifer need him to entice her back into the land of wakefulness. It had happened a couple of times when she'd got stuck in a dream, and it was a terrifying and dangerous glitch in the process. They couldn't figure out why it happened. But as long as the trigger words Nathan whispered in Jennifer's ear worked, they didn't worry about it. Jennifer would feel a lot more secure in her employment if they did.

Miriam was retained as a psychiatrist in case Jennifer experienced or saw something she couldn't deal with without professional help.

When she first helped them with her dream-spying, Jennifer wasn't convinced she could do it, but she ignored her doubts. She told Saul Mueller she would be their official remote viewer or lucid dreamer as long as he promised to get her husband out of Syria and back to Israel.

He did as she asked, and she realised she had signed her life over to the Israeli Secret Service. She had come a long way from being an interior designer who decorated hotels and holiday resorts and planned homes for elderly couples who had retired to Cyprus.

Jennifer got her husband back, so she couldn't complain.

But it wasn't as simple as that.

Thanks to her, Ilan came home. But he came back ragged and exhausted, both mentally and physically, after spending eight months posing as a Muslim named Jamal while infiltrating a terrorist network. The well-funded group of terrorists had planned to send a couple of dozen jihadis into the world. In the few days leading up to the Christmas holidays, they wanted them in the major cities of Europe and North America. But they weren't suicide bombers or gunmen, nor did they plan on flying aeroplanes into buildings.

A terrorist called Sayeed Qahtani hatched the plan to infect these men with a mutated strain of pneumonic plague. He said it came to him in a vision and called it Allah's Will. The mutation was resistant to antibiotics and had a longer incubation period than lesser strains. It made it capable of infecting the greatest number of innocent people. The first infected would go on to give it to everyone they came in contact with. The plague would spread exponentially through the populations of every city. His plan was to kill hundreds of thousands of people and wipe out as many enemy states as possible.

Ilan's job was to stop Qahtani and destroy the virus by any means.

It was a suicide mission. But Ilan, and Saul Mueller, concocted a scheme that might, at a pinch, save his life. If it came down to it, they planned to use Jennifer to remote-view Ilan at the terrorist base in Northern Syria. She'd find out what was happening, obtain his exact location and tell the military where to strike.

Jennifer succeeded beyond their wildest dreams. She infiltrated their operation at the planning stage and found out what they would do. Later, she pinpointed their location. The most important step to her was discovering the pick-up point Ilan had chosen so that she could direct the rescue to him. She forced them to go out of their way to rescue him, and as a bargaining chip, she promised Mossad she'd continue working for them in the same capacity. Her husband was brought home to her.

That was why Jennifer woke up in a strange bed at seven-thirty in the morning in her nightwear at the Mossad building in Tel Aviv.

'I'm sorry it didn't work. I don't know if it's something to do with the subject or if it's my fault. Maybe I wasn't focused enough when I went to sleep.'

Saul narrowed his eyes as he scrutinised her. 'Is something on your mind and distracting you, Jennifer?'

'Nope. Nothing more than usual.'

Don't you dare go there, Saul.

Saul took a deep breath. Ilan and Jennifer were having problems with their marriage. She knew it was probably common knowledge by now. The bastard knew what

30

he'd done to them, but it wasn't something he would be likely to comment on. It was between them. However, if it impacted her work, that was a different matter. She knew he'd be all over her, telling her to sort it out and concentrate on her work. Her track record had been good until now, and he told her he believed the issue was with the target and not Jennifer. The problems between her and Ilan hadn't made a difference previously, so there was no reason to think it should impact her work now. At least not yet.

'Can I go now?'

'Yes, of course.'

She stopped at the canteen and bought a coffee on the way out for the short journey home. She waved to the guards operating the electric gate as they hit the button that slid it open and smiled as one of them saluted her. He was young and new to his post and didn't recognise everyone who came in yet.

Someone needs to tell you that you don't have to salute civilians. But it's nice that you do.

She gave him an extra smile as she drove through the gate. She was almost home when she remembered Ilan had reminded her to pick up some groceries on her way back.

He can buy beer and whiskey, but he can't bring a few groceries in.

Muttering a curse under her breath, she swung the car around to drive back to the supermarket.

She walked up the aisles, adding the basics to her shopping cart. Milk, bread and butter. Then salad and vegetables, a whole chicken and a pack of chicken fillets. She added two steaks and fish, ingredients for a cheesecake and some other processed desserts. Her favourite wine was on offer, so she loaded four bottles into her shopping trolley, and she grabbed cat food and a bag of cat litter. It was enough to keep them and the cats in food for the next week.

While she waited at the check-out, Jennifer saw some customers were wearing masks. Other people wore disposable gloves. The news was all about the flu virus rife in China and spreading to other countries. Italy had reported a high number of cases. And were showing news clips on the hour with the shattering stories about their first deaths.

She put her groceries on the conveyor belt and thought it was strange to see people wearing medical masks inside a supermarket in Tel Aviv. She shuddered at the thought of this virus spreading around the world.

Jennifer parked in the driveway and sounded the horn when she got home.

The least he can do is help me carry all this inside.

Ilan appeared as if he'd been waiting for her behind the door. He took the shopping bags and leaned forward to kiss her. Jennifer turned her face and offered him her cheek at the last second.

'Did you get my e-cigarette juice?'

'Yes.' She had bought it the evening before on her way to work.

'Three bottles of the pineapple flavour?'

'Yes. You told me that's what you wanted, and that's what I got.'

'Todah.'

Jennifer shrugged and carried the rest of the shopping into the house. She made a point of ignoring Ilan but hated herself for her attitude. He was bringing out the worst in her.

I need to get over this. It was my decision to do what I had to. It was that or lose him. He might have gone behind my back and necessitated that decision, but the choice was mine when it came down to it.

Chapter 4

Ilan had been home a day and a half when Jennifer dropped her bombshell. She told him that she would be working with Saul Mueller on his new project within the next week.

Dream Catcher wasn't Saul's choice of name, but it was a favourite among the team and the one or two people who knew about it. The programme was almost up and running and was scheduled to start as soon as the first target was identified.

Jennifer felt sarcastic and offered to design a logo with a woolly sheep and a cloud above its head. 'We could put it on coffee mugs and pens. We could be rich, Saul, with pillowcases, duvet sets, jammies and nighties. Rich, I tells ya. The merchandising possibilities are endless.'

Saul was already frowning at her suggestion, but it turned into an angry glare, and she had shut up, but not before making a zipping motion across her lips.

'Why did you agree to do it?' Ilan asked her.

'I had no choice.'

'Did Saul force you?'

'Not really. It was mostly my idea.'

That stopped Ilan in his tracks, and he stared at his wife.

Well, at least he's looking at me.

Jennifer kept her head bowed as she tidied the living room. It felt good beating a scatter cushion to death.

From the minute they arrived home and stepped through the front door, life had been uncomfortable for them. Ilan was battling his demons and was confused and hurt by his wife's icy attitude towards him. Jennifer, despite her anger, was wracked with guilt because the coldness was her fault. No matter what he said or did to make up for his absence, she couldn't forgive him. And now this.

'What do you mean — it was your idea?' Ilan's eyes narrowed.

'Saul wasn't going to wait for you to make your escape to the pick-up point. He threatened to extract the coordinates from me by whatever means necessary. He was going to launch the attack as soon as he got them. I told him I was giving him nothing until he promised he'd wait until you got away. He had to arrange a team to pick you up to get any intel from me. He threatened to throw me in prison for not cooperating. Apparently, my lack of cooperation could have been seen as treason, so I had no choice but to promise to work for him as a remote viewer. I thought I'd pulled a fast one on him, but it was the other way around. You should have seen the gleam in his eyes when I said I'd work for him indefinitely as long as he got you to safety. I agreed to do what he wanted, and he agreed to do what I wanted. Then I gave him the coordinates. Win-win situation, everybody's a happy bunny—and I'm fucking ecstatic.'

Ilan swore in Hebrew, and Jennifer ignored him. She stood for a minute and breathed to regulate her mood. Gathering up yesterday's newspapers, she took them to the recycling bin in the garage, where she slammed the lid in her temper.

It wasn't like her to be this angry, but the sense of betrayal was overpowering, and she couldn't think it through with a rational mind. Her emotions put paid to that. She had spent three years without worrying about her husband. He was tucked safely behind his desk in his comfortable office. Then, he informed her he was going on a mission out of the blue. And that hurt. She thought he was bored of her, though he probably just wanted to do what he was born for.

Ilan had risked his life and hers as well. But between him and Saul Mueller, they'd cooked up the scheme, and that pissed her off. He knew she wouldn't refuse Saul. Not if it meant losing him.

And that was the crux of the matter. Jennifer still loved him and was relieved to have him home relatively un-scathed. It would take him a while to adjust to ordinary life. It usually did, but he always got there in the end and was the loving, funny man she'd always known.

And I wish I could tell you all this, Ilan. I want to sit you down and explain my feelings to you. But I can't because I don't understand them myself.

Jennifer had to try. She couldn't hide in the garage ignoring him or go in to make his dinner pretending nothing was wrong. She had to clear the air between them, or she was likely to poison his fish supper.

They couldn't move on until she sorted it. And there was another matter. The incident in her dream where he'd stuck his gun in her ribs and pressed his arm across her throat. He almost choked the life out of her, terrifying her in the process. But it hadn't happened. It was a manifestation in her dream, not in real life. Ilan would never harm a hair on her head. He was the gentlest, most loving man in the world, and he'd give up his life before risking hers.

Since that night, every time she looked at him, Jennifer felt her throat tighten, and she struggled to breathe as the memory from her dream flashed in front of her eyes. There was anger on his face. She heard his threatening words and felt the gun in her ribs and pain in her throat as she fought to get a breath. She couldn't forget it.

'What's wrong, neshama?'

Ilan's words interrupted her rambling thoughts as she saw him standing in the doorway.

'Nothing.'

'I don't believe you. When you say nothing with that bright smile on your face, I know you well enough to know you mean the opposite. Please tell me.'

The look on his face tore Jennifer's heart in two, and all the fight went out of her. Her shoulders slumped, and she covered her face with her hands. She couldn't hate him. She loved him too much.

'I missed you every single day. I couldn't sleep or eat for worrying about you. It was hell. I spent eight months waiting. But I was angry too.'

Ilan took a step forward to take her in his arms, but Jennifer stepped away from him. 'No, let me finish.'

'I'm sorry, go on.'

'Saul approached me and told me what he wanted to do. I was sceptical. I didn't think it would work, but I agreed and well, here you are. But how could you, Ilan? How could you put all this on me, not even knowing if it would work? How could you take a chance like that?'

'Jennifer, I'm sorry. I believed in you. I knew if anyone could find me, it would be you.'

'But to take such a chance?'

'There was no other option,' Ilan said as if that was the end of the matter.

But it wasn't. And here they were. Three months on, and she still couldn't forgive him. She couldn't put her arms around him and kiss him or show him she meant that she was glad to have him home.

She was glad to have him home, but anger and sarcasm were her default mood. Even when she finished unpacking the groceries, and saw Ilan with a bouquet of red roses in one hand and a bottle of her favourite Prosecco.

'Happy birthday.'

'What?' Jennifer frowned and glanced at the calendar.

'It's your birthday. Have you forgotten?'

'Not really.'

'You did forget, didn't you?'

Jennifer gave a rueful laugh. 'Yeah, okay. It sorta slipped my mind.'

'Well, I thought we could go out. I could take you to a restaurant I know that you'll enjoy, and we can drink this at home later.'

'And how could I go to work tonight with a bottle of wine in me?'

Ilan's face fell. 'I thought you were finished with the case.'

'Well, I'm not.'

She hated herself for being so bitchy when he was trying to make an effort.

He'd been making an effort to please her since he came home. He gave her space when she needed it, and he worked through his own problems when he could, without involving her. He spent hours tidying the garden and did his share of the housework. He took her hiking, shopping for new clothes and sightseeing. He would make her a coffee or pour her a glass of wine without her having to ask. He was doing a hundred little things he knew she liked to win her over. It was a shame they weren't working.

Jennifer took a deep breath. It was time she tried to meet him halfway.

'I'm not finished with this case. In fact, I'm getting nowhere with it. Saul told me to take a break and try tomorrow night, so I'd love to go out tonight, Ilan. And thank you for the roses. They're beautiful.'

She found a vase and arranged the flowers. 'They are gorgeous. Where should I put them?'

'On the small table by the window. Did you mean what you said?'

'I don't understand.'

'About going out. With me.'

'Of course,' Jennifer smiled, determined to make an effort to be nice to him. 'It is my birthday.'

See. I'm being good. I'm making an effort like I promised I would. I thanked him for the flowers, and I agreed to go out with him.

It was the best she could do for now. But she knew it wasn't enough.

Jennifer did her best to keep a cheery smile in place as she thanked Ilan and gave him a peck on the cheek before she put the vase of roses on the table where he suggested. Then she told him she'd have a quick shower and would love to spend the day doing something together.

'If you want to, that is.'

'I want to,' Ilan told her. 'And I even have something in mind.'

'So where are we going? And why did you tell me to wear comfortable shoes?' Jennifer asked as they walked out of the house.

'It's a surprise. And I think you will love it.'

'What if I don't?'

'I'm confident you will.' He unlocked the car and motioned for her to get in.

It didn't take long to drive through the city, and in no time, they were on the main road to Jerusalem. Jennifer had never been to the Mahane Yehuda market but had mentioned wanting to go there a few times. She loved shopping, so what was not to like about one of the best markets in the world? Ilan decided her birthday was the perfect excuse to spend time there.

They found a space in the multi-story carpark servicing the market and walked the short distance to it, taking in everything and doing their best to ignore the crowds of tourists. Jennifer noticed that some of them were wearing masks. There were only a few, noticeable because there weren't many.

This was the second time in the last couple of days that she had seen people wearing masks. It seemed they were taking the threat of the virus from China seriously, even if the authorities weren't.

I'm not going to think about it. It's a nice day, and we have some shopping to do.

Jennifer put her serious shopping face on and looked around. The market was spread over parallel streets and connecting alleyways. It was partially covered and part open to the elements. She marvelled at the bustle of the place. Most of the noise came from the vendors shouting their offers and informing everyone that they had the best bargains in the city, if not in the whole world. This was counteracted by customers' voices as they haggled the sellers down to accepting a realistic price.

Jennifer went crazy. She couldn't help herself. She splashed out on herbs and spices for the kitchen, several scarves, an ankle-length skirt and two pairs of sandals. She found cheap sunglasses when Ilan thought she was done because she'd forgotten to bring her good ones and a brass incense burner. Then three packs of incense to go with it. She inspected every stall and marvelled at the colours and smells.

With every purchase, her purse grew lighter but so did her heart. The mere act of doing something normal—that she enjoyed—made her eyes sparkle, and she felt the weight of the past months lift. Her shoulders were lighter as a smile lit up her features. It had worked if Ilan planned this to cheer her up. Years of coming home from a mission, exhausted and traumatised, had taught him the best recovery was found in the normal. Everyday life and doing simple things he loved helped — hiking, swimming, enjoying fresh air or just lazing in good company. In Jennifer's case, a morning browsing a market and spending money was the perfect remedy. She smiled at his thoughtfulness.

Ilan walked beside her. He carried her new things and didn't complain once as she added to the weight he was carrying.

Finally, she stopped and caught the enticing scent of fresh coffee. Jennifer realised she needed coffee more than she needed air.

'My feet are killing me, and I'm hungry. Can we take a break and maybe get a coffee and a snack, please?'

'Great idea. I know just the place, and it has the best coffee I've ever tasted,' Ilan said as he shifted the shopping bags to one hand. He took Jennifer's hand, and they ducked under an awning and down a narrow alleyway that led into a small, crowded courtyard. Jennifer faltered and pulled back for a second as memories she thought were buried came to the surface. The place Ilan was leading her through reminded her of her dream. It was about the courtyard and the large room where she saw somebody being killed. She'd thought it was Ilan.

Claustrophobia and fear gripped her, and her mood darkened as the memories returned.

Her sharp intake of breath stopped Ilan, and he looked at her.

'What's wrong, neshama?'

'I'm sorry. It reminds me of somewhere.'

'I know. I can see the resemblance too.'

'So, why doesn't it bother you?' Jennifer asked.

'I don't permit it to.'

'How can you not be affected by it?'

'I refuse to let it bleed into my life. It's just another irrelevant part of my past. I played a role in carrying out my mission, and it's not who I am now.'

'But how can you shut it off? You lock things away so easily. Every time I close my eyes, I see that courtyard and the door I walked through. I still see you being shot and killed by him. I know it wasn't you. It was your friend, Etan, and it was you who shot him. But I can't stop seeing it.'

43

Jennifer closed her eyes as she forced the memory away. That other one came with it, and she pushed it away. It was the one causing all the problems in their marriage, and she didn't dare mention it.

'I was trained in how to do it, Jennifer. You weren't. Come on. Let's get that coffee.'

Still holding her hand in his, Ilan walked her through the small courtyard. Jennifer huddled close to him, glad of his size and strength. She expected to see Qahtani or one of the armed guards who were in the room that night when she'd dreamed her husband had been killed. She shuddered at the memory and pushed it away. Ilan wasn't dead. He was beside her holding her hand. He led her through the streets and alleyways to the café he promised sold the best espresso in the world. He was alive, and they were shopping. It was a normal day, and Qahtani was dead.

It was a dream, remember that. Yeah, but that other part was a dream, too, and I can't get past that bit any more than I can forget about this.

Jennifer held on to Ilan's hand as she followed him through the courtyard, so similar to the place in her dream.

They ducked under the awning of a stall selling rugs. Jennifer tried to stop. Her fears were forgotten as she was tempted by the colourful designs on sale, but Ilan held her hand, and his forward motion carried her past the seller, deliberately, she thought. He confirmed her correct guess and said he didn't much like the idea of lugging the weight of a rug back to the car.

'I would have settled for a small rug, you know.'

Ilan threw his head back and laughed as he led her away from the stall. He turned left, down a narrow alley, and they were in another courtyard square. It was more open than the one in Jennifer's memory, made from a quadrant of bustling shops and cafés, and there was even a restaurant. However, it was closed at this time of day. All the nearby shops and cafés were open and packed with people, eating, drinking, and laughing. They were normal people enjoying their day. There were no jihadis or terrorists with guns on their backs and hatred in their hearts. Just normal people, like them, enjoying themselves.

Ilan led her to a café on the corner of the square. A waiter appeared and placed two menus on the small table. He pulled out a chair and invited her to sit down. Jennifer felt a tug at her heart as she remembered the café in Cyprus where Ilan had taken her on their first real date. She turned her head to hide the tears threatening to fall.

What is his game plan? He always had one. Is he trying to recapture the old feelings we had for each other? I think he wants me to fall in love with him again. You don't have to do that, you know. I'm still in love with you. I just need to learn to like you again. But—that's the hard part.

Before she had a chance to tell him that she was hungry and looking forward to a good lunch, Ilan placed the order. He went for Espressos and some kind of light pastry. Jennifer forced a smile and let him think she was happy that he'd ordered for both of them even though she was starving. She wanted a salad, or maybe a sandwich and a bowl of soup. The pastries wouldn't be enough to stave off her hunger. She was a big girl, she'd had a shock, and he took charge, but she was okay now—and more than capable of ordering her own food.

Jennifer took a sip of her coffee, licked her lips and nodded her approval. It was as delicious as Ilan promised, and it was strong. She took another drink and smiled as she felt the caffeine hit her system. It woke her up and lifted her mood. She pushed the new sunglasses onto her head, closed her eyes, and felt relaxed for the first time in a long time. Or as content, as she could be these days. She breathed in the heady aromas of people and spices, freshly-baked bread, coffee, and the every day scents of a diverse market in an old city. She allowed the noise to wash over her—the hum of conversation mixed with louder voices and laughter that was musical and told the real story of the market around her.

It was loud and confusing. Under other circumstances, it would be annoying, but Jennifer loved it. It spoke of life and living, fresh air, food and clothing. She was surrounded by all humans' basic elements, food, shelter, and warmth. She had it all and basked in it. Only one thing was missing, and that was love. But that wasn't true. She had love. And it was right there beside her. He was within touching distance. All she had to do was reach out her hand, and everything lost would be hers again.

So why don't I? Just take his hand, and everything will be okay. We'll go back to how it used to be, and we'll be happy again. It isn't difficult—do it. I only have to make an effort.

46

The temptation was strong, and Jennifer almost gave in to it, but something held her back. Part of it was the sense of betrayal when she looked at him. But mostly, it was the dream where he almost choked her to death. She couldn't get beyond that memory and couldn't repair their relationship until she did. Not yet. Maybe in time, it would fix itself. Perhaps it wouldn't. But either way, Jennifer couldn't find it in herself to make a move.

'You're deep in thought. What are you thinking about?' He knew, and his voice was quiet.

'Nothing. I'm not really thinking about anything.' The lie slipped off her lips as easily as coffee froth. She lowered her sunglasses to cover her eyes and looked at her husband. 'I was just enjoying the coffee and listening to everything going on around me. This place is remarkable. I love it. How come we've never been here before?'

'No particular reason. It never occurred to me to come here instead of the market in Tel Aviv.'

'Is there much more to it?'

'There is.'

'I want to see it all. Let's go,' Jennifer slung her bag over her shoulder and got to her feet. She set off through the market and studied what the stalls offered. It was the perfect way to avoid what could be another uncomfortable conversation and one she would have to face soon. Asking Saul for the night off seemed like a foolish idea now.

Despite forgetting about it earlier, Jennifer was determined to make the most of her birthday. She checked out as many stalls and shops as she could, buying things they needed and several items she wanted. Ilan kept his credit card at the ready, insisting he'd pay as it was his idea to come, and he wanted to treat her.

When they couldn't carry any more herbs and spices, fruits and vegetables, meats and fish, plus the summer clothes and shoes, the second-hand books and everything in between, they called it a day. Laden down with bags that cut into their fingers, they walked back to the car—and the distance seemed twice as long as when they came.

'What are you going to do with all this?' Ilan asked as he eyed the results of her shopping spree—clothes, shoes, custom jewellery and books. They carried numerous bags in from the car and dumped some on the table. Before they could have coffee, the perishable food—the meat and fish, the fruit and vegetables, had to be stored in their proper places. But all the condiments she bought

48

were still sitting on the kitchen counter. 'Are you going to set up your own market stall?'

'I could, couldn't I?' Jennifer looked at the pile on the table, the one on the couch, and even the floor. There were books that she knew she would never read and a scarf that had looked beautiful in the market but now seemed garish under the kitchen lighting. 'Bloody hell. Why did you let me buy all this?'

'What? Come between a madwoman and her shopping spree? I'm not brave enough.'

She looked at her husband and grinned, and at that moment, something loosened inside her. A pressure valve released, and a bit more anger left her. It helped ease the tension she had felt as it dissipated. It wasn't all gone, but it was a beginning, and maybe now she could be more civil towards him.

'Let's stay here this evening, Ilan,' Jennifer suggested as she finished packing the food away and started on everything else she'd bought.

'Wouldn't you like to go out for a meal to celebrate your birthday?'

'Not really. I mean, yes, of course, it would be nice, but it's warm enough to eat outdoors. I can open a bottle of wine, and you can have beer or whiskey if you prefer. We could grill the fish, and I'll make a salad. What do you think?'

'Sounds good to me.'

'Unless you want to go out.'

'No. I'm good either way.'

'That's settled then. We'll stay in. What the hell am I going to do with all this junk I bought?'

'Like I said, set up a market stall.'

Chapter 5

They weren't the only ones who had spilled out of the building. The canteen was deserted, and the seating area was packed with workers thankful to be outdoors during their break. The three of them had taken advantage of sitting outside and appreciating the pleasant weather. Miriam Melandri tilted her head towards the sun before answering Saul Mueller's question. Nathan Cohen was vaping beside her, and she caught the whiff of the flavoured e-juice he was using—something fruity, she couldn't define it. Watermelon possibly, but she couldn't be sure.

'There's nothing wrong with Jennifer,' Miriam said.

'Then why isn't this working?' Saul asked, and Miriam heard the impatient annoyance creeping into his voice.

'Because it isn't an exact science,' Nathan said from behind his watermelon-flavoured cloud. 'It was never going to be. We knew that.'

'You told me Jennifer's a natural remote viewer.'

'She is to a degree. And before you go off on one, Saul, let me explain,' Nathan added.

'Go on.'

'From what I've read about them, a remote viewer—the kind we used back in the day—was normally awake during the process. Jennifer is different. Whatever it is in her brain, and we're nowhere near understanding even a fraction of it, activates when she's asleep. We direct her to what she'll dream about. In truth, it's a combination of the two—remote viewing and lucid dreaming—because she uses her directed dreams to view and observe her subject.'

'Yes, I know all that, Nathan. What I don't know is why isn't it working this time?'

'There could be several factors at play,' Nathan said as he took a long drag from his e-cigarette. Jennifer had recommended it to him as Ilan used a similar one. It was the Lamborghini of e-cigs.

'Such as?'

'The subject might not be sleeping,' Nathan said as he did his usual disappearing act in a cloud of watermelon mist. 'Or maybe he only flits in and out of REM sleep. Making it hard for Jennifer to find him in her dreams.'

'Or could Jennifer herself be the problem?' Saul asked.

'I don't understand.'

Saul turned to the woman beside him. 'Is there a problem with Jennifer, Miriam?'

'Not as such,' Miriam replied.

'Would you care to elaborate?'

'She's having difficulty adjusting to Ilan being home. I can't go into the details because of patient-client confidentiality.'

Saul rolled his eyes. 'She works for us. You work for us. In your capacity to assess her mental state concerning the operation, such confidentiality does not apply. So tell me.'

Miriam had no intention of telling her boss what Jennifer confided to her one afternoon when they met up for a coffee. Miriam had noticed how subdued Jennifer was and asked why.

'Because I'm afraid of Ilan,' Jennifer had said. She'd taken a deep breath that turned into a sob and wiped away the tear on her cheek.

'In what way?' Miriam had kept her voice quiet and calm, hiding her shock at the words. She was surprised Jennifer blurted it out the way she did. It was obvious the woman needed her help. The speed with which Jennifer had offloaded told Miriam that she needed someone to confide in.

'I never told anyone this, but he tried to kill me in one of my dreams when we were searching for him. I know it was only a dream, and I'm being stupid, but I can't forget it. It was when I was trying to convince him I was real. He had me by the throat and was choking me and every time I look at him, I remember his hands on my throat and the look of hatred on his face.' She wiped away another tear and fished in her bag for a tissue. 'It's like I can feel him choking me again every time I see him. I hate feeling this way, but I can't stop it.'

'Go on,' Miriam said quietly.

'This is off the record? Right? You won't say anything to Saul? And definitely not to Ilan?'

Miriam spread her arms in a placating gesture and smiled. 'Of course not. We're just two work colleagues having a chat over coffee. Do you see an office and a couch? And even then, what you say would be in the strictest confidence.'

Jennifer had laughed uneasily. 'No, but you work for Mossad.'

'So, I'll run to them and relay every word of every conversation you and I have? Is that what you think?'

'I don't know.'

'Jennifer, I wouldn't do that. If it relates to your work, if Ilan was demanding you quit, then yes, of course, I would have to discuss it with Saul. But this is not work-related. This is between you and Ilan, and I promise it will go no further.'

'Thank you,' Jennifer had said, and Miriam could see the relief on her face. 'But I really don't want to go into detail. Maybe some other time, if you don't mind.'

Miriam nodded. She wanted Jennifer to open up about what was going on with her and Ilan, but she knew not to push her. Instead, she had switched the topic and delighted Jennifer with a lengthy tale about her husband's escapades in the Antarctic.

That conversation was a week ago. Miriam hadn't found another opportunity to talk to Jennifer about her feelings.

'Her mental state is fine, Saul,' Miriam said. 'Like I said, she has a few minor problems adjusting to having Ilan back home, which is natural. But other than that, she is well.'

'I repeat. Why is she not getting results?'

'I don't know. Maybe it's the subject. He could be innocent. Has that ever occurred to you?'

Lost in a cloud of vapour and not wanting to be a part of the conversation, Nathan kept his head down while Miriam and Saul went at it. Their words were acrimonious as neither gave an inch. Saul wanted results, and Miriam was concerned about Jennifer's mental well-being. They were incompatible colleagues. Nathan knew Saul enough to know that he would stop at nothing to achieve his aim and bugger the consequences. Nathan only met Miriam when this project began, but he realised she was also a force to be reckoned with. Although Saul was a good man at heart, and what he needed from Jennifer was all for the greater good, Miriam's motives were more humane.

There was no doubt in Nathan's mind that keeping his head down until they had finished was the best course of action, and that's what he did.

'What evidence do you have that it's him?' Miriam asked.

'That's classified,' Saul replied.

'Oh, I bet it is.'

'What are you implying, Miriam?'

'It's always classified. Classified is your way of saying you don't know.'

'We have good intel. Our source is impeccable.'

It went on. They argued but said nothing. Nathan had enough and stood up.

'Cheers, guys, but I have to say, I've had better coffee breaks. You pair can continue your not-so-pleasant chat without me. I'm getting back to my paperwork before I go home.

Chapter 6

The subject of the argument between Saul and Miriam was sitting alone on her patio, also enjoying the late February sunshine. She was figuring out how she'd manage to get through the rest of the day in her husband's company.

And the night. Don't forget the night. A pleasant evening usually led to hot sex. I should have stayed at work. Maybe I would have cracked it tonight. Yeah, right. Tomorrow night then, or the next. It would have been better to keep trying than come home. What's wrong with me? It's my birthday. And he's trying to make it special because he loves me. I should be happy. Why aren't I happy? Why can't I just get over it?

Jennifer heard Ilan rummaging around inside. He was opening drawers and cupboards as though he'd lost something.

Me? Is he looking for me? The real me.

Then there was silence, and Jennifer wondered what he was doing and if he'd found what he was looking for.

She lifted the thriller lying face down on the table and stared at the words.

Her concentration had deteriorated over the past months. She had been a voracious reader, devouring books to the point of buying them in bulk online and in second-hand shops. The same applied to television shows. Jennifer would download box sets and binge-watch them until the small hours of the morning, only crawling into bed beside Ilan when her eyes ached too much or when she had finished the series.

As far as books were concerned, the words made no sense no matter how many times she read them. And the TV shows didn't capture her attention—the plots didn't make sense, and the actors seemed to speak words she did not understand. Nothing went in and stuck.

Jennifer was worried about it and wondered if it was to do with her head injury or even a side-effect of her interactive dream adventures. During one of their unofficial sessions over a glass of wine, she mentioned it to Miriam. However, she wondered how much of their off-the-record conversations ended up in her medical file.

Miriam dismissed Jennifer's concerns and told her it was a natural consequence of Ilan being away from her so much.

'How do you expect to concentrate on a television show when worrying about Ilan is uppermost in your thoughts?'

'He's home now, so I don't have to worry about him, but I still can't concentrate,'

Miriam smiled.

'What?' Jennifer asked.

'The choking thing.'

'What has that got to do with me not being able to concentrate on the latest Laura Lyndhurst book?'

'Well, it makes sense. You're uncomfortable around Ilan because of that. You know he didn't choke you, and he would never hurt you, but you remember how it felt in your dream.'

That was the crux of the matter, and Jennifer knew Miriam was right. In reality, Ilan would never hurt her. But she couldn't forget the anger in his eyes, the gun pressed against her ribcage and his hand on her throat.

It didn't happen. It was only a dream, and I need to remember that. I need to let it go.

It was a mantra Jennifer often repeated these days, and she needed a better one. Something more motivating.

Her eyes were drawn to the book in front of her. The words taunted her, and Jennifer shook her head to clear the fugue. She turned the pages back and read from the beginning of the chapter.

Half a page later, she gave up and put the book down as she heard the sliding patio door open. Ilan appeared beside her, his vape pen clamped between his teeth, a bottle of wine tucked underneath his arm and two wine glasses in his hand.

'Though you might like a glass of wine to toast your birthday,' he mumbled through his clenched mouth as he sat down beside her.

'I'd love one. Thank you,' Jennifer smiled and reached for the glass he poured for her.

Ilan clinked his glass with hers, wished her a happy birthday, and took a sip. It was cold, crisp and delicious.

'I have a gift for you.' He reached into his pocket, retrieving a black box.

'The keys to my new Lambo?' Jennifer asked with a grin.

'No. Sorry. They didn't have it in your colour.'

'Any colour of Lambo is my colour.'

Ilan gave her the box, and Jennifer opened it.

'It's beautiful.'

She took the necklace out and stared at it. Two rose gold hearts linked together hung from the chain. One was large, masculine and solid. The smaller one was more delicate and feminine and embedded with tiny, perfect diamonds.

Jennifer smiled, and, at the same time, tears welled in her eyes. This was Ilan at his best. Not that he had spent a considerable amount of money on her, but he had bought something meaningful. Despite their problems, their hearts were and always would be linked together, and this was his way of showing her he meant it. A tear trickled down her cheek.

Ilan cupped her face with his hand and wiped the tear away with his thumb.

'Don't cry,' he said.

'I'm not. Not really. I just never expected this. I love it. I love—Thank you so much.'

'So, you're not disappointed about the Lambo?'

Her tears forgotten, Jennifer smiled and shook her head as she watched Ilan puffing on his e-cigarette while a white cloud smelling of strawberries surrounded him.

Jennifer took another sip of wine, closed her eyes and sighed. While all her problems hadn't gone away, she felt more comfortable with Ilan than she had for a while. At least she did right now, and she wondered whether it would last.

'Do you want to put it on?' Ilan asked, and Jennifer heard the hope in his heart.

'Maybe later—or tomorrow.' She felt the distance crawl into her being and stretch between them again with her words.

His silence spoke volumes, and Jennifer couldn't stop the words. She couldn't change the dialogue of their unspoken conversation, and she couldn't even try.

'You know, today was wonderful,' Jennifer said. 'I enjoyed it so much. And that market—wow. I could go there every day. It was amazing, and I can't thank you enough for taking me. But, if you don't mind, I'm going to have a long soak in the bath and an early night. It'll be nice to put my head down and not worry about accidentally disconnecting all the cables they hook me up to.'

I'm looking forward to a decent night's sleep in my own bed.

Jennifer's plans for the rest of the evening were met with stony silence from Ilan. She gave him time to see if he'd respond and when he didn't, she stood up. She left the box with the necklace on the table, picked up her glass of wine and went indoors. She looked back to see Ilan sitting there, sipping his wine.

Chapter 7

After his impromptu discussion with Miriam regarding Jennifer's state of mind, Saul put her out of his mind and spent an hour locked in his office. While the Dream Catcher Programme was the main operation on the go, he still had other equally-as-important assignments to deal with. Some were even more pertinent to the organisation. Several new projects needed his approval, and he studied their details. He approved two immediately and rejected the third one outright. The remainder, five in all, were returned with a request for more information and supporting data. The next file he looked at had been concluded in the last few days. He read it quickly and was pleased with the successful outcome. He signed off on it. And another small-scale but still important battle in the fight against terrorism was officially closed.

Saul worked steadily on updating the reports for two hours. The final one he looked at had just been initiated, and it wasn't up and running but looked promising. If she got her act together, it might require Jennifer's skills. He made a note to that effect and, satisfied with his work, he decided he'd done enough for the day. It was time to make his escape before anything else landed on his desk, and he probably had a five-minute window before that happened. He knew Gavi Levin was looking for him. His curiosity about Dream Catcher was never-ending, and it was only a matter of time before his colleague caught up with him. Saul didn't want to be on the receiving end of Gavi's curiosity, coupled with his superior interrogation skills.

The coast was clear, and Saul got in his car and reversed out of the parking bay. He breathed a sigh of relief when he'd cleared the security gates and turned out of the complex to join the throngs of civilian traffic. He could relax.

He wasn't unhappy with the results they'd received since Dream Catcher went live—Jennifer's ability was remarkable. They were still gathering amazing intelligence and information regarding subjects and situations—but he knew those who controlled the purse strings would always want bigger and better. A few more concrete results, especially a positive outcome from the operation they were currently running, would work wonders for his budget.

But the rest of the day and the evening were for relaxation, Saul decided as he pulled into his driveway. There was a spring in his step that hadn't been there in a long while. He switched off the engine, and at the same time, he mentally switched off from work.

Saul's good mood deflated when he saw the state of the living room. Cardboard boxes were strewn on the floor, and piles of books were everywhere. All kinds of books. He stepped over children's learning books, horror stories and romances. Then he had to circumnavigate crime thrillers and mystery dramas, fiction and non-fiction. The books were scattered over every surface. But it wasn't all bad. He couldn't see any cruise brochures or garden catalogues, and his mood lifted. He was okay as long as she wasn't sorting through reading material to take on a cruise she'd booked as a surprise.

His thoughts were interrupted when his wife Rachel stepped out of their small kitchen. She scrunched a small towel that she was using to dry her hands and looked at Saul with a startled smile.

'Oh, it's you. I heard the door opening and thought it was one of the kids.'

'Are you expecting any of them?' Saul asked. They had five children between them, two sons and three daughters. One daughter from his first marriage, a son and a daughter from Rachel's and a son and a daughter of their own. They were grown up and had children of their own—and all but one of the grandkids were teenagers now. Babysitting was no longer a grandparenting requirement, much to Saul's relief.

'I don't think so. But you know how they show up whenever they feel like it. Especially Yael. She'd be here every day if she could—for the free food. Why are you home so early?'

'No particular reason,' Saul shrugged and glanced around the room with a questioning gesture.

Rachel smiled. 'Sorry about all this. I wasn't expecting you yet. These are donations for the charity book shop we're opening next week, and I've been sorting through them to see which are fit for resale and which ones have to be thrown out. If you give me half an hour, I can clear them away.'

'I'll do it for you. Where do you want me to put them?'

'Thank you. In the spare bedroom would be great. So, you're in a good mood. What are you up to?'

'What? You think I can't be in a good mood without a reason?'

'I didn't say that, Saul. Last year I was convinced you were on the brink of retiring, but now you definitely have a new zest for going to work. But you can't deny there hasn't been much of a sparkle in your eye for the last few weeks. Are you having a workplace affair or something?'

He knew she was joking, but she was right about his mood. She didn't need an answer from him, so he kissed her on the cheek and cleared all the books away for her to sort out later.

When the last pile of books had been banished to the spare room and Saul had reclaimed the couch, Rachel handed him a cup of coffee and sat down beside him. She put her feet up and breathed a happy sigh.

'Do you have to go in tonight?' she asked.

'No. I'm here until tomorrow evening. Why?'

'Just curious. Maybe tomorrow we could go out for the day. I'm feeling good this week and want to go to the garden centre, but I'm not sure I could manage it on my own.'

'Of course,' Saul hated that Rachel suffered from arthritis, and every year it progressed. This past winter had been hard on her. Seeing her swollen knuckles, the stiffness when she walked, and the pain etched on her face broke his heart. But spring and summer were coming, and the dryer air lessened her symptoms. The heat altered them to the point where she could live an almost normal life until winter came around again. The better weather, her prescribed medication, and the CBD oil she took regularly managed the worst. The oil helped her the most, and he often heard her on the phone with her friends, telling them about it and laughing like she used to.

'Without telling you what I'm doing at work, I want to tell you about what I'm doing at work.' He took her hand in his.

'That sounds intriguing. You're going to have to tell me now.'

'It's something different. It's old school and a bit out there. It's so unbelievable that you'd laugh if I could tell you what it is. And you'd worry about my sanity. But I can tell you it is real. It's fascinating and exciting, but at the same time, it's nerve-wracking. You'd love it, Rach. I wish I could tell you about it.'

'But then you'd have to kill me.' Rachel smiled.

Saul laughed. 'Yes. Then I'd have to kill you.'

'I remember the old days so well,' Rachel said as she thought back to her own days in Mossad. She was based extensively in Europe as an agent runner—and an agent herself. 'Mostly because that's how I met you, but also because of the rush. I miss that adrenaline high. I couldn't get enough of it.'

'Yet you quit.'

'Yes. I quit. I fell in love with you and realised that I had to choose between you and my career. It cost me my first marriage, and I couldn't let it happen again. And let's face it, Saul. The job does kill relationships.'

'But not ours, never that.'

'It would have if I'd continued working.'

'Do you ever regret leaving?'

'Always. But it's only as a passing regret. Maybe a bit more than usual today, after seeing the gleam in your eyes and what you've just told me. Without actually telling me anything.'

'I wish I could.'

'I kind of like this thing I do called breathing. So, I'd prefer you tell me nothing. You can take me plant-buying tomorrow as a penance.'

Gardening was Rachel's passion. In her youth, with her sisters—Naomi and Sarah—she had been a lover of all things involving flowers and shrubs. They had all been blessed with green fingers and were often called by friends to rescue neglected plants. They loved to spend an afternoon explaining to a neighbour why his hydrangea wasn't flowering as well as the one two doors down. Said neighbour tended not to ask again. The three sisters weren't averse to taking souvenir cuttings from plants and shrubs whenever they visited formal gardens and parks. Their beds were often well-stocked with their special souvenirs.

But between Rachel's work and raising five children, she had little time to tend to a garden, let alone plan one. But when she retired, and the last of their brood left the nest, she'd taken up her old hobby.

The arthritis was a hindrance, and Rachel got frustrated and angry because she couldn't put as much work into it on her bad days. Saul, who didn't know a dahlia from a dandelion, indulged and helped her as much as he could. Still, he shied away from any interest other than admiring what she created. It was more about relaxing in her garden than understanding how she made it work so well.

That was why he was happy to drive her to the garden centre. He'd display enduring patience walking with her as she decided what she wanted. He'd help her fetch and carry her treasures when she was done—and usually enervated. It could take her three days to recover after planting them out.

'Your wish is my command, my love,' Saul told her and planted a gentle kiss on her cheek.

Chapter 8

The wine, the fresh air, and the warm, relaxing bubble bath she spent an hour luxuriating in made Jennifer drowsy. She was propped up in bed watching a movie on Netflix, but she struggled to keep her eyes open and nodded off every few minutes. A few minutes later, she'd jerk awake in response to a surge in the soundtrack. This time, fifteen minutes had played since the last time she had fallen off the cliff. She tried, but she'd lost it, and the plot made no sense to her. She hit the remote to kill the TV, switched off the bedside light, and lay down, hoping sleep would catch up with her again.

Although she was on the brink of drifting into a light sleep, she was aware of Ilan tiptoeing into the room and slipping into bed beside her.

Jennifer sensed he was naked under the covers. She turned to face him. She wanted to reach for him. But instead of putting his arms around her, he grabbed her and pressed his arm against her throat, cutting off her air.

He demanded that she answer his questions. 'Who are you? Why do you look like my wife?'

Stop it. He didn't choke you. Ilan wouldn't do that. Then why did he try to kill me? That wasn't him. And it isn't him now. You're reliving the dream. I'm not. I'm not even asleep yet. Yes, you are. You do this every night, and it's time for you to get a grip of yourself and get over this. I'm trying. Then do it.

'Do you want a divorce?' Ilan asked. His voice was quiet in the darkness but deadly serious.

'What?' Wide awake, Jennifer's eyes flew open. Any chance of sleeping had flown out of the window with the dream and his words. She pulled away from her husband, sat up in bed, and switched on the lamp.

'What sort of a question is that? Why would you think I want a divorce?'

'Because you can't talk to me. You can barely look at me these days.'

'And that's a reason to divorce you?'

'Maybe. If it's what you want.'

Jennifer heard the sadness in his voice, and it broke her heart.

'I don't want a divorce, Ilan. We've just spent a lovely day together having fun and enjoying ourselves. How can you say I don't talk to you or look at you? I haven't stopped loving you, Ilan. I'm not going to leave you, and I don't want you to leave me.'

'What's wrong then?' Ilan asked.

It was on the tip of Jennifer's tongue to tell him everything. She had no idea how to tell her loving husband

71

how physically frightened she was of him each time she remembered him choking her. It was only her dream, and Ilan didn't know anything about it, and he'd be shocked if she told him. Ilan considered any man who would strike a woman his enemy.

'But you're right. I'm angry and hurt at what you and Saul did. You concocted this scheme between you. I don't know which of you came up with it, but that doesn't matter. The fact that you planned it without a word to me annoys me so much.'

'But it was a successful result. I'd have died if you hadn't come on board with the plan. Saul's plan, by the way. And we successfully foiled a terrorist plot. I don't understand why you can't accept that, celebrate the win and move on.'

Jennifer thumped the pillow with her elbow and glared at him. He didn't get it.

'I know that. But it was the sneaky way you did it that annoys me. You treated me as if I was an agent the pair of you were running. Saul inveigled me into doing it. He played on my love for you, and he only told me what I needed to be told. I didn't know anything about his plan to sacrifice you as long as the mission was completed.'

'But I survived. Thanks to you. I came home. Does anything else matter?'

'You don't understand,' Jennifer punched the pillow again. 'You see everything in black and white. I'm not complaining about you coming home. It was the way I was persuaded to help. You could have been upfront and said you were going on a dangerous mission, and you'd need my help if it all went pear-shaped.'

'Pear-shaped?' Ilan looked confused.

'Yeah. Pear-shaped. It's an expression. It means to fail and go horribly wrong. My dad says it all the time. I'd have been there for you, Ilan. You know I would.'

'Pear-shaped.' Ilan repeated it a few times, trying it on for size. Jennifer suspected he would use it at the first opportunity.

'Do you understand what I'm trying to say, Ilan? I would have been okay with it if you'd told me.'

'That wasn't possible.'

'Why not?'

'You didn't have security clearance.'

'Oh, come on. Saul had me cleared in a couple of hours once I'd signed his precious NDA. Or Official Secrets Act. Or whatever you call it.'

'Yes, but that was after the fact,' Ilan said as he sat up in bed and folded his arms in front of him. 'The mission was coming to its conclusion, and because your role was vital, you were cleared and included.'

'Whatever. I still would have preferred to have been told upfront.'

'I couldn't tell you.'

'Are we going to go back and forward with this all night?' Jennifer asked.

'I'm not. Are you?'

They glared at each other, and Ilan caught her hand and brought it to his lips. He held it as he pressed his lips against her warm skin.

'Please try and understand, Jennifer.'

'I do understand, you know. I just felt so screwed. But I get it, too.'

'Can we go to sleep now?'

'I'm not sure I can. I'm wide awake.'

'Try,' he said as he slid down the bed and turned his head on the pillow.

Jennifer felt proud of herself in the darkness because she hadn't flinched when Ilan put his arm around her again. She switched off the light and lay down with her back to him, not expecting him to hug her. His arm was still there, and she wondered if he was asleep.

'Ilan?'

'What?'

'I think Saul is disappointed with me.' She said it in a quiet voice.

'Huh? Why?'

'He's not getting the results he expected from me.'

'Saul always aims high. He can't expect a hundred per cent success rate from you all the time.'

'I think he does,' Jennifer said and linked her fingers with Ilan's. 'But I'm lucky if I score fifty per cent.'

'It must be more than that.'

'Maybe sixty-five, but that's not good enough for Saul. It's this current case I'm dealing with in particular. I'm getting nowhere with it, and I can't figure out what's wrong.'

'Tell me about it,' Ilan said.

'I can't, or are you cleared for me to read you in?'

'Yes,' Ilan said. He chuckled at the expression she used. To read someone in was a common term in Intelligence Services, but it wasn't widely known in civilian circles. Although with so many spy movies and TV shows, it was more common than he realised. 'I can assure you that I'm cleared for you to read me in. My security clearance is a lot higher than yours.'

'Is this a mine-is-bigger-than-yours contest?' Jennifer asked.

'No. You can tell me, and you won't have to kill me afterwards. Unless you want to kill me?'

In the darkness, with her head on his shoulder and his arms around her, she told him about the case that was frustrating everyone.

'The target's a mid-level diplomat,' she began in a hushed voice. 'He has some access to classified material. Saul and the team are convinced he's been turned and is passing on the material. Saul didn't tell me who he was passing it to, though. Apparently, telling me too much can skew my interpretations of the dreams. Anyway, I've been trying hard to find out what he's up to, but all I'm getting are fragments of normal things. He dreams a lot about fishing and writing a novel one day. He has the occasional nightmare of being in a plane crash. Apparently, he is scared of flying—it was in his file—and it seems to be a flashback nightmare that stems from a turbulent flight when he was younger. He doesn't dream about passing anything on to anyone. Which makes me think he isn't doing it in real life.'

'If he is, why would he dream about it?' Ilan asked.

'Because the dream process is the brain dealing with the multitude of experiences bombarding it every day. It compartmentalises everything into it needs and files it all away like a storage computer. It would overload if it didn't. And something like this, being a traitor, would definitely be something he'd dream about.'

Jennifer remembered her dream in which Lucy had a conversation, first with her doctor and then with her best friend, Claire, about the same subject. Claire commented about the brain doing its housework and tidying everything away. Jennifer thought it was an apt way to describe the process.

'We dream more than we realise, Ilan. And we dream things that we don't understand. That's why the ones we do remember can seem so mixed up. The brain knows all the details, but we only get the edited highlights. That's where I come in. I can sneak into somebody's dream, poke around and find out what their brain is collating.'

'Does your subject have to be asleep? Perhaps he suffers from insomnia?'

'Nearly always. But once or twice, I've seen somebody who isn't asleep. It's tricky, and I'm not very good at controlling it. Although I did it with you, I didn't do it intentionally. But it happened when I thought you'd been shot. You were awake, and I was able to watch what you were doing. Okay, I got it wrong, thinking it was you on the receiving end of the gun. Trust me to get it arse-about-tit. But, I said, I'm not good at controlling it when my subject isn't asleep.'

'How is that possible?' Ilan asked, and Jennifer could hear awe or fear in his voice.

'I don't have a bloody clue. Maybe Nathan could explain it, but I can't. It just happens. One little bump on the head, and the next thing you know, I have a superpower. If I was a character in a cartoon, I'd be called Daphne DeDreamer, and I'd wear a lacy nightgown instead of a cape.'

'Now, that I can imagine.' Ilan kissed her shoulder. His hand rested on her hip, and Jennifer could almost feel the old desire for him awakening in her. Almost.

'But superpower or not,' Jennifer said. 'I still can't get a handle on what this guy is up to.'

'Is he married? Does he have a family or close friends?'

'Yeah, he's married. I don't know about close friends, though. He's got three kids, but they're all under ten. Why?'

'Maybe it's not him. If everyone dreams, and he isn't dreaming about passing on classified materia, in that case, he's innocent, and someone else is obtaining the information from him, most likely without his knowledge. Check out his wife. Or, indeed, anyone he is close to.'

'Oh, you are a bloody genius,' Jennifer said as she gave an impressed whistle. 'I can see why they made you an officer.'

'No. I've just been in this game a lot longer than you,' Ilan told her, and his arms tightened around her. 'Now, can we please get some sleep?'

Chapter 9

Jennifer smiled. She had been watching her subject from behind a rack of summer dresses for the last twenty minutes, and although she was enjoying herself immensely, she needed him to make contact with his handler. If he didn't do it very soon, she'd be getting arrested for loitering. She kept an eye on him as she pretended to browse the dresses, flicking through them and lifting one off the hanger, holding it out in front of her and then against her as though she was considering whether to buy it. It wasn't her style or colour—in truth, none of them was—so she put it back and pretended to check out a different style.

Her subject was an elderly man. He was in his late sixties or early seventies. He was short—about five foot six with stooped shoulders and an unruly, almost demented, mop of white hair that no comb could ever control. He put Jennifer in mind of Albert Einstein, and the resemblance was enforced by the fact that he was wearing a black suit. He resembled an old black and white photo of the German-born theoretical physicist. The only difference was that Einstein had a moustache, and this guy was clean-shaven. Plus, Einstein was not the kind of guy to wander through a clothing store, bypassing the men's section, and make his way to the women's lingerie rails. He would wait for his handler there and pass on classified and extremely sensitive government secrets.

Jennifer considered the possibility that her Albert Einstein lookalike wasn't a traitor giving away vital secrets but just an old pervert. Perhaps he enjoyed the feel of a pair of lace panties between his finger and thumb. But while he looked as though he was rifling through the various underwear sets on display, Jennifer noticed how his eyes darted around as though he was looking for somebody. And that somebody had not made an appearance yet.

While she was watching Albert, she saw the sales assistant was hovering nearby and paying attention to her. Jennifer frowned. An imaginary person in Albert's dream could see her. It wasn't the first time it had happened, but it was rare, and she didn't know why it popped up every now and then. She would prefer not to experience it, but there was nothing she could do apart from ignoring it. She rummaged through another rack of dresses, lifted one and held it against her body. She admired it, then frowned and put it back. Her hips swayed as she checked the length, colour and style and pretended to decide whether it would suit her. She caught the woman watching her again, and she smiled and shrugged her shoulders in an, I can't make up my mind, gesture.

The woman smiled back in understanding and went back to her place by the sales counter.

It's not like she's busy. She's probably just bored. It's a pity because a few more customers would keep her watchful eye off me. God, I feel like a shoplifter. I'm actually beginning to feel guilty.

With one eye on Albert, who was frowning and seemed to be muttering to himself as though debating which nightgown to buy, Jennifer moved to another section where she could still keep him in her peripheral vision but look as though she was browsing. Two more customers came in—a woman and a man. Jennifer's senses pricked up, and she watched them discretely as they walked towards Albert.

After a quick glance at the clothing, the woman frowned and screwed her face up. When they veered off, it was obvious that she was just another shopper who couldn't decide what to buy.

Jennifer was outstaying her welcome. Soon, she'd have to buy something or leave—shit or get off the pot. She pretended to look at shoes, handbags, scarves, coats, jackets, dresses and trousers. She was running out of options and would be in hardware if she kept moving back. Not to mention out of sight of Albert. And all the while, people came and went. Some bought items and left carrying bags with the name of the department store blatantly advertised on both sides. Others couldn't make up their minds and left empty-handed. But none of them came near Albert. He didn't make contact with anyone—neither eye contact nor verbal contact. Not even a 'Hello,' or an 'Excuse me.'

While Jennifer enjoyed a shopping spree, this one was losing its appeal. She couldn't actually purchase anything because this was a dream. Even if she saw something that she liked, it probably didn't exist in real life and was just a figment of Albert the Possible Perv's imagination. She was getting nowhere with her target, and she was bored. Added to that were frustration and annoyance because it looked like she would have another failure to take back to Saul.

Jennifer was about to call it quits and walk back through the door—in this dream, it was the fire exit to her left. She'd wake up and try to explain another dream that produced no results. Her ruminations stopped, and she was on alert. She saw a man striding towards Albert—he was moving too fast. Was this going to be a hit? It looked as though he was going to take the old man out. She put the jacket she was holding back on its hanger and watched him. Then something told her this was Albert's contact.

The man was the opposite of him. Whereas Albert was small and elderly, this guy was big and young. He was overweight but not obese. His hair was black and tidy compared to Albert's wayward white mess. His features reminded Jennifer of the actor who played Tony Soprano. It was an unlikely combination—the physicist and the Mafia boss.

Albert stopped dawdling. He moved with purpose and made his way to the men's coats, where he tried one on for size. Jennifer let out a sigh of relief. Albert was very aware of the other man because Jennifer saw him glancing at him and keeping him in his line of sight. But he didn't seem concerned or alarmed by him. He shrugged his shoulders, tugged the sleeves, buttoned the jacket up, and put his hands in his pockets. He turned in front of the mirror. His hands were still in the pockets. Mark made—his decision not to buy the coat was also made. He unbuttoned it, hung it up, and walked out of the shop.

Jennifer knew from her briefing to ignore the man she called Albert and concentrate on the new guy—Tony Soprano. He played the same game for a few minutes, and she followed him with her eyes as he checked out the shoes and the hats. He glanced around the store once, then went to the men's coats, where he selected the same one Albert had tried on. He didn't try it on. It wouldn't fit him, but he slipped his hand in the left pocket, withdrew something, and slipped it into his coat. He put the jacket back on the rack and left by the same door.

And that is it. God, that got boring very quickly. Time to wake up and put them all to sleep with the details of my exciting dream.

While Jennifer was dreaming her way through a large department store, Saul sat down and sorted the files he wanted to deal with this morning. He switched on the desk monitor. Jennifer was still asleep, but it was seven-thirty, and she would be awake soon, hopefully with good news. They needed a result. Something concrete to justify the money they were spending. They'd had three amazing results recently and several good tips that led to arrests. Since then, they'd only picked up a few useful snippets that were nothing world-changing. It wouldn't help his argument for increased funding, especially now that the world was on the brink of shutting down. The Covid-19 pandemic was spreading across the globe at an ever-increasing rate. It was this, rather than terrorism or crime, that was uppermost in everyone's thoughts. It was all people talked about and was the subject of every department meeting.

It will blow over soon. In a week or two. Maybe a month. Hopefully.

Or would it? Saul couldn't say if all the worst-case scenarios and disaster movies over the years were correct, and 2020 was going to be the year the world changed forever.

At some stage, the government would have to decide what to do. But, at the moment, they were only initiating a fourteen-day self-isolation rule for travellers coming from certain countries. It might be enough if people were sensible and did what they were told—stay indoors, avoid contact. The same advice as would be given during an ordinary flu outbreak.

Despite this threat, life carried on. The trains were still running, the sun still rose in the east and set in the west, and the war on terror still raged.

Movement on the monitors caught his attention. He saw Jennifer yawning. She was waking up, and he sent off a text message to Nathan that their subject was sitting up and wondering why nobody had brought her a coffee. This was Nathan's cue that Jennifer didn't need his assistance, and he could go home.

Nathan replied with several emojis, and the only one Saul could identify was a smiley face and possibly a little car. He had no interest in attempting to interpret the rest of them, but he got the gist of the message—Nathan was delighted to be going home.

Saul went to the sleep room, where Jennifer was dressed. She'd made a pot of coffee and was already at the workstation and about to type up her report. She smiled as he walked in the door.

'That was boring, Saul. Where are the fast cars and gun battles you promised me?'

'I never promised you anything of the sort.'

'I know. I'm just messing with you. But it was boring. Want a coffee?'

'Yes, todah,' Saul nodded. 'Did you get a result?'

'I did indeed,' Jennifer said, and she spent the next ten minutes telling Saul everything that had happened in her dream. He laughed when she described her subject as an Albert Einstein lookalike but was confused when she called the other man Tony Soprano.

'I'll buy you the box set.'

Jennifer laughed as Saul gave her a blank stare.

'It was a television show about a mafia boss called Tony Soprano and his family. Ilan and I binge-watched the whole series, and we loved it.'

'And you say our subject's contact looked like the man in this television series?' Saul brought the conversation back to the matter in hand.

'Yeah, up to a point. I mean, he wasn't a dead ringer, but I thought of that actor when I saw him. It's a trick Ilan taught me. Since I was fast-tracked into this, I had to learn some basic spycraft. He taught me to look for recognisable characteristics in a person's facial features—hairstyle and colour, eyebrows, jawline shape, and stuff like that. But he said that because it takes a while to learn, I should look for something familiar in my subject, so that's what I do. I see who they look like rather than building up a photofit description because I'm not trained enough to do that. So, last night, I saw Albert Einstein and Tony Soprano in my dream. I know it sounds daft, but it works for me.'

'Actually, that makes perfect sense. So, Ilan is helping you with this? How are things with you two? I expect you're glad to have him home again.'

'Everything's great. Just super. He's home safe and well. Now that he's retired from service, I don't have to worry about him getting into danger,' Jennifer said, with a cheerful smile as false as the alien autopsy footage. But less grainy.

She knew Saul was aware she was lying and was tempted to question her, but it was none of his business if it didn't interfere with her work. She would tell him that if he opened his mouth to ask.

'Okay,' he said. 'As soon as you type up your report, you can go home.'

'Great. I'm afraid it isn't going to make for exciting reading, but at least we got a result.'

'We did. This time. But we're getting nowhere with your other case.'

'Actually, Saul, I want to talk to you about that. Can you spare a few more minutes?'

His hand was on the door handle, but he stopped, and his long-suffering sigh was only a small one. 'Go ahead.'

Jennifer explained what Ilan had suggested—how the subject might have passed information to an acquaintance without even realising that he was doing it. And it was very possible that this was how the data was being leaked.

'Ilan said we should look into his family and friends,' Jennifer told him.

'Good point. I'll have someone look into the backgrounds of the people around him. Thank you, Jennifer. Oh, just one other thing. I trust you haven't discussed your involvement here with anybody else?'

'Of course not—and only with Ilan because he has high-level clearance.'

She had the impression he would say more and regretted letting him know that she'd discussed the details of her work with her husband.

I should have pretended it was my idea, not Ilan's. Bugger that. Why should I? Ilan has a much higher security clearance than me. Why shouldn't I talk about my work at home? It's not like we're blabbering about it in a crowded restaurant.

But Saul merely gave her a nod, opened the door and left her alone to finish her report.

Jennifer turned back to the laptop and typed. Her fingers flew over the keyboard as she rushed to get it down. She only paused to refresh her memory of the dream or take a sip of coffee, which was cold.

Her dream had been uneventful, apart from the actual meet, drop, or whatever the correct term was in the language of spies. So, her report consisted of a page and a bit. She saved it to the relevant, password-protected folder, where Saul would read it, and powered down the laptop. A quick wash of the coffee mugs, and she was ready to go.

But where? Home?

Jennifer sighed as she put on her jacket. The thought of going home and seeing Ilan, even though things were better between them, still didn't fill her with much joy.

Chapter 10

The mug of coffee stopped halfway to his mouth as Ilan read the alert on his phone with a frown.

'What is it?' Jennifer asked.

'Turn on the television. There's something, an update maybe, about this virus, and the Prime Minister is about to speak live.'

Her coffee forgotten, Jennifer picked up the remote. Ilan perched on the arm of the couch on the opposite end and scrolled through his phone.

'It's something about restrictions on movement,' he said as they waited for the press conference to come on.

'Do you mean putting us into a quarantine? Like they've done in Italy?'

'I don't know, possibly.' Before Jennifer could ask him what he meant, he disappeared into the kitchen and returned with a fresh coffee and his vape pen. He parked himself back on the arm of the couch.

Jennifer's leg jiggled with nerves as she waited. The international news had been terrible for a few weeks. Only a couple of cases were reported in Israel. It seemed to be under control, and the general opinion was there was nothing to worry about. And then the cases increased.

Is it serious now?

She didn't know, but she had a feeling it wasn't good. She chewed a piece of skin on the side of her thumbnail and then progressed to the nail itself. She realised what she was doing and dropped her hands to her lap, where she tried to keep them still but failed.

Aware of her agitation, Ilan slid down onto the seat and shuffled over until he was beside her. He caught her hand and gave it a reassuring squeeze as the prime minister appeared in front of the cameras. Jennifer grabbed the remote, turned up the volume, and listened to what he had to say in a tense silence.

'Well, that wasn't so bad,' Jennifer said as she muted the volume. 'As it's a virus, it makes sense to keep a safe distance. Less cross-contamination means it'll run its course, won't it?'

Ilan grunted non-committedly.

'Won't it?'

'I don't know, Jennifer. We can only wait and see how it plays out.'

He got to his feet and patted the pockets of his jeans, then frowned.

'What are you looking for?'

'My wallet.'

'It's on the cabinet in the bedroom. Why?'

'Make a grocery list of all the things we'll need if we stay indoors for a week or two.'

'You're kidding. Right?'

'No. We should go to the store and stock up on essentials. You heard what he said.'

'Okay. I'll get my coat.' He was taking this way too far.

It's just a nasty flu bug, hardly the apocalypse. But if I don't go, he'll be off on a survival rant, and I'll do it if it keeps the peace. Besides, we're out of a lot of groceries.

Three hours later, Jennifer gave a sigh of relief as she closed the door on the over-stuffed cupboard and wondered if it was too early for a glass of red.

She had followed Ilan as he pushed his trolley—he insisted they had one each. They trudged the aisles, and she tried her best not to laugh at the image of her secret agent husband awkwardly steering a shopping trolley. Domestication did not sit well on his shoulders.

But he was determined to buy as much as possible, and the trolley was brimming. They prioritised canned goods, including cat food and dry goods like pasta and rice. They bought multi-packs of toilet rolls, household cleaning products, anti-bacterial wipes, and hand sanitiser gel.

'This many toilet rolls? Seriously?'

He nodded at other shoppers, grabbing the toilet rolls off the shelves. As Jennifer looked around, she saw more people in the store than usual. Everybody had a trolley filled to the brim, and most people were wearing disposable masks.

Maybe Ilan is right. We should stock up, just in case.

She made for the alcohol section and selected several bottles of her favourite wines and a good selection of beer and whiskey for Ilan. Then she added a bottle of gin and several bottles of tonic.

Essentials. Right?

After they'd packed their shopping into the car, Ilan suggested getting lunch nearby.

'Are you sure? Don't you want to get back to the bunker before the hordes of zombies cut off our escape routes and bear down on us?'

He tapped his phone and told her they still had an hour before the infected turned.

'Lunch it is, then,' Jennifer smiled.

Every cupboard in the house was filled to the brim with food. Stacked against a garage wall were boxes with both wet and dry cat food and several bags of cat litter. It was enough to last a couple of months, and Jennifer reckoned they'd only need to go out again for fresh food. There was enough booze, and Ilan had stocked up on his vape juice flavours. Anything else he could buy online. He sat on the sofa, with his feet on the coffee table and his laptop balanced on his legs. She looked over his shoulder to see what he was doing. The numpty was ordering a new freezer, so he could stock up on meat and frozen vegetables if necessary.

This is crazy. You do this if you're expecting a cruel winter in Montana or waiting for a nuclear war. The government had limited gatherings to no more than a hundred people—that was it, nothing else. But the world had gone mad—viral, even.

I can't believe Ilan is going over the top on this. Does he know something the government isn't telling us?

Jennifer sat in front of the television and switched on the evening news. She surfed all the channels, giving each five minutes before selecting the next one. It wasn't good news. Every programme talked about the virus and speculated about infection rates and death tolls. It made for grim listening, and she curled up underneath a throw as she watched.

'We'll be okay,' Ilan handed her a glass of wine and sat beside her.

'I hope so. The reported cases are predominantly people returning from cruises. Those ships are floating Petri dishes for bugs at the best of times. As far as countries are concerned, the worst-hit nation is southeast Asia, so it's not as if it's rife here in Israel. They should quarantine all the visitors and let the rest of us get on with our lives. Part of me thinks this is blown out of proportion because it's only travellers who've been infected, but it still feels disturbing and very frightening. We've seen it in movies, and we know real life isn't like that. Or at least it wasn't until now. It's not that serious, is it? Like disaster movie serious.'

'It probably isn't,' Ilan said. 'But it makes sense to cut back on social interaction for a while.'

'At least I don't have to work for a day or two unless Saul calls me for something urgent, so we can hunker down here.'

'He won't want you in. He'll be busy with this trouble, so let's wait and see what happens. Do you want some more wine?'

'Yes, please.'

Ilan filled her wine glass to the brim. His was filled with whiskey and one lonely ice cube. They might as well make an evening of it watching the news and getting nicely drunk.

Chapter 11

Saul said the restrictions didn't go far enough, and someone in the government agreed. Four days later, the limit
on meeting people was reduced from a hundred to ten,
and they were advised to keep a distance of no less than
two metres apart.

Life went on, albeit within the necessary restrictions in
place. It had to. And Saul had no intention of postponing
their work with Jennifer. It was vital to the country's
security, and he would do what he could to ensure it
remained classified as such. To that end, he had a meeting
scheduled with the director the following day. They had
no operations listed for the next three days, and Saul
would spend the time at home with Rachel to allay her
fears.

He caught her watching him from her favourite place
in the garden. It was where she sat in the sunshine, surrounded by her beautiful flowers, and where she went
when she needed peace. This corner of the garden had
all the colours and scents, the birds and the insects. Some

shrubs shaded her from the sun's heat and sheltered her from the cold in winter. It was her happy place—her Eden. She would sit with a coffee and a good book. Today she was using the Kindle he bought her for her birthday. She was dubious about whether she would like it. She preferred a good old-fashioned paperback. But, when he showed her how to buy and download books, she loved it

Her garden corner was much more than just a place to relax. It was where she came when she was troubled and afraid for the future and when she was in pain. She insisted there was something magical in the earth at this corner of their garden, and it healed her spirit and eased her aches and pains. She said it settled her mind and her soul.

She had been sitting out there for two hours. Saul knew she was concerned by the news bulletins. She hadn't said much, but he could tell by the pinched lips and the worried frown.

He turned away and went into the kitchen. He couldn't say anything to ease her mind, so he did the next best thing and made a cup of her favourite herbal tea.

He took it out to her with a crocheted shawl.

'Oh, thank you,' Rachel said.

'I don't want you to get a chill.'

'Where's your tea?'

'You expect me to drink that hippy muck? Not a chance. I'm having this,' Saul said as he pulled a beer bottle from the back pocket of his trousers.

'It's not even two o'clock in the afternoon, Saul. Isn't it a bit early?'

'It's five o'clock somewhere in the world, and it is only a beer. The sun is over the yardarm or something. What are you reading?'

'It's called *Waiting in Wattlevale*. I bought it ages ago, but I'm only getting around to reading it now.'

'And?'

'It's about a retirement community in rural Australia.'

'And do you like it?' Saul asked with a raised eyebrow. Rachel's taste in literature ranged from spy novels, where she could laugh at the inaccuracies, to historical novels and some of the classics. And a lot of non-fiction books.

'I love it. It's funny and sad, and I feel I know the characters. The descriptions of life in Australia—I'm not sure where, but it's a rural setting—are amazing. Why didn't we ever visit there? It's a shame we never got around to it.'

'We might. One day.'

'We could take a cruise.' Rachel's eyes danced with laughter as she watched his reaction to the word cruise. It never failed.

'Hell would freeze over before you got me aboard one of those floating Petri dishes. Especially now.'

'What if I held a gun to your head?' Rachel smiled.

'I would prefer to be shot. I think it'll be a long time before anyone travels by sea or air again. There's talk of them closing the ports.'

'Will you stay at home for a while now that we're in lockdown?'

'No. We're still operating as normal but under strict procedures—masks, hand sanitisers and social distancing, at all times.'

'Please be careful, Saul.'

'Of course,' he said and patted her hand.

Chapter 12

'Shit.' Jennifer muttered under her breath as she peered around the corner and saw the car's tail lights reversing out of the car park. There was no way she could follow him. Not on foot.

Then she remembered the object in the pocket of her jacket. She pulled it out but struggled to see it in the darkness. She turned it over, and it felt similar to her own car key. A remote keyless entry device. She pressed one of the buttons with her thumb, praying it wasn't the alarm. Two short beeps sounded a few meters away, and the orange indicator lights of a nearby parked car flashed once.

Bingo. Jennifer opened the door and climbed in. A grin worthy of a delighted Cheshire cat spread across her face as she sank into the Ferrari's luxurious leather seat.

Despite the circumstances, Jennifer felt a thrill that was definitely sexual. She pushed the start button, and the 3.9-litre twin-turbo V8 engine came to life with a deep, throaty rumble that hinted at power and speed.

It was brand spanking new—with less than a thousand kilometres on the clock. It was the height of supercar luxury, and it was drop-dead sexy.

She would never admit it to anyone, not even Ilan, but she was aroused. Well, maybe she would admit it to Ilan. He loved fast cars, so he'd most likely get it.

That's all very well sitting here thinking sexy thoughts about a car, but I have work to do. I have to catch up to this guy and find out where he's going and what he's up to.

Jennifer reversed out of the parking place and left the car park. She took a left turn, the same direction as the man she was following, and floored the accelerator pedal.

The powerful engine did what was asked of it. The specifications said it took three seconds to reach sixty miles per hour from zero. Jennifer was flying down the road. The sleek beauty lived up to what the sales brochures promised. The top was down, and the wind was in her hair. She wished she was wearing her red dress and her diamond earrings. A fur coat, fake, of course, and a platinum credit card in her purse wouldn't go amiss either. But she was wearing her jeans, a lightweight jacket and trainers. She didn't look like someone who should be driving a super-cool Ferrari. Heels and a sexy dress were useless for following someone on a cold night, and she had taught herself to dream that she was dressed appropriately.

The car's top speed was a hundred and ninety-nine miles per hour. There was little or no traffic around, and Jennifer would love to have floored the accelerator to take it to the limit. She had grown up around cars and watched people racing them. She always wondered what it felt like to control a vehicle at its top speed. But she'd never dared do it and didn't trust her ability. She'd been given a birthday voucher from her brother for a two-day rally course. Leaping at the chance, she'd spent the first day driving an old rally MK11 Ford Escort around a gravel track as the instructor shouted instructions at her into her helmet radio, and thankfully, he didn't scream in terror too much. The second day was the same—he told her what to do and when to do it as she tried to go fast around the track. She was in a modern Mitsubishi Evo this time, and it was easier to drive than the Escort but not as much fun. It was more a rally experience event than an actual training session, but it was fun and very cool. She had learned some things about driving from the gruelling two days. The most important lesson she took away from the experience was that she hadn't, and never would have, the talent to ever contemplate racing in any form. There was no shame in being a spectator.

Nothing from those two days many years ago was useful to Jennifer now, but that didn't matter. She was on the road with no other traffic, and the car she was in stuck to the surface like glue. She had to keep her foot on the accelerator pedal and steer—simples. The powerful engine, the near-perfect suspension and the traction control did the rest for her. She spotted the car her target was driving, and she concentrated on catching up to follow him.

When the car stopped, the driver got out, walked a short distance, and then turned a corner into an alleyway.

Jennifer had no choice but to pull over and abandon the Ferrari at the side of the road. She followed her subject on foot.

After fifty metres, he stopped and turned as though he'd changed his mind and was going back to his car. Jennifer ducked into a doorway beside a rancid-smelling dumpster. While he couldn't see her, she had a clear line of sight, and she breathed through her mouth to avoid the stink of rotting meat and vegetables while she watched him.

Under the glow of the street lights, she saw her subject appear indecisive. He seemed agitated and nervous. She watched him scratching his head and glancing at his watch, looking furtive.

Well, doing what you're doing—betraying your country—will make you nervous. All that guilt and the fear of getting caught isn't good for the constitution, sweetheart.

But it wasn't the guilt or the fear of getting caught that made him nervous. Jennifer saw it was anticipation. She realised it as soon as his handler stepped out of the shadows, and the two men embraced. Her eyebrows shot up in startled surprise when she watched the embrace turn into a lingering kiss, and she felt a moment of sadness for the man who was betraying his country for love. Or for what he perceived love to be.

Jennifer waited for the handover.

Why do espionage and sex go hand-in-hand so often? I have to watch lovers in a steamy embrace, knowing that one is only there to garner knowledge and the other is being led up the garden path.

It was something that had crossed her mind on several occasions. Even in spy movies, it always boiled down to sex, no matter what the situation. Someone wanted it, and someone else used it to get something they wanted. She tried not to think of Ilan working that way. Had he ever seduced someone to gain knowledge? If he had, and most likely he had, she didn't want to know.

It's best not to go there. Ever. Those thoughts are dangerous.

While she was trying not to think about Ilan having to seduce some woman—or man—in the line of duty, Jennifer watched her target and his lover. They had stopped smooching and were engaged in muted conversation. Her target reached into his pocket and withdrew what looked like a compact disc.

How very old fashioned. All the best traitors use flash drives these days.

He handed it over, and his lover slipped it into the inside pocket of his jacket. The lover walked away, but Jennifer's target grabbed him by the sleeve and pulled him back. The lover shook him off in anger. She could tell from their body language that her man didn't want the rendezvous to end, but his lover was having none of it and prised the fingers off his jacket. He must have said something because the fight left her man and his shoulders slumped in defeat. The lover turned and jogged away. He had what he came for.

Jennifer stepped out from behind the dumpster, opened the rear door of the nearby restaurant, and walked through it.

Chapter 13

Jennifer opened her eyes and sat up in bed as the morning light sneaked in through a gap in the heavy blinds. It wasn't real, but she fancied she could still smell the dumpster and its contents in her nostrils and on her skin. She put the coffee on to brew and hit the shower.

Feeling clean and refreshed, she sat at the desk and sipped her coffee. She typed her report, and as always, she was amazed at how much detail she remembered. She felt sad for the guy who thought someone loved him but was only using him for his own ends.

She finished her report with a note about how driving a Ferrari, even if it was only in a dream, was great fun and emailed it to Saul. He'd told her the previous day that he wouldn't be in the office that morning.

Finished in record time, Jennifer took a few moments to relax over her coffee and thought about her dream. She didn't normally do that and preferred to forget. The mission stayed in the building when she left and it didn't do to take the dream memories home with her. Once finished, she was done until she moved on to the next case Saul gave her. This dream left her feeling melancholy, and she thought about the man meeting his lover who abused him to obtain state secrets.

She marvelled at how detailed the dreams were. It was amazing how much people who felt guilty for something dreamed about it.

She had mentioned it to Miriam when they met up for socially-distanced coffee once a week after the lockdown ended. Although Jennifer kept her conversations about Ilan vague and casual, they chatted about the weather, the pandemic, and their husbands. She was still reluctant to divulge her issues with the therapist. Miriam was happy to talk about her husband. He had been home for a while before disappearing to the Antarctic again.

'I put it down to guilt,' Miriam told her after their coffees were served and the waiter was out of hearing.

'How so?' Jennifer asked.

Miriam flicked her long dark hair over her shoulder as she thought about how best to answer Jennifer's question.

'Well, it's speculative because nobody knows exactly why we dream. Several theories, such as the evolutionary one, suggest dreams are a safe way to learn how to deal with challenging situations. Then there's the memory-consolidation theory which suggests they are a by-product of organising your memories in response to what someone has learned throughout the day. Both theories have one big common denominator. When we're anxious, we dream more or remember our dreams more often. It's a way of coping with stressful circumstances and new information. This is in line with another theory of dreaming known as the mood regulatory function of dreams theory, where the purpose of dreams is to problem-solve emotional issues.'

'This is fascinating. But how does it relate to my subjects dreaming so much about their crimes?'

'Freud came up with the idea that dreams are a window into our subconscious. They reveal your unconscious desires, thoughts and motivations. It isn't hard to extrapolate that your subjects use their dreams to deal with what they're going through in their lives. If someone is selling state secrets, their guilt is buried when they're awake, but it manifests in sleep. And so they dream about it. Somehow it normalises it in their minds. They compartmentalise it to cope, and it lets them get on with their lives in a way that doesn't eat them up.'

Jennifer nodded. 'I can see that makes sense. I just didn't think they'd dream about their guilt in so much depth.'

'I'm not an expert, and dreaming isn't something I've studied in-depth. But I've been reading up on it since I met you and got involved in Dream Catcher. Another theory is that the purpose of dreams is to help store memories—important ones—and dispose of anything irrelevant. They sort through complicated thoughts and feelings, which tie in with my assumption that dreams help alleviate the dreamer's guilt.'

'So how am I dreaming their guilt?' Jennifer asked. 'I get into their minds when they sleep and see what they are doing in their dreams? And why? Why me?'

'Honestly? I have no idea, Jennifer. I'm not an expert on dreams. I hardly know anything about them other than what I've read. They're not my field. But I've spoken to a few people, in confidence, about what you are experiencing, and they think lucid dreaming and remote viewing is a latent trait in all of us. They reckon your head injury activated something in your brain. It allowed your mind to open up and be accessible to installing yourself in other people's dreams and experience what they are dreaming. Tell me, have you ever tried it outside of Dream Catcher? Maybe with Ilan?'

'Why on earth would I go into Ilan's dreams?' Jennifer wondered why Miriam was taking their conversation in this direction.

'No reason other than curiosity. I'm speaking as a friend right now. I know you want to try and mend your relationship with him. You've said things are better, but you're not there yet. Maybe, if you went into his dreams, you could see how he's feeling, and it's possible you could find out how troubled he is because of the issues you're going through.'

'Or I could find out that he's pissed off and thinking of leaving me.'

'That is highly unlikely, my dear. He's told you he loves you and he bought you that lovely necklace for your birthday. The one you're wearing today and, correct me if I'm wrong, but don't you wear it every day?'

Jennifer smiled as she touched the necklace with the two entwined hearts.

'I guess so.'

'Those aren't the actions of a man planning to leave his spouse,' Miriam continued. 'But a little poke around in his subconscious might be interesting. Even fun.'

'No. I won't be going into Ilan's dreams. No way. I'd be afraid of what I might find. In some cases—especially in my case—someone's thoughts and feelings are best left in their dreams.'

Miriam grinned. 'Which is kinda the antithesis of Dream Catcher, and I wouldn't let Saul hear you saying that.'

Jennifer finished her coffee, and her mind was still on what Miriam had said during their last get-together a few weeks ago. The government restrictions to slow the rising cases of Covid-19 meant that all but the basic facilities were closed again. They couldn't meet up for their weekly chats anymore, and Jennifer missed the psychiatrist. They talked on the phone, and between phone calls, they sent texts and WhatsApp messages. Jennifer and Miriam spoke almost every day, but it wasn't the same. The women had become best friends, and Jennifer felt alone without her company. She missed the delicious coffee and lunches in the tucked-away cafés that Miriam always found for them.

At least they had some contact, and it was a welcome break from the constant news reports regarding the pandemic sweeping the world. Although they were getting on a lot better, it was a welcome break from Ilan.

They had to. Being cooped up in the house together with only each other for company, they realised they had no choice. So, after a few days of arguments over what to watch on television, which room to re-decorate first or whose turn it was to cook, they settled down into a routine that worked well for them.

Jennifer discovered reading again, and she bought dozens of eBooks online. So many that her old iPad was running out of space and hardly worked properly. She downloaded them onto Ilan's device, and he complained that he had to spend ages searching through them to find his own books.

Ilan had nipped out after lunch to get fish and fresh vegetables for dinner, and when he came home, he handed her a carrier bag. Jennifer looked inside. It was a new device for reading.

'It's a good one,' he said. 'You can read outside in the sunshine, and there's no glare from the screen. Look, I've transferred all your books onto it for you.'

'Oh, Ilan, thank you,' Jennifer smiled and gave him a kiss on the cheek. 'I hated squinting and trying to read in the sun. Thank you so much.'

Then Ilan's arms were around her, and the gift he bought her was forgotten as she felt the warmth of his body against hers. He pulled her to him, his lips found hers, and he kissed her tenderly. Jennifer tasted a mixture of mint toothpaste and coffee, and she felt her body responding to the demands of his mouth. She was about to break free from his embrace and lead him to their bedroom when her phone rang.

'Shit.' They both uttered the word simultaneously as the moment was ruined by the insistent tinny sound of her ringtone.

She reluctantly broke away to answer it and saw the bulge in Ilan's jeans that told her how much he wanted her. Her body said the feeling was mutual.

She caught his hand and held on to it, not letting him put any distance between them, as she answered the phone and tried not to sound out of breath.

'Saul? Hi. No, I wasn't doing anything important.' She rolled her eyes.

Like hell, I wasn't. I was only about to get into bed with my husband and make love to him for the rest of the afternoon.

'Um, no. If it isn't urgent, can it wait until tomorrow night? I've had a few glasses of wine.'

She hadn't, but the lie was believable. Everyone drank away their lockdown afternoons these days.

'No. It isn't urgent. Tomorrow it is then. I'll see you at nine for the briefing,' Saul replied.

Ilan was laughing when she cleared the call.

'What? What's so funny?'

'You won't see him tomorrow night if I kill him first.'

'I know. His timing. Maybe later?' Jennifer suggested.

'Why not now?'

Saul had killed the mood. Even though she wanted Ilan for the first time in a long while. And what annoyed her was that it had been spontaneous. It wasn't planned, forced or contrived. It had just happened, and she was ready for it. But one second after her phone rang, the moment passed.

But at least I wanted him. And he wanted me. That's a beginning. Isn't it? Of course, it is. Okay, the call from Saul ruined it, but there's a lot to build on. We'll just wait for the right moment again and go for it.

'I'm sorry. Saul might as well have thrown a bucket of cold water over me. Let's have a relaxing afternoon and a tasty dinner, then we can pick up where we left off this evening. A slow burn and a hot date. How does that sound?'

'You could wear your Daphne DeDreamer superhero costume,' Ilan suggested with a leer that set Jennifer's pulse racing again. This was the old Ilan. He was sexy, funny and suggestive. And most of all, loving. He was loving her.

'Until I can get one, and that might be tricky, can you close your eyes and imagine me in it?'

'I already am.'

But the moment had passed. For now.

Chapter 14

'What are you reading?' Jennifer asked as she slipped under the covers beside Ilan. He was staring at his screen, deep in concentration. Seriously deep in concentration.

'One of your books that I forgot to delete. It's called—- *Covid Blues and Twos*. It's very erotic.'

'Is it? I haven't read it yet. So don't tell me anything about it. I thought you were reading that spy drama—- *Operation Palmetto*.'

'Yeah. I finished it earlier.'

'What did you think of it? I loved it. The guy—Karl—made me think of you. A younger version of you.'

'I enjoyed it, but he was nothing like me' Ilan frowned.

'Oh, I dunno. He was sexy and a bit headstrong,' Jennifer said with a grin. 'He tended to act first, think later sometimes.'

'I am not like that,' Ilan growled and returned to the book he was reading.

'Maybe not now, but I bet you were when you were younger.'

Jennifer leaned her head on his shoulder to see what he was reading. A grin spread over her face as she read the page on the screen.

"She slipped her other hand between her legs to check that she was ready and felt the wetness of her soft flesh."

'Oh, my,' Jennifer whispered as the words danced in front of her. The sudden heat she felt could have been emanating from the screen, but it wasn't. It was inside her. As though the powerful, erotic words were a key that had unlocked her senses.

She continued to read.

"Jessica pinched and rolled her nipple between thumb and forefinger. At the same time, she eased her toy into her vagina. She watched Chris' eyes in the darkness for a sign that he was watching."

'Oh, my.'

'Hey.' Ilan tilted the screen away from her. 'I thought you didn't want any spoilers.'

'Just a sneak preview.'

She reached for the iPad, but Ilan playfully batted her hand away, and despite her arousal, she gave up and went back to her own book.

Ilan's hand snuck under the bedcovers, and his fingers stroked her inner thigh. He pretended to do it without thinking as he concentrated on the book he was reading, but Jennifer noticed he hadn't swiped to the next page. The tension between them was electric.

Her book was forgotten. An involuntary moan escaped Jennifer's lips as she parted her legs in invitation. Ilan's fingers kneaded the muscle of her inner thigh as they travelled up to her panties and everything that was there for him to take.

Their eyes met, and Jennifer stared at her husband before sliding down the bed. She let the paperback fall to the floor.

Ilan closed his iPad. He pulled the covers back and exchanged his left hand for his right. The kneading motion was driving Jennifer wild.

'Yes?' His voice was gravelly as he pulled the thin cotton of her underwear to the side.

'Yes, please,' Jennifer whispered. She closed her eyes and opened her legs to him with a sharp intake of breath.

His finger dipped inside her, feeling the slick wetness, and his mouth found hers. Jennifer threw her arms around his neck and pulled him closer to her as his lips crushed hers. Her pulse was racing, and it felt as if she couldn't breathe. She wanted to have him inside her—like before.

His kisses were insistent, and Jennifer returned them with a fervour that bordered on hunger. Because it was a hunger. She had been starved of his affection for so long.

Not his fault. Mine. All mine.

Ilan's mouth and tongue were relentless. Probing her. Tasting her. Driving her wild. His fingers sought her clitoris. They slid over the sensitive button. Teasing and tormenting her in ways that she had almost forgotten. Just as she thought he was keeping a steady rhythm that would bring her to orgasm, his finger slid away, dipping inside her. Exploring her. His finger went as far inside her as it could, massaging her cervix, then moving forward to seek out her G-spot and settling there for a while as she arched against him. Trying to force him deeper, she wished it wasn't his finger.

He had two fingers inside her. Stretching her. Then his mouth left hers. Tracing a line of kisses along the line of her jaw and down her neck.

The neck he had tried to strangle in her dream.

No! Don't think of that.

Jennifer squirmed and moved her head away from him.

'Go lower,' she said. 'Suck my nipples. Please.'

Ilan was happy to oblige, and he traced a line from her shoulder to her left breast with his mouth. His tongue circled her erect nipple, sucking gently. His hand was still between her legs, and his thumb worked her clitoris in rhythm with his fingers. They were slick with her wetness, and he explored her vagina.

Jennifer pushed against the fingers inside her and reached for him. Feeling his hardness and size encircled in her hand, he was rock hard. Her hand slid the length of his shaft and back, pumping him.

It's his cock I need inside me. Not his fingers.

She needed him. All of him, she put her lips to his ear and whispered. 'Please. I need you inside me. Now. Please.'

Ilan pressed his erection against the side of her thigh, and Jennifer detected a steady rhythm as he moved his hips against her leg.

He's humping my leg like a horny dog.

She bit her lip to keep from giggling.

His fingers slid out of her, and Ilan raised onto his arms above her.

She was still wearing her panties, they were sodden now, and Ilan pulled them down, over her knees to her ankles, and they were off with a deft movement. He threw them onto the floor, out of his way, and positioned himself over her.

She spread her legs and waited for him to slide into her. But he didn't.

'I want to taste you,' he said.

He lowered his head, and his tongue found her. Tracing the tip of his tongue along the outline of her labia, he lightly brushed the tip against her clitoris. Just for a moment before he left to circle around it. He was sucking and lapping up her juices. He wouldn't give her enough to satisfy her. He was enjoying tormenting her.

For now, she hoped.

She groaned as she pressed her sex against his mouth.

'Please, Ilan. Please. I need you inside me. Please.'

But it was his tongue that was inside her. Not his cock. He returned to her breast and sucked her nipple as though he was starving while his finger worked around her clitoris. It kept teasing and circling in endless patterns. She wiggled her hips to push his fingers onto the place she wanted—needed—to be touched, but he deftly counteracted her every move and avoided the one place that would tip her over the edge. He teased her with ecstasy and drove her insane.

'Please. I need to come.'

'You will.' His voice was muffled as his finger slid inside her, hammering against her walls. She clenched her internal muscles against the probing fingers, trying to hold him inside her and wishing a different part of him was there.

Jennifer felt his mouth on her stomach. He dropped gentle kisses on her skin that made her tingle all over.

Then, nothing.

It seemed he wasn't even there for a second or two, and Jennifer wondered if she had dreamed it and sat up.

Before she could take the thought any further, he pushed her down, spread her legs and entered her.

She gasped as he pounded into her. She hiked her legs around his back to allow him deeper inside her.

Buried inside his wife, Ilan was still as Jennifer clenched her muscles around him and rocked her hips as though she dictated the movement. Not him. She revelled in her moment of dominance before he pulled back, almost out of her, and plunged in again as hard and deep he could get. Jennifer grunted as he repeated the movement. She sensed he was close, and she was ready. Her body gripped him and forced him deeper inside her with every thrust until he groaned, and with a last, hard movement, his orgasm burst like a dam, and she felt his hot liquid filling her.

She gasped. Her body surrendered to his weight as he collapsed, breathing heavily and unable to move on top of her.

'You didn't come,' he said as his breathing returned to normal.

'You were too quick. You hit the accelerator pedal, took off, and left me standing by the side of the road. All alone.'

Ilan laughed at her fast-car analogy.

'I'm sorry. It's been a while, and I was desperate for you.'

'Don't apologise. You can make it up to me,' Jennifer smiled as she reached to open the bedside drawer and took out her vibrator. She switched it on, lay back with her legs spread, and put the pulsating toy in his hand.

Chapter 15

'Jennifer. Good morning,' Saul glanced up as she poked her head around the door. 'I thought you would have left by now. Have you finished your report already?'

'Not really. It's time-sensitive. I need to speak to you about this one.'

'The possible bank robbery?'

'Yes. And it's not just a possibility.'

'Grab a seat and tell me what you found out.' Saul indicated the chair opposite his desk.

'Okay. This guy was amazing. He was so focused on what he was planning that his mind was still going over it in his sleep. He was checking for flaws and working out all the possible outcomes. He even tweaked his idea in his sleep. This could be the most detailed dream I've ever experienced.' Jennifer told him with awe in her voice. 'It was amazing.'

Saul nodded. 'Go on.'

'The robbery is happening today. This afternoon, I think. That's why he was dreaming about it so much.

He was probably stressed and worrying about it going wrong. Anyway, I could see everything. I saw him looking at the plans he had drawn up, with diagrams and entry and exit points. Although the bank has a state-of-the-art alarm system, four new on-site security guards started working there three weeks ago. Their credentials look impeccable. They are impeccable, but all four of them are working for our friend. Not willingly, though. As an added incentive, these guys have family members who have been threatened, and they were told that, should they fail, their family members will be killed.'

Jennifer saw the shock on Saul's face.

'So,' she continued. 'You have to stop the robbery, and according to my subject's dream, it involves a serious amount of money, many millions, I believe. You'll have to put in measures to identify and protect the family.'

'Do you know who they are?' Saul asked.

'No, sorry. All I could get was an elderly parent, and one was a child. I got this because my subject feels bad about killing innocent people, especially the elderly and children. Still, he's firm in his resolve and in his mind, they won't be killed if the guards do their job.'

Jennifer could see from Saul's face that this would take some doing. They had to prevent the robbery, but that was the easiest part. Identifying and locating the families at risk was near impossible when they had no idea who they were.

'Will the guards be carrying out the robbery?' Saul asked.

'No. They're support staff. Their role is to disable the alarms and cameras and let the team of robbers in. He has five geared up and ready to go. The guards will assist them in accessing the vaults, but their main job is keeping the public out of the building and the remaining bank staff under control while the robbers empty the vaults.'

'Did you get the impression our subject will be an active participant in the robbery?'

'I can't be sure, but I don't think he is. He's the brains behind it but doesn't want to get his hands dirty. At least that's the feeling I got.'

'Okay. That's valuable. Good work. And, this robbery is definitely taking place this afternoon?'

'I'm afraid so.'

'Jennifer, thank you. But now I must ask you to leave. Go home and rest.'

'I haven't written my report up yet.'

'No need. You did the right thing coming to tell me. If need be, you can do it later, but I doubt we'll need it. I'm sorry to be so abrupt, but I need you out of here to get everything organised. We don't have much time. Oh, and thank you, Jennifer. Thank you so much.'

Saul's abrupt dismissal prompted her to get out of there before all hell let loose. Before driving home through the morning traffic, she considered another coffee but decided against it. She was too wired from her dream about the bank robbery. Besides, Ilan had promised to make her a special breakfast.

Later that evening, as was his habit, Ilan sat down with his glass of whiskey to watch the news. Because of the constant reporting on the Coronavirus outbreak, he decided to forego the twenty-four-hour rolling news and said he'd only watch it twice a day. First thing in the morning and then again at nine or ten o'clock. It wasn't because he was bored with it, but the headlines every hour were too repetitive. Mornings and evenings were enough. Jennifer agreed with him because it was too disturbing.

She had just finished emptying the dishwasher and was wiping down the kitchen worktops when she heard the newscaster mention something that stopped her in her tracks.

'What's happening?' Jennifer asked as she followed the voice on the television into the living room and sat down beside Ilan. She reached for her wineglass on the table.

'There was an attempted armed robbery at one of the banks in mid-town. The cops were waiting for them, and they were all caught and arrested. The police think a man on the inside tipped them off.'

'Or it could have been a woman,' Jennifer said quietly, and there was a touch of pride in her voice.

'What?'

'It might have been a woman. Someone you might even know,' she said. 'Maybe she had a dream that the robbery would take place.'

Ilan stared at his wife as the words sunk in. Jennifer couldn't help herself as she smiled smugly and raised her glass in a toast.

'That was you? You found out what they were planning through a dream?' Ilan turned away from the television to stare at his wife.

'Yep. It was me.' There was still pride in her voice. She took another sip of her wine as she enjoyed her moment of quiet celebration.

'That is so cool. So amazing.' Ilan looked at his wife with awe and admiration.

'I'll tell you, it was bloody close. I only got the dream through last night, and when I realised they were planning to do it today, I went straight to Saul and lit a rocket under him. Four guards had been threatened by the criminals. They were going to kill their families if they didn't comply. I'm so glad they put a sting in place to catch those bastards.'

'You're amazing.' Ilan's voice was soft. 'And I am so proud of you. That money could have been used for anything. Terrorism, probably, judging by the names of the people captured.'

'Yeah. It would have. We suspected it. But it was only when we got more intel on the guy I was dreaming about that it was confirmed.'

Ilan raised his glass and smiled at his wife before taking a mouthful of whiskey. 'Well done, you.'

Jennifer was happy. The admiration on his face and in his voice melted her heart. She snuggled up beside him while they watched the rest of the news before returning to a series they were binge-watching.

A couple of hours later, Jennifer reached for Ilan in bed and pulled him towards her. Her lips found him, and she kissed him. He was still for a moment, then he wrapped his arms around her, and just like last time a few nights ago, the passion was there again.

Chapter 16

'Let's go out for the day,' Ilan suggested between mouth-fuls of fruit and muesli.

'Sounds like a lovely idea. Where to?' Jennifer looked up from the sketch she was drawing. It wasn't a design for the inside of a house—just something for pleasure. Her time as an interior designer belonged to another life she had once lived, but not one she wanted to go back to. However, she still enjoyed sketching. This was a pencil drawing of Holly, asleep on the chair near the window, and she was bathed in warm sunlight tones. As the sun moved around the house, so would she, following its path and its warmth.

'We could go to the market again. Then maybe lunch somewhere,' Ilan said.

'The market?' Jennifer grinned. 'Are you sure about that? You almost wrecked your back carrying all my stuff last time.'

'Well, what about going for a hike?'

'Only if it's a short one.'

'It is.'

'It's a date then. But where?'

'You'll see,' Ilan smiled.

Five minutes later, they were dressed for walking. The day was hot and sunny, and they only needed light clothes—T-shirts, shorts and sturdy walking boots.

Jennifer packed some bottles of water and snacks—dried fruits and nuts, which was her homemade, healthier version of trail mix—into the backpack with her camera. She wasted a few minutes searching for her sunglasses, and then they were out of the door and into the car.

They drove up the coast, heading north. Jennifer relaxed and enjoyed the scenery as Ilan motored at a steady pace along the highway. She would have loved the journey to take longer, but they arrived at their destination in no time when they left the city behind. It was only twenty minutes away. Fifteen when the traffic was light.

They talked to each other as they travelled. The days of stony silences were in the past, and their conversations were relaxed and no longer forced.

'Do you remember that guy I told you about?' Jennifer put her bare feet up against the dashboard.

'What guy?'

'The one we thought was passing on info, but no matter how many times I tried, he wasn't dreaming about it. I told you about him and how frustrating it was. You suggested we look at the people around him.'

'Vaguely. Yeah.' Ilan pulled out to overtake a slower car.

'Well, you were totally correct. He was completely innocent. His missus, not so much. I went into her dreams and discovered she was up to no good.'

Ilan smiled.

'Aside from the fact that she was having an affair, two actually, she had been getting stuff from him for a while. She's a real good-looker, and she takes lovers like she's in training for the sex Olympics. She's had more bloody flings than I've had salads. And it was all about the excitement for her. No ideology. No just cause. Spying on her husband and passing on classified information was all about the thrill of the game. Most of it was when she listened to his work conversations, but she would also sneak into his home study, download stuff off his laptop and pass it on to her handler. It wasn't high-level, but it was serious enough. She's now sitting in a cell somewhere, and he got fired for being a stupid dickhead.'

'I'm surprised he isn't in jail too.'

'Ah, I know. I was surprised too, but he probably didn't think he needed to be more careful around his wife. Anyway, we got her thanks to you.'

Ilan turned into the carpark. Being a workday morning, it was almost empty, and tourists hadn't returned to the area because of the pandemic. Although places were opening up again and things were returning to normal, Jennifer didn't like being in crowded places anymore. She considered the emptiness of the place one of the hangover benefits of a partial lockdown and restricted movement.

Ilan paid the parking fee, and Jennifer retrieved her camera out of the backpack and wore it hanging around her neck. Ilan hoisted the backpack over his shoulder, and they set off.

'It's been ages since we've been here. I adore this place,' Jennifer said as she slipped her hand into Ilan's, and they walked along the designated path.

Even though he had told her it all before, Ilan gave her a local history lesson again as they walked. A path that hugged the cliffs took visitors to view the remains of the old fort, and it offered a spectacular view of the coastline. She nodded when he reminded her that Apollonia was the ancient Greek name of what had been an ancient city on the Mediterranean coast, situated on the Sharon plain. The township fell to the Muslims in 640 AD, and in 1101 it was conquered by the Kingdom of Jerusalem and was a strategically important stronghold. Jennifer was fascinated to learn that in 1265, the fortified city and the castle fell and were destroyed by the Mamluks. Ilan explained that this referred to non-Arab, ethnically diverse slave soldiers and formerly enslaved people. The Mamluks were assigned military and administrative duties and served the ruling Arab dynasties in the Muslim world. Looking over the sea and hearing Ilan's words brought the history alive again for her. She imagined the people of those times. She loved hearing him talk.

Jennifer loved the scenery of their country. Less than half an hour from their home, the ancient site is now in the Herzilya municipality, just north of Tel Aviv. It was extensively excavated in 1994. Today it was their national park, and it was opened to the public in 2002.

It wasn't the only archaeological site in Israel situated on the coast. Most of the ancient sites of the Torah had been located and excavated at some point. But the planners of this park worked around the existing ruins. They'd used the natural landscape to create a unique and wonderful experience for locals and tourists alike.

Jennifer already knew much of the history of this lovely place from her last trip, but she let Ilan talk, and his words were soothing as she imagined the lives of the past. They were fortunate to have this remarkable piece of history almost on their doorstep. The first time Ilan brought her here was a few weeks after she was released from the hospital. She'd been advised to get plenty of fresh air and exercise to regain her strength and fitness. They said it would help with her mental well-being recovery as well. Despite his love of lying on the couch watching sports all day, Ilan was a great believer in exercise, and he took her on many hikes. But this was her favourite and the one that healed her the most.

Maybe it was the stunning views of the Mediterranean Sea, with Cyprus somewhere on the horizon. It was out of sight but still there, pulling on her heartstrings, even though she knew she would never go back. It was okay to say goodbye to Cyprus and her life there. With its beautiful scenery, ancient history, and its promise of a future, this place spoke to her and told her she could make it her home.

And Jennifer did that. Six months after leaving Cyprus, she sat on a rock, gazed out to sea in the direction she'd called home, and whispered goodbye to it. A few tears had fallen down her cheeks, and the pain was unbearable. She'd wanted to scream at its unfairness, but Ilan was beside her, and he'd put his arm around her. He didn't say a word. No words were needed because Jennifer knew they would make a new life together here. She would always miss Cyprus, but she had her memories, and it was okay because she had new memories to make here with Ilan.

They'd made a lot of memories since that day.

Always by her side, Ilan had shown her the beauty of the land of his birth. He saw it anew through Jennifer's eyes as she marvelled at some areas of contrasting harshness sitting beside the lush verdant greenery. The ancient ruins had been preserved and protected while modern, bustling towns and cities grew up around them. The life and vibrancy of the people drew her to love them. The beauty, the history and her husband gave her a new anchor. And Ilan helped her with the language when she struggled with it. The ancient and the modern melded with her new life and rolled into one.

All this was when they first moved to Israel. Jennifer didn't want to make it her home when they fled Cyprus but Ilan took her out every day and showed her the ancient land steeped in history beside the modern development and innovation. With the rugged beauty and the urban sprawl, Ilan basked in the beauty of his country. He had shown it to her, and then he gave it to her, so it belonged to them both. She accepted his gift because he came with it.

'Oof. I'm getting old. I love this place so much, but it's hard work when you're out of shape,' Jennifer said as she grasped Ilan's outstretched hand and let him help her up the steep path. When it levelled out and was wide enough for them to walk side by side, she leaned into him, and he threw his arm around her shoulder.

Even though she was wearing sunglasses, Jennifer squinted in the sun's brightness as it reflected off the white limestone. A gentle breeze carried away all the dust they stirred up with their feet. She could smell the scent of the plants and wildflowers growing around them as they passed by. She was assuaged with peppery and pungent tones one minute, gentle and sweet the next. She inhaled the infusions, capturing them in her memory and soul. She wanted to grow the same plants in her garden and recreate these scents.

I must ask Rachel for advice. She'd know.

She'd overdone the inhaling part of her experience and sneezed violently. Once, then twice. Then several loud, explosive sneezes in quick succession. They were the kind of sneeze that nearly burst her eardrums— and those of everyone in the vicinity.

Ilan pulled a paper tissue out of his pocket and handed it to her.

'Sorry. I don't do polite, genteel nose-blowing. Thanks.' She blew her nose into the tissue.

'No. You certainly do not,' Ilan chuckled as he handed her another tissue.

Her sneezing subsided after a few minutes, although her eyes were watery and her nose was blocked.

'Stupid pollen,' she said.

'Stop sniffing the flowers then,' Ilan told her. 'If you sneezed like that in town, everyone would think you had Covid and run away screaming. Next time we're in a busy supermarket, you should do it, and we'll get through the checkout a lot faster.'

'Ha, bloody, ha,' she sniffled and gave her nose another good, hard blow. 'Now, less of the sarcasm and more of the hiking, if you don't mind.'

They stopped at a restaurant for a bite to eat on the way home. Jennifer ordered the lamb kebabs, and after some indecision, Ilan selected the same. She was tempted to add a glass of white wine to her order but decided on sparkling water. Ilan did the same as he was driving.

Despite the heat, they sat outside at one of the tables, partially in the shade. They took their drinks and sat facing each other, waiting for their meal. Jennifer switched on her camera and scanned through the photos she'd taken in the park.

'I got some lovely shots.'

She looked up to find Ilan staring at her.

'What?'

He reached across the small table and took both of her hands in his. He seemed to be searching for the right words, and Jennifer's stomach flipped. There was a darkness in his look, a hint of something. Not anger, though. Confusion, maybe? Jennifer didn't know, and it made her uncomfortable. She wanted to pull her hands out of his and hide them under the table.

He's going off on another mission. And he's trying to break it to me gently. I know he's been in contact with Saul. Oh, Ilan. How could you? After you promised me last time really was the last time.

'Are we okay?' Ilan asked.

'What do you mean?' Jennifer frowned. It wasn't what she was expecting him to say.

'The last few weeks. I'm confused. The sex has been great, but are we okay?'

'And days. Don't forget about the days—the mornings and the afternoons.'

Ilan laughed, but there was little humour in it. 'No, I haven't forgotten. But that's just it. For ages, you seemed to be doing your best to ignore me. You pretended that I didn't exist. It was as if you hated me or were angry with me about something. I felt as though I was losing you. When I couldn't stand it any longer, I'd ask you if you still love me. Every time you said you do—but your eyes didn't believe what you were telling me. You were polite when it couldn't be avoided and friendly even, but that's all there was. And I understood. It was wrong of me to do what I did, but I thought you would accept it and move on. Then suddenly, things have changed again, we can't get enough of each other, and I need to know, is it just sex?'

Jennifer knew what he meant. She'd wondered the same thing. They'd gone from weeks of sniping to hours of biting. Biting and grabbing and kissing. And screwing.

Exchanging bodily fluids and orgasms like there was no tomorrow. But was it just sex? Was that all that was left between them now? Just a physical attraction? Was the love gone, or was it hiding while they got their rekindled passion out of the way? She hoped it was the latter.

'Maybe it's all those sexy books we're reading?' She grinned to break the intensity of his mood and end the subject.

It was true. Since that first night, they had downloaded a couple more and read them together. The sex afterwards was amazing. The last one was a sexy romp involving a hot firefighter. He was the kind that saved kittens and posed for the annual charity calendar. Every woman would want to set fire to their beautiful homes just to have him rescue her from a burning building. Jennifer loved it, and Ilan was happy to read it, but he wasn't enjoying it as much as the first one.

'Oh, don't be so flippant, Jennifer.' A scowl flitted across his face, and he pulled his hands away from hers. 'I'm serious.'

'I know. I'm sorry.' Jennifer took a deep breath. It was crunch time, and while she hadn't planned on having a serious conversation with him here and now, her hand was being forced. She had to tell him the truth.

'I do love you, Ilan. But I've been so angry with you for so long, it became my default setting.'

'Yeah, I got that. The way you look at me sometimes, it's as if you want to kill me. What did I do wrong? Was it because of Saul? Because he forced you to work for him, and I told him to get you? I've apologised for that. I don't know what more I can do.'

'I know that.' Jennifer snapped back. 'That's only a part of it, and I'm over that part.'

'Then what? What have I done to make you look at me as though you hate me?'

Before she could speak, a waiter appeared beside them with two plates. Their lunch arrived, and Jennifer didn't know if she was glad of the temporary reprieve or disappointed that she didn't get her confession off her chest.

It didn't look so appetising now, and she wasn't sure she wanted it, but Ilan tucked in as if he hadn't eaten for days and he hadn't a care in the world.

Eat first. Fight later. Fine. I can do that.

She took both ends of the skewer in her hands, lifted the kebab to her mouth and took a nibble. It was okay. It was probably wonderful, but the conversation with Ilan had already left a bad taste in her mouth, and she dreaded the one they had coming. She put the skewer on her plate and waved to catch the waiter's attention.

'May I have a glass of wine, please? A large one?'

'Isn't a bit early to be hitting the booze, neshama?'

There wasn't much Jennifer could say in response, so she didn't say anything. She took a defiant sip and smiled at her husband. Besides, one large glass wasn't even close to hitting the booze. His disapproval stung.

Her appetite was long gone, so she sipped her wine, pacing herself and watching Ilan as he ate. All the while, her heart was pounding in her chest, and her stomach was in knots. Jennifer felt the heat rising as she remembered his hands around her throat, and she prayed she wasn't blushing.

What on earth would be going through his mind if I started blushing? He'd be convinced I was having an affair or something.

She took another sip of wine and tried to think of the best way to answer his question. He would ask it again. There was no doubt about that.

And true to form, Ilan pushed his empty plate forward and folded his arms on the table.

She got in first. 'I don't hate you, Ilan. I was pissed off with you over the Saul thing. But it's done. I work for the Mossad, and there's no going back. I'm not angry anymore. Well, not about that.'

'Then what?'

'It's hard to explain.'

Jennifer tried to smile and failed. She wanted to tell him this was the most difficult thing in the world.

He won't see it that way. He'll think it's trivial. He won't understand.

'Do we have to do this here? In public?' she asked. 'Can we go home and talk properly?'

Ilan looked around the outdoor seating area of the restaurant. They were the only people there.

'We'll do it here and right now.' he said.

Jennifer sighed. There was a hardness in Ilan's demeanour that she'd never experienced before, and it was directed at her. Could she blame him? No, it was her fault. She caused this, and it was up to her to fix it.

Ilan motioned to the waiter and ordered a whiskey for himself and another glass of wine for her.

'You can't. You're driving,' she said and hated the hushed, timid voice. Even to her ears, she sounded scared of him.

'We can get the bus home and come back for the car tomorrow.'

'Fine.'

They sat in silence until their drinks arrived. Ilan waited for the waiter to leave before taking down half the whiskey.

'Start talking,' he said.

Jennifer took a deep breath first, then another sip of her wine.

'When you were in Syria,' she began, 'Saul made me go into a dream to find you. You won't remember it because it was a dream, but we met in a bar. It was a classy place, an old hotel. I was dressed up to the nines, and you were there, drinking. We had a couple of cocktails, and then I did what Saul asked—I questioned you. You didn't like it, and you were angry. Then you grabbed my arm and hauled me outside and down an alleyway beside the hotel. I thought you were going to—well, I thought we would kiss and maybe have sex, but you were so paranoid. You didn't believe it was me. And then you choked me.'

Jennifer paused, and a shiver ran through her as she remembered the dream. Every last detail played in her mind. From the red dress, she wore to the anger in Ilan's eyes in the dirty alleyway. She lifted the glass of wine to her lips but set it down again without taking any.

Keep a clear head, Jennifer.

'You pressed me against the wall and stuck a gun in my side, against my ribs. Your forearm was against my throat, like this.' She lifted her arm to show him. 'And you pushed hard, choking me. It was agony, and I couldn't breathe. You kept screaming at me. You demanded that I told you who I was.'

Ilan's face was a rigid mask, and Jennifer couldn't tell if his expression was shock, disbelief, or anger. He stared at her, then muttered a string of swear words in Hebrew. Jennifer knew most of them, but there were a couple that sounded like real fireballs.

'I had to convince you. But I was terrified because I was afraid something might happen to me in real life if you killed me in a dream. I begged you, and then, when you wouldn't stop, I whispered our secret phrase in your ear. You took your arm away from my throat and your gun from my ribcage. It was only then that you believed me.'

Jennifer took a mouthful of wine. She couldn't meet Ilan's eyes, so she had another gulp. For something to do, she picked up a piece of lamb. It was cold and greasy, but she put it in her mouth. It tasted like crap or the congealed lump of cold meat it was. She spat it onto her palm and put it back on the plate.

'Why didn't you tell me this?' Ilan asked.

'I couldn't, Ilan. I don't know why. It terrified me, and even though I knew it wasn't real, I relived it every time you came near me. It came back when you looked at me or put your arms around me. I know it was only a dream. I know that. But it was so vivid that I couldn't help myself. Miriam said it would fade in time, but it would go away much quicker if I talked to you. I wanted to, but I couldn't. I didn't have the words.'

'You spoke about this with your shrink? Yet you couldn't talk to me about it.'

'She isn't my shrink. We're friends, and we only talked about it in conversation, not in a professional patient-psychiatrist way. She knew something was upsetting me, and she asked. So I told her. Eventually.'

'And what did she say about it?'

'She said that, even though I know you would never hurt me, the dream of you choking me still felt real, and that being near you triggered flashbacks of it. She said I shouldn't bottle my feelings up and insisted I talk to you about it.'

'Shit,' Ilan shook his head. 'I thought you were having an affair.'

'What? Are you nuts? Who the hell would I be having an affair with?'

'I don't know. Nathan Cohen, maybe. You're always talking about him. Nathan did this, and Nathan said that. You mention him every day. Then you bought him that vape kit like mine for his birthday.'

Jennifer burst out laughing. She tried not to, but she couldn't help herself.

'Nathan? Nathan Cohen? Oh, Ilan, that's funny. You don't know Nathan that well, do you?'

'I've met him once or twice, but I don't know him. Why?'

'Aside from the fact that he's nearly fifteen years younger than me, Nathan is gay. He has a husband. That's why they went off to Cyprus in February. They got married, you goof. I thought I mentioned it to you. Mind you, if he was straight and I was looking for someone, he would be high on my list. Definitely in the top five. Maybe even in the top two or three.'

Ilan stared at her over his glass. His eyes were brooding, and she melted. He still had that effect on her. More so, after the last few weeks and the wild lovemaking.

'Are you still afraid of me?' Ilan asked, and Jennifer could hear the worry in his voice. It brought a lump to her throat, and she felt tears welling in her eyes.

She shook her head. Unable to speak.

Okay, maybe a just little bit. I was half an hour ago.

'Do you still love me?'

Oh, yes. With all my heart and soul.

She nodded. Still unable to speak.

'You should have told me, Jennifer. You know I would never hurt you. I couldn't.'

Jennifer was silent until she could get her voice under control.

'I know. I wanted to tell you. And I'm sorry I didn't say what was wrong and why I was angry—afraid—of you. It was on my tongue many times, but I thought you'd laugh at me because it was only a dream. Even though it was real to me. And it frightened me. Very much.'

139

'And now? Do you feel the same? Are you still afraid of me?'

'No. Definitely not. This past while, I've realised how much I love you. I know it sounds silly and maybe a little cheap, but the books and the sex made a difference.'

Ilan's arms were resting on the table again, and his glass was in one hand. He raised it to his lips.

'Maybe we should try it without the steamy books?'

'Oh yes, please. I'm tired of the hot firefighters and the women who love their husbands and ex-boyfriends at the same time. In the same bed. Well, not really tired of them. I still enjoy them, but I have three good murder mysteries and a thriller that I want to read instead. After we, you know, try it without the books,' she grinned. 'The safety net.'

He finished his drink, and the look in his eyes told Jennifer that he wanted her as much as she wanted him.

Then her phone beeped with an incoming text message. It was from Saul.

Jennifer read the text and grimaced. 'I'm sorry, but we'll have to put it off for another time. Saul wants me in work tonight, and it's urgent.'

She stared at the half-full glass sitting in front of her.

'And I've used up my—too many glasses of wine—excuses, so that won't fly.'

'What is that man, the fucking special agent of contraception? In the morning then, when you get home?' Ilan asked.

'Yes. It's a date. Now, you find out when the next bus is due, and I'll pay for the meal,' she said.

140

'No, I'll pay. My treat. And we'll get a taxi. It'll be quicker than the bus if you're working later.'

Chapter 17

'So, what have we got on that's so urgent you need me tonight?' Jennifer asked as she dropped her overnight bag on the chair. She had planned a movie night curled up on the sofa with Ilan, only to have her phone ring just as she was about to open a bag of potato crisps and pour them into a bowl. Or potato chips, as Ilan called them.

Whatever they were called, they were still in the bag in the cupboard at home, and she was here.

'Nine people have been taken hostage in a private home. I need you to enter the dream of one of the victims and see what you can find out. Apparently, a birthday party was going on when the attackers stormed in.'

'I dunno, Saul. If I was being held hostage, I doubt I'd be able to curl up and fall into a contented sleep.'

'They've been held for twenty-four hours. Some of them will have fallen asleep through exhaustion. We just need one asleep that you can connect with. It's a long shot, but it's all we've got.'

'Hey,' Jennifer smiled. 'Long shots are my thing.'

She made herself comfortable at a spare workstation and opened the laptop files on the hostages. She selected one—a woman—and read her history to get a feel for her. She'd be invading the lady's dreams. The least she could do was get to know her a bit. But she wasn't happy about it and didn't think it would work.

'Do we know anything about the kidnappers, Saul?'

'No. Even if we did, they would probably be awake. Why?'

'Just a thought. Okay, I'm going to go for this one,' she said, pointing to the face on the screen. 'Hopefully, she'll be asleep. If not, I'll try somebody else.'

Jennifer opened the door a few inches and peeked in. The room was large, modern and well furnished. Three of the nine hostages—two women and a man—were on the floor by the back wall. Only these three were in her direct eye line. Their hands and feet were lashed together with cable ties, and their mouths were bound with grey tape. All of them were dressed to the nines. It was a posh party, the kind Jennifer only got to attend once in a blue moon. These weren't your average scumbags, and she wanted to help them. It was a well-to-do house in a good neighbourhood.

I should have worn my red dress.

The hostages' best clothes didn't look so glamorous now. One man's shirt was torn, and a woman had a broken heel. There was a urine stain on the man's trousers, and his eyes were wide with terror.

All three were wide awake. The fear on their faces was obvious, and all had been badly roughed up. The man had a gash on his forehead, possibly caused by being assaulted or knocked down, and one of the women had a red mark across her cheek. Her eyes were swollen, and she was crying. It looked as if she'd been punched in the face.

I can't say I blame her.

Jennifer wished there was something she could do to help. If not by freeing them, then comforting them and trying to allay their fears. But that was impossible. She was only there to observe.

Jennifer stepped forward and scanned the expansive room for the rest of the hostages. A woman was in a comfortable chair. Her hands and feet were tied, and tape covered her mouth. She appeared to be asleep, or maybe unconscious, and Jennifer realised it was this woman whose dream she was in. This woman was hostage number four, and she found number five—an elderly man—lying behind the massive three-seater couch. There was a pool of blood surrounding him on the polished wooden floor. Jennifer couldn't tell if he was alive and wounded—or dead.

Five hostages were accounted for in this room, and Jennifer wondered where the other four were being held. And why were they kept somewhere else?

144

Even in her sleep, the woman was agitated, and Jennifer felt the effects of her agitation. Her mouth was dry, and her hands were clammy. The fear was palatable, and even though she knew it wasn't real, Jennifer felt uncomfortable. She was frightened. She did her best to shake it off.

One hostage-taker stood guard. In accordance with the guidelines of the day, he was standing in the corner of the room, with his back to the wall, while he guarded the hostages. He was masked and practising social distancing—it seemed ludicrous in this situation.

He couldn't see her, much to Jennifer's relief.

Of course, he can't. I'm not here. Yeah, but some people can. But he can't, so I'm okay.

She studied him. He was young, from what she could see of his face. And he had dark eyes that flitted around the room. This kid was nervous. She saw the tremor in his hand by the way the gun he was holding shook. He'd been left there to guard the hostages, and he was ready in case they rushed him. Jennifer hoped, for their sake, they didn't, as any movement could set him off. There was only one thing more terrifying than a terrorist—and that was a terrorist with a gun and the tremors.

Jennifer left him and the five hostages and went to find the remaining kidnappers and the four hostages who were still unaccounted for. She stepped out of the room, but she didn't wake up like she usually did. The remote viewing aspect of her ability came to the fore. It was something she had been practising for a while, and it allowed her to leave the woman's dream and walk along a spacious, minimally-furnished hallway. To her left were two double wooden doors—large and heavy looking. She made a mental note of this being the way into the building. The SWAT teams going in would need to know the layout from the inside.

She turned towards the staircase. She considered checking out the upper floor but decided to leave it and go down the hallway to what, she presumed, was the kitchen.

The lights were on, and Jennifer heard muffled voices coming from the open door. She stood still and listened.

'Do as you're fucking told.' It was a male voice. Angry and threatening. 'If you don't, your loved ones will die.'

Jennifer stepped into the doorway and surveyed the scene in the kitchen. In her subject's dream, the party didn't seem to have kicked off yet. Plates of nibbles, still covered, sat on one of the worktops. Bottles of wine, spirits, and mixers were everywhere, with good quality cut-glass goblets and tumblers nearby. Knives and forks had been wrapped in linen napkins and placed beside stacks of plates. The ovens were on, and the smell of food wafted from them. Hot food would burn the place down if it wasn't taken out soon. Not that the kidnappers cared if the quiche was overdone. Although they might if the kitchen exploded and the fire department showed up to join the party.

There were two kidnappers in the kitchen. Both were armed, and one—the angry one —was standing in front of the central island. He put the handgun on top of the polished granite surface. He was still shouting. The terrorist repeated his threats that their friends and family would be killed if they didn't do what he wanted.

The remaining four hostages stood in front of him, almost at attention, except their arms were raised. Their hands were clasped behind their heads in an arrest pose.

Jennifer folded her arms and leaned against the door-frame. She eavesdropped on Johnny Shouty—the nickname she had given him. He wasn't yelling at the top of his voice, but he was making sure that he wasn't ignored by the four people in front of him.

He explained that the five people in the other room would die slow, very painful deaths if they didn't do what he told them to do.

You mean four people, Johnny. I think one of them is already dead.

She watched the four hostages. They were all men, and like the others, they were well-dressed and didn't look as if they had ever gone hungry. They were nervous, terrified and kept their eyes downcast as they concentrated on the floor and tried not to wince at Johnny Shouty's words.

He motioned to the other kidnapper to keep an eye on them and ducked into a room just off the kitchen—it looked like a pantry.

Five minutes later, he walked out, followed by a third kidnapper. That made four in total, three in here and the other with the five hostages in the living room. Jennifer's blood ran cold when she saw what they were carrying. Even if it was only a dream.

Suicide vests. Four of them. One for each of the people in the kitchen.

Jennifer knew what to do. She walked through the house like a ghost, counting the rooms and checking the entry and exit points. Once she had a mental picture of the layout, she walked through the front door and woke up.

'Could someone get me some paper and a pencil? Quickly.' Jennifer spoke into her phone as she balanced it between her ear and her shoulder. She pulled on a pair of jeans and manoeuvred a long-sleeved top over her head and arms.

'Coming right up. What have you got?' Saul said.

'Everything you need except the location. But you should find it through aerial photos when I draw the shape of the house.'

'Don't worry about that. We already know the location, but we need to know what's going on inside.'

Jennifer quickly sketched the ground floor layout, including the front doors as Saul appeared at her side.

'Okay. They are all on the ground floor. Go in through the double doors, and they are down a hallway. This way.'

She pointed to the doors and drew an arrow along the hall.

'Five hostages and one guard are in this room.' She marked it with an X. 'The rest are in the kitchen. Here.'

She made another X mark on the paper.

'They have suicide vests and are ready to suit the remaining four hostages. Only three kidnappers, but they are armed and angry. Johnny Shouty especially, and he is the one running the show. The hostages in the first room have been roughed up, and one is definitely unconscious, maybe dead. God, I hope he's not dead.'

Saul scanned the sketch again and picked up his phone. He looked at Jennifer.

'Thank you. You have been a great help to us.'

Jennifer refused to let his insincere words of thanks and obvious dismissal rankle as she turned on her heel and walked out of the office. She had a hot date with Ilan.

Chapter 18

Much to her annoyance, Ilan was nowhere to be found when she arrived back at the house. She checked the bedroom and found the bed in its usual untidy mess. He wasn't on the patio or in the garage. And he hadn't left a note as he normally would.

And there was I looking forward to a morning in bed.

She fed the cats. Ilan had probably fed them, but they pretended he hadn't and let her know they were neglected and starving. Once they had settled down to a bout of after-breakfast personal grooming in their favourite places—Holly on the windowsill and Possum on the sofa—Jennifer made her own breakfast.

Because she'd left work without coffee that morning, she made it her first job. Then she cracked eggs into a bowl, whisked them, added some herbs and put them in a pan. Her phone let her know she had a message while she stirred the scrambled eggs.

"Meeting Saul for coffee. Back soon."

He'd added two x's. Jennifer would prefer real ones like he'd promised her.

Surely, Saul was working on the hostage situation. What are you up to, Ilan? You'd better not be trying to get Saul to reinstate you. If I get even a whiff of you going on another secret spy mission, I'll be very annoyed.

Ilan was oblivious to Jennifer's irritation. He stirred his coffee, reading the morning newspaper while he waited.

It wasn't an appointment as such, more a get-together—a catch-up. They were just two colleagues who were old friends, doing what friends do. It was a while since they'd seen each other. They'd have coffee and spend a pleasant hour catching up on their news and gossiping.

Ilan glanced at his phone to check the time. Saul was running late, but he wasn't annoyed as it was a pleasant morning—sunny but not too hot yet. And he was enjoying the chance to be alone with his newspaper. He inhaled his vape, enjoying the sweet flavour, as he worked on his crossword.

Saul was thirty minutes late. Ilan spotted his car across the street as he parked. He signalled the waiter to bring two coffees and watched Saul dodging the traffic across the busy street.

They did the greetings and the 'You look well' niceties while drinking their coffees. Then they moved on to the 'Have you heard the news about so and so?' until Saul stopped talking and stared at Ilan.

'Listen to us. You and me, Ilan. We sound like a couple of old gossiping fishwives. No?'

'Less of the old, please,' Ilan said with a grin.

Saul's shoulders shook with mirth, but his eyes never left Ilan's face. Searching, scanning, studying the man in front of him.

'So? Do you want to come back to work? I have plenty of work for you. We have a potential terrorist cell in Berlin under surveillance, but we could use someone on the inside.'

'Nothing like that, Saul. I'm enjoying my retirement too much to be tempted. That's not why I'm here. I want to talk to you about my wife.'

Saul's eyebrows went up in surprise.

'Jennifer? Is this an attempt to save your marriage?'

'My marriage doesn't need saving. However, I'm worried about Jennifer.'

'She does not strike me as a lady that needs saving, Ilan.'

'You do not see her like I do. She's exhausted and traumatised by the things she has seen. She can't sleep, and the work you're asking her to do is overwhelming. She needs a break, Saul. It's time for her to switch off for a while, or she'll burn out.'

Ilan was lying through his teeth. Jennifer was fine. She was happy they'd resolved their differences, and she loved what she was doing, too much for his liking. He wanted her to quit, but he knew she wouldn't. Talking to Saul was his second option. If he took her away for a couple of weeks, she might find she loved spending time with him instead of working. That, and the idea of a second honeymoon, appealed to him. After what they'd been through, they needed it.

'And what do you propose?' Saul asked.

'I'm asking you to give her some time off, a month at the most. Let me take her away somewhere. She needs sand, sea, and some relaxing nightlife. The world is opening up. We can travel again.'

'As can those we hunt,' Saul reminded him.

'I know that. But she needs a break. I want to take her somewhere different where she doesn't have to think about work and remember what she sees in her dreams. She needs to recharge her batteries.'

Saul seemed to be mulling it over. He put his cup down and looked at the people going about their lives. These were his citizens, the people he was charged with protecting. With deliberate slowness, he turned back to Ilan.

His face hardened. 'No.'

'No? Just like that? Why not?' Ilan wasn't surprised by his refusal, but he didn't expect it to be so definitive and abrupt.

'I need her. I have several projects coming up for her. They are vital, and none of them can be postponed while she jets off on holiday.'

'I asked you out of common decency, Saul. You can't stop me from taking her if it's what she wants. And if I think she needs it.'

'You won't get beyond airport security,' Saul replied. He didn't try to disguise the threat.

'Ben-zona,' Ilan swore. His anger was palpable as he stood up and grabbed his keys. He walked away without looking back.

'Where were you? And why did you meet Saul?' Jennifer demanded.

She was on the patio, enjoying her book when Ilan's car pulled into the driveway. She waited until she heard him come into the house before rushing in to confront her husband.

Ilan put his arms around her. He pulled her close and nuzzled her neck, just below her ear.

'You smell good,' he whispered.

'Don't fob me off with kisses and cuddles, Ilan. Why were you meeting Saul?'

'Just catching up with him, that's all.'

'I don't believe you. Are you asking to work again? I can't stand the thought of you on another undercover mission.'

'No, definitely not. We were just chatting. Things came up in conversation, and I asked him to give you some time off because I wanted to surprise you with a trip—perhaps a second honeymoon? But he said no. He needs you at work and can't spare you.'

'What did you say to that?' Jennifer asked.

'I called him a son of a bitch, got up and left—dramatically. And I left him to pay for the coffee.'

Jennifer laughed at the mental image of her husband throwing a strop and storming off.

'Saul's right, though. I am busy. But I want that second honeymoon sometime soon. In the meantime, we could have some fun here.' She took him by the hand and led him to the bedroom.

Chapter 19

'This is a straightforward case, Jennifer,' Saul explained as she picked up the file.

Saul didn't mention what happened with Ilan, and Jennifer decided she wouldn't bring the subject up. She was okay with not travelling. It would be nice to go somewhere different but staying at home was fine, especially now that her relationship with Ilan had improved. Covid was still here, and it loomed large in people's thoughts.

Jennifer read the brief.

'A missing person? What's so special about this guy? It's not our usual fare, Saul.'

Saul stepped over to the window and stared outside, muttering something under his breath.

'I'm sorry. What did you say?'

'No. It is not our usual fare as you put it. This one has a personal element. He's a good friend of mine.'

'Oh, I see. Does that mean we're keeping this case off the books?'

'No. It is as official as any case we deal with. His wife is a government liaison officer to the military, and she deals with a high level of sensitive information. We are concerned. He hasn't been seen or heard from for forty-eight hours.'

'Where does he work?' Jennifer asked.

'He's a used-Subaru salesman.'

'So, no connections to the government or the military?' Jennifer fumbled with the file until she found the relevant line. 'Other than his wife, Sharon.'

'None whatsoever.'

Saul paced the small office before returning to the comfortable chair. He leaned back, crossed his arms and looked at Jennifer.

'You are deep in thought,' he said.

'Yeah. Something's nagging me. Why him? I mean, she's the one with the important job, and he sells second-hand Scoobies. Why not her?'

'Good question, Jennifer. We presume someone has taken him to put pressure on her,' Saul replied.

'And that's what we need to find out, isn't it? Which is why I'm needed?'

'That, of course. But we also need to find him.'

'I knew something else was bugging me. He's been missing for two days. Didn't anyone notice? Why didn't Sharon raise the alarm when he didn't show up for dinner?'

'She was out of town at a conference. She tried his phone a few times, but it went to voicemail. That's not unusual. He has a habit of forgetting to charge it, so she didn't consider it out of the ordinary.'

'They have a daughter. She didn't notice her dad missing either?'

'The same applies. Their daughter was away for a few days.'

'Gotcha. Right. I'll get ready and see if his dreams can shed some light on his whereabouts.'

'Thank you, Jennifer,' Saul nodded.

Jennifer opened the door but paused and turned around. 'Is he a close friend of yours?'

'You could say that. He's Rachel's nephew.'

Jennifer opened the door and walked into a small café empty of all but one customer. Rachel's nephew was sitting at a table near the window. His back was to the café, and a latte was on the table beside him. She saw a large envelope with half of it ragged and torn where he'd ripped it open. Obviously removed from the envelope, a set of photographs was fanned out in a semi-circle. He was looking at them and seemed worried.

The same young woman appeared in all the images. They were candid shots, and it didn't look as though she knew she was being photographed.

The view outside the café was rural. It was on the grounds of a farm by the look of it. Jennifer saw some horses in a paddock where they grazed while they swatted flies with their tails. One, a chestnut, was away from the others. It slurped water from a trough that was leaking on one side. The horse finished drinking, raised its head and whinnied.

As though in response to the horse's call, her subject's shoulders slumped, and he pressed the palm of his hands against his eyes. Jennifer could see his obvious distress. More than that, she felt it. The man was in a pit of despair. He was terrified of what would happen if he didn't meet their demands. Who are they? She wondered. But that was for Saul to find out and deal with. Her job was to find this man through his dreams. Here he was, but she didn't know where they were. It could be a real place, but it could also be somewhere his imagination had conjured up. In most cases, people dreamed about real-life locations—but not always, and it had tripped them up before.

Jennifer hoped this was a real place as she looked for something that would pinpoint his location.

Eight hours later, Jennifer walked out of her bathroom. She had dressed in a hurry to go and find Saul, but he was already waiting for her. As usual, he was pacing the floor.

'Oh, good. I was on my way to see you. It took me a while, but I know where he is, and you need to get someone there immediately.'

'What's wrong?'

'He's in a bad way, Saul. He's thinking of killing himself. Their daughter is called Laurel, but she prefers Laura, and she's at university. Correct?'

'Yes. Laura is studying to be a vet.'

'Okay. He's been threatened and told that his daughter will be killed if he doesn't obtain the details of something called *Operation Calamari*. They sent him photos of her on the campus, in the coffee shop she frequents, and even shots of the horse-riding farm she goes to at the weekend. They're saying they can get to her anywhere. I have no idea what *Operation Calamari* is, but I'm guessing it's something his wife's working on.'

'It is,' Saul told her. 'Where is he at the moment?'

'He's near a place with horses. Maybe a ranch or an equestrian centre.'

Saul nodded. 'That makes sense. The family take vacations at a guest ranch because Laura and her mother have a passion for horses.'

'That's where you'll find him. He's camped in a rugged area nearby. He dumped his car miles away. It's well hidden under some trees, which is why you've had no sightings of it. He's hiked a good distance from any locations where he's likely to be seen. I'm not sure which ranch he's near. I'm assuming there's more than one. And there's a small café overlooking a paddock, if that helps?'

'It does. He's Rachel's late brother's only child, and you don't know what this means to us. Thank you, Jennifer.'

'Just go. I don't think you have much time.'

Chapter 20

Jennifer looked around the house. It was as clean as a whistle because she'd spent the morning catching up on housework and laundry, and while she was pleased with her hard work, now she was bored.

Ilan was on a sea fishing trip with some of his old army buddies—they'd collected him at eight o'clock. She suspected there wouldn't be many fish caught. After an hour, they'd give up and have a great day drinking beer and relating old war stories. With every telling, the reports would become more exaggerated in proportion to the beer consumed. They would laugh as they reminisced about things they'd done in their youth. There would be a couple of sombre moments as they remembered comrades that were no longer with them but, generally, it would be drinking and having a good time with old friends under the pretence of catching fish for dinner.

Then the doorbell would ring sometime around seven or eight, and she'd open it to find Ilan, propped between two mates. He'd be grinning, and out of his tree from all the beer he'd put away. Ilan was a happy drunk and was never mean or maudlin. He wouldn't quite be standing when she opened the door. He'd be swaying and possibly singing or trying to sing. Her husband would grab her in his arms and kiss her, telling her how much he loved her. The beer on his breath would almost knock her out, and she'd help him onto the couch where, depending on how drunk he was, he'd fall asleep.

If he wasn't too drunk, he would be horny.

Horny would be good, though.

Since their conversation the day they went hiking, things had been better between them. They reset their relationship to the way it was before he went to Syria, and it was as good as it had been when they lived in Cyprus.

The Covid pandemic and lockdowns helped. Jennifer had worried that close proximity, their issues, and being stuck in a house together would hurt their relationship.

If anything, it had improved over lockdown. They had to make a go of it, or they could hate each other and split up. Maybe even trashing the house while they fought it out. Jennifer did tend to throw things when she was angry, although she usually managed to curb the tendency.

Regardless of their motives, they enjoyed each other's company, growing closer with every day and finding the spark of passion they lost for a while.

There were days when they got on each other's nerves like everybody does. She still had to work a couple of times a week as the Dream Catcher Programme remained operational. It was controlled under necessary Covid compliance restrictions. But when she wasn't working,

Jennifer opened a bottle of wine at lunchtime. Despite a few snide remarks, Ilan usually poured a beer or sometimes a whiskey. Their monthly grocery bills were massive due to the amount of alcohol they bought.

They weren't alone. An epidemic of hard-drinking was running parallel to the Covid epidemic. Saul told Jennifer that he was concerned that Rachel's afternoon tipples would interfere with her medication. Jennifer noticed that when her mother video-called her from Australia, most of the time, she was drunk.

Stuck in the house, they watched a lot more television. Their viewing comprised movies, complete TV shows that they sometimes binge-watched over an evening, and sports, motorsport in particular. Jennifer loved watching motorsports when she could. On one rainy Sunday, the Grand Prix was on. Ilan plonked himself beside her and watched the whole race.

After a few races, some MotoGP thrown in for good measure, and some classic race videos they found online, Ilan was hooked. But he wasn't an expert and was amazed at how Jennifer knew a car needed to pit for tyres before it was called by the pit crew. Regardless of his lack of knowledge, he was an enthusiast and promised her they would go to a race someday when they could travel again. Jennifer vowed to hold him to the promise.

They managed to survive the worst of lockdown between motorsport and books, sunbathing, good food and alcohol. They came out of it closer and more in love than they had been in a long time.

And the sex was out of this world.

But, although Covid hadn't gone away completely, the restrictions had been lifted, and life had more or less returned to normal. Ilan was on a fishing trip with his friends, but Jennifer was bored and wished he was home. She decided that if he could spend the day drinking with his friends, so could she. Although her friends were mainly the characters in the books, she read.

Her current read—*Leverage* by Katherine Black—didn't have a main character Jennifer would like as a friend. She was as creepy as fuck, and worse still, she was called Jennifer. And that seemed even creepier because every mention of the name made Jennifer think of herself. It was a hell of a page-turner, and she couldn't put it down.

With her sunscreen slathered on and her sunglasses perched on top of her head, Jennifer poured a large glass of white wine. She tucked her e-reader under her arm and went to the patio.

With her feet up, her book, a glass of wine, and plenty more in the fridge, Jennifer was happy—right up until her phone started ringing.

It was Saul.

She was tempted not to answer as she wasn't scheduled to go into work that night and was planning on enjoying a few drinks, but he would keep trying until she did.

'Hello, Saul.' She tried her best not to let him hear the sigh in her voice.

'Jennifer, I'm calling to thank you.' Saul got right to the point as usual. 'Or at least the family are. He is under professional care, and enhanced security has been implemented for his wife and daughter. I didn't explain how we found Nevan, but they asked me to pass on their thanks for everything the team did for them.'

'That's good to know. It was nice of them, and thank you for letting me know.'

Now, go away and let me enjoy my wine.

The was silence, and Jennifer wondered if he would say something else. Maybe a word or two about the wonderful work and how much she was appreciated. Even if her work went unnoticed by everyone except the few who knew about Dream Catcher.

'Right then. Enjoy the rest of your day,' he said, and the line died.

She wasn't going to be awarded a medal or a good citizen award. That was obvious, but his call was a rare pat on the head, so she took it in the spirit intended.

'Oh, I plan to enjoy my day,' she said aloud as she got up off the sun lounger and went back into the house for another glass of wine.

Jennifer was so engrossed in the book that she didn't realise how much of the day had gone by. When she heard the car pulling up outside and the raucous laughter spilling from it, she realised it was early evening. She was glad she remembered to slap on some sunscreen earlier.

Ilan was home earlier than normal, and she was surprised until she heard the other occupants of the car pleading with him to join them for dinner and some serious drinking.

She heard Ilan turning down their invitation and telling them he'd go next time.

There were a few jokes about him getting too old for a night out, but it was good-natured banter. Jennifer heard Ilan laughing with them and reminding them that they were the same age as him. But he was wiser, he told them.

They accepted defeat. The car door closed, and it drove off. Jennifer wondered which one was the designated driver and sympathised with whoever had been selected this time. It was a miserable task, drinking something non-alcoholic while the voices got louder and the jokes got dirtier, and no one wanted to drink up and go home.

She had the front door open before Ilan pressed the doorbell.

'Hello,' he said with a grin.

Jennifer stepped back to let him in, and Ilan swung one arm around her waist and the other underneath her knees. Jennifer squealed in surprise when he swept her up off the ground and planted a kiss on her lips with a loud, smacking sound.

They stayed still for a moment, and she caught the look in his eyes.

'Oh, no,' she wrinkled her nose at him. 'No way. Not until you've showered.'

'I thought you liked it dirty,' Ilan said as he lowered her to her feet but kept his arms around her.

'We need to work on your definition of dirty. You stink of fish. Does that mean you actually caught some today?'

'I did. And I—, shit, I left them in Dani's cool box.'

'Never mind. We won't starve.'

'I'm starving now,' Ilan said and pulled her into a tight embrace. He trailed his lips up her neck to her ear and licked her earlobe. 'I'm starving for you.'

He kissed her ear and neck while his hands found a route underneath her blouse and to her breast.

'I know what you mean, but you aren't getting even a nibble until you shower. Now, go.'

Ilan showered quickly, and when he'd dried himself, he went into the bedroom naked.

Jennifer was lying in bed with her elbow on the pillow and her hand propping her head up. She smiled and threw back the covers to show him her nakedness.

'Now, how about some dinner?' She patted the empty space on his side of the bed.

Ilan moved so quickly that Jennifer thought he had time-jumped. He was that hungry for her. His mouth locked on hers as his fingers travelled down her body, stopping to wait until she parted her legs for him.

Chapter 21

Jennifer wished she'd worn a warmer jacket. And a woolly hat, a scarf and a pair of gloves. She was freezing as she stood in the cold winter's night, pretending to be waiting for a bus. She promised herself that, in the future, she would try and dream that she was dressed more suitably for the occasion because her light sweater and jeans weren't cutting it on this frosty night.

Next time I'll dream that I'm wearing a padded jacket, and if I end up somewhere sunny, I can take it off.

But it rarely worked because she never knew where a dream would take her, and she had no control over it as it wasn't her dream. She had walked through the door into her subject's dream and she was in London, of all places. It was a surprise considering the mark was Chinese.

Saul had briefed her that they believed he was stealing financial secrets from the UK government.

Jennifer frowned when he told her. It didn't sound like something the Mossad would be interested in, and she questioned Saul about their involvement.

'In this case, it's China. But, like all governments, we are interested in what China and Russia are up to. And our friends in MI6 asked us to assist them.'

'They couldn't investigate it themselves?' Jennifer asked.

'They didn't give a reason, but they'd prefer to keep their fingers out of this particular pie. And they asked us because there's a lot of chatter within the intelligence communities about the remarkable results we have been getting recently—their words, not mine.'

'You mean from me? They're talking about me as far away as London?'

'They are indeed. Naturally, they don't know who, and they certainly don't know how, but they think we've been on a hard-hitting and successful recruiting campaign. I suspect they have asked us for two reasons. They genuinely need our help, and secondly, they hope that by bringing us in, they'll be able to nab some of our recruits—namely, you.'

Jennifer saw the gleam in Saul's eyes, and it didn't go unnoticed by the Dream Catcher team that Saul walked around with a spring in his step, which hadn't been there for a long time. It was obvious that, although this wasn't a return to the old-fashioned, tried and trusted methods of spycraft, it was something similar, and it was lucrative.

And Saul relished it.

Jennifer enjoyed it too. Some days she felt a buzz of excitement just to know she was a part of something this big and powerful, and, although she was coerced into it, she thought of it as a vital part of her life.

It would be nice to tell people what she did for a living, but at least she could talk to Ilan about it.

'So, I'm famous but not famous, then?' Jennifer grinned with pride.

'You could say that,' Saul replied, and he still had that gleam in his eyes.

Here she was, shivering on a footpath on a cold night, somewhere in London, as she watched her subject from across the street. Jennifer stamped her feet and blew into her cupped hands to warm them, and she noticed that her subject didn't look as cold as she was. He seemed cosy in his heavy, woollen coat. He took his phone out of his pocket, tapped it to open it and checked the time before scanning the street in both directions. He was waiting for someone, and she hoped that someone didn't arrive in a car.

After a few more minutes and another glance at the time on his phone, he picked up his leather briefcase and walked along the deserted footpath.

Jennifer dashed across the road to follow him. She didn't have to worry about traffic as the street was deserted. There weren't even any parked cars or people. There wasn't a soul walking, cycling or even sitting in the window of a bar. It was like the stage set in a movie that had closed for the night. She wondered if her subject was a solitary person in life because his dreams were bleak and devoid of people.

It was something she must remember to ask Miriam when they met next.

Jennifer was glad to be on the move. She was warmer and had stopped shivering. She followed the Chinese man for fifteen minutes as he meandered through the streets. His step was brisk, and his briefcase swung in his hand, occasionally striking his leg as he walked.

He ducked down a narrow side street. Jennifer caught up to the corner about ten metres behind him and stopped. She didn't want to turn into the road to find him waiting for her. She leaned against the nearest building wall and ducked her head around it to see where he was. Most people couldn't see her, but sometimes they did, so it was better to be cautious.

She hoped he hadn't stopped for a pee or met someone for a quick shag in a dark alley.

It happened often enough not to surprise her, but she preferred it when she didn't have to watch intimate moments or listen to them. Neither scenario was out of the question.

But he wasn't relieving himself or having sex. He was doing the same thing he did earlier, standing with his briefcase on the ground at his feet. And he was impatient because every few seconds, he pulled out his phone and checked the time.

He did it a few times, and Jennifer thought the meeting wasn't going to happen when car lights cut through the darkness as they turned in from the other end of the street. Her subject turned in that direction to check it was the person he was meeting. He picked up his briefcase and stepped to the edge of the footpath as though he was going to flag down the passing car.

The car pulled up alongside him, and he climbed in beside the driver—the only occupant.

From her vantage point, Jennifer caught a clear view of the man driving when the door opened and the interior light went on.

She gasped in shock when she recognised him.

It can't be.

But it was, and that was all Jennifer needed. The well-known driver passed a thick file to her subject. By his stupidity in not switching off the light, he confirmed who it was selling secrets to the Chinese.

The why didn't interest her, although she wondered about his reasoning. It was the who that was important. This was what the authorities—those secretive, shadowy civil servants at Vauxhall Cross in London—needed to know.

Jennifer walked to the nearby building with the blue door. She opened it and walked through.

'Bloody hell, Saul. That was shocking. Beyond shocking.'

173

Jennifer decided not to email her report to Saul to pick up when he came in, but she waited for him. This was something she had to tell him in person. She had showered and dressed, made coffee, and drank it while waiting for him to arrive. Like her dream subject, who was impatient to meet his contact and felt the need to check the time every minute, Jennifer tapped her phone every now and then as she waited.

Normally prompt, Saul was twenty-five minutes late this morning. Jennifer was about to email her report to Saul on her phone and go home when the elevator door opened, and he rushed along the corridor. He apologised, unlocked the door and invited her in. He had barely taken his seat when Jennifer related the details of her dream.

'I can't believe it's him. That MP. The guy who works for the British government? He's always on television talking about how great the economy is doing, despite the virus and the high gas and fuel prices. He says the NHS will be okay, and there will be no shortages in the super-markets. He quotes numbers and figures, shows graphs and projections, and tells the viewers that everything is hunky-dory. And all the time, he's a traitor.'

Jennifer shook her head in disbelief.

'Why?' she asked. 'What's he giving to the Chinese?'

Saul shrugged. 'We can only assume he's giving them the true figures, and they'll move in with what will look like a fantastic trade deal and later it turns out to be a buyout. Maybe the British health service. Maybe the energy companies. Maybe both.'

'What will happen to him?' Jennifer asked.

Saul scribbled notes on a sheet of paper on his desk. He stopped writing, set his pen down and looked at her.

'What happens to him is not our concern, Jennifer. It is not our fight. We were asked to investigate by MI6, and we did so. Our findings will be passed on to them and what they do with this knowledge is up to them. We'll have no more part in it.'

'So, basically, you farmed me out to another secret service. I got what was needed, and that's it?'

'In a nutshell, yes. We owed them a favour.'

'But this is big, Saul. I mean, massive, and I think someone should be in on it.'

'No.' Saul raised his hand to stop her. 'It is not our concern. We did what they asked, and now I will give them what we have. What they do with it is of no concern to Israel. It's not our fight, Jennifer.'

'I know, but it's not right.' Jennifer hesitated. What Saul said was true, but she found it hard to reconcile his words with concern for the country of her birth.

'They will deal with it as they see fit.' Saul seemed to read her mind. 'Now, go home and get ready for the party with your husband. Rachel and I will see you later. Do you need us to bring anything?'

'Just yourselves,' Jennifer replied as she got up to leave.

Chapter 22

On the way home, Jennifer stopped to pick up some shopping—last-minute items she needed for the party, which would be huge. Friends and family were coming to eat, drink and enjoy themselves, and she had invited most of their neighbours.

'They can't complain about the noise when they're the ones causing it,' she said to Ilan when he'd questioned why she was inviting them.

They had considered throwing a party a while back but hadn't made any plans until Jennifer told Nurit when they had dinner with her and Reuben. Nurit had jumped on the idea and persuaded Jennifer to start planning.

Jennifer's friendship with her step-daughter had been sealed when she'd offered to design the interior of the house Nurit and her husband built.

Nurit was by her side as she helped find Ilan when he went missing working undercover in Syria. They'd held one another and cried together when they thought he'd been killed.

Ilan was rescued and returned to them, and Nurit had hugged her stepmother, told her father she loved him and stepped back to give them privacy. Her experiences in the army taught her that a soldier needed time to find himself again, which was true of her father.

The virus struck, and the world went into lockdown. Nurit, Reuben and the kids were at home while Jennifer and Ilan stayed in their place. They only left the house when Jennifer had to go to work and when Ilan went running in the mornings.

As cabin fever set in, Nurit and Jennifer would meet from a safe distance while out for a run or a cycle, and that was the closest social interaction the two families could have until the restrictions eased.

A couple of weeks before, the restrictions had been lifted, and the thought of a party was still only a vague idea. Until Nurit and Reuben had come over for dinner. They brought their three children, two toddlers, Gal and Hannah, and their six-month boy, Noah. Nurit asked her if she'd thought any more about a party.

'Still considering it,' Jennifer had replied.

That first get-together after months apart had been a lovely evening with Jennifer and Nurit drinking wine and catching up. Ilan was the happy grandparent until the two older children were sleepy and less interested in playing with him. But it made Jennifer think more about having a party. Nothing formal—just a get-together with lots of food and drink. She planned it all out the next day.

The food was prepared, and the caterers had done an excellent job. It was Ilan who suggested hiring someone to make it all. Jennifer hesitated, preferring to do it herself, but he warned her that she'd be working all day cleaning and getting everything just right, and she'd be exhausted and not in the mood to party.

He opened his wallet, pulled out his credit card and gave it to her. Jennifer took it with a smirk, pretended to blow the dust off it and skipped off to phone some catering companies.

She smiled in appreciation of all the work they'd done and how they had adhered to her requests. The spread consisted of mostly different salads and cold meats. Falafel and dips with tubs of hummus and salsa standing by. There were vegetarian and vegan options, fruits and assorted nuts. Dessert consisted of sweets like baklava and halvah and other chocolate and sugar-filled pastries for anyone with a sweet tooth. There was wine, beer and spirits, mixers, and soft drinks for the designated drivers. Bowls of potato chips—Jennifer still called them crisps—were covered and waiting to be dished out with salted peanuts and popcorn.

She took a look around to make sure nothing had been forgotten, poured a glass of wine and went to the patio to join her husband.

Taking a seat beside him, she breathed a relaxing sigh. They sat together, surrounded by the scent of the flowers and a glow from the fairy lights dancing in the breeze. Music from Ilan's playlist came through the Bluetooth speakers. It would be turned up as the party progressed, but it was background noise for now. Although it was tempting to get up and indulge in a slow dance with Ilan, Jennifer was content to sit with him. They sipped their wine and enjoyed a few calm moments alone before their guests arrived.

'You're so beautiful, neshama,' he said as he took her hand, raised it to his lips and left a kiss there.

Jennifer smiled at the familiar endearment. Although it translated as *my soul*, it was commonly used to mean darling or sweetheart, and she preferred the literal translation.

They were dressed for comfort—smart casual. Jennifer wore white cargo pants and a red sleeveless top. Ilan looked amazing in tight jeans and a loose-fitting white linen shirt, making his dark skin look swarthier. His hair, although grey, suited him, and he'd trimmed his beard to the designer stubble she preferred.

Her hair was still in her distinctive short and spiky style, and she'd kept the white-blonde colour she loved and added some turquoise highlights. There was grey underneath, but that was her secret. Her diamond earrings sparkled in the candlelight, and she only wore a hint of make-up on her tanned face—red lipstick to match her top and dark, smoky-eye makeup. It enhanced the blue of her eyes.

'I love you so much,' she said, and her voice was a hushed whisper as though she had a secret to tell him. Her desire was strong, and she wanted to be in his arms for the rest of her life.

Jennifer promised that she would never let them lose one another again. They had come close, and she'd been ready to give up, but they found their love again, and it was stronger now. They knew how precious it was and how easily it could slip away. She vowed to never let that happen again.

This is the best. I've never been happier, and Ilan is comfortable and relaxed. I don't ever want this perfect day to end.

She saw the gleam in Ilan's eyes and his smile, and she knew what he thought before he even said it.

'I want you now, my love. Perhaps we should cancel the party?'

Jennifer bit her lip as she considered the idea. It was tempting, but she shook her head and gave him a rueful smile.

'Too late,' she said. 'But later, when they've all gone home.'

'I will have to be patient,' he leaned towards her, and his lips brushed hers with a promise.

Jennifer closed her eyes and soaked up the moment.

This is what it's all about. The simple things we take for granted every day—friends and family. Having someone to love who loves you back and living life at an easy pace. Perfection is watching the sunrise and sunset, enjoying a tasty snack and a glass of fine wine. It's all there in the normal, mundane, day-to-day things we hardly even notice. This is how to shut out the bad stuff.

The doorbell rang, and the spell was broken. With a smile and a regretful shrug, Ilan went into the kitchen to open his bar duties while Jennifer took another sip of wine before welcoming their first guests.

Two hours later, the party was in full swing. The music, though loud, was still within a reasonable level of tolerance, and no one had reported them to the police yet. Jennifer reckoned there probably wasn't anyone left to call the cops. The neighbourhood was all in her house or the garden—including some off-duty police. Reuben must have mentioned at work that his father-in-law was throwing a party, and they had invited themselves. She wasn't sure who half the people were as she smiled at them and asked if they wanted another drink or some food.

The smokers were out by the garage, and Ilan had joined them, a bottle of beer in one hand and his e-cigarette in the other. Someone had cleared the patio furniture, and four couples danced to a slow tune. The hum of conversation varied between their thoughts on an upcoming international football match and whether Israel stood a chance of finishing top in their group and last weekend's motorcycle race. Jennifer was amazed at how much Ilan had learned about a sport he'd never followed. She listened to him debate the pros and cons of the tyre choice of the rider who had been expected to win but only finished sixth.

Their eyes would meet, and Ilan smiled at her to remind her that they had plans for later.

Jennifer smiled back at him as she poured wine into someone's glass and had a vague conversation with a couple she thought she recognised. Maybe they were neighbours, friends of Ilan's, or friends of friends of Ilan. They discussed the rising price of lamb, or it could have been fine art or even second-hand cars. Later, she wasn't sure.

Nurit and Reuben were one of the couples on the dance floor, and she had linked her arms around Reuben's neck. Nurit looked stunning. She was wearing a black-strap top and black jeans that she must have had to prise herself into, and she didn't look a bit like an army captain and the mother of two toddlers and a baby. Her long hair was piled up on top of her head, and a few strands had fallen loose around her neck and shoulders. Reuben's hands were resting on her hips as they swayed in time to the music. While they danced, he whispered into her ear, and whatever he said must have been funny because she was giggling like a schoolgirl. Or maybe he was tickling her, Jennifer couldn't tell, but they were enjoying their dance.

She excused herself from the strangers she was talking to and made her escape into the kitchen for wine. She had poured out a glass earlier and then set it down to do something, and when she returned, it had disappeared. That was the second glass she had misplaced, and she realised that she hadn't even finished the one on the patio earlier with Ilan. It might still be there. It might not.

She dropped a couple of ice cubes into the glass, half-filled it with chardonnay and went out, ducking people until she found a less populated part of her garden. And best of all, a chair that had been abandoned. She plonked herself on it before anyone else could claim it and took a big mouthful of wine. Her feet were aching, and she slipped out of her shoes with a sigh of relief. She sipped her wine and took a few moments to relax from her hectic role as hostess. She glanced around and admired her surroundings—familiar for the most part but different tonight. She'd lit candles in glass jars and placed them all around the patio and garden, where they burned brightly and gave the area a soft, ethereal glow. The wind chimes hanging from some of the taller shrubs and trees tinkled in the gentle breeze and added to the feeling of magic and serenity. They dulled the noise of the music and people laughing. The sounds blended and created a memory Jennifer would treasure forever.

It had been hard work getting everything prepared and ensuring everyone had enough to eat. Their drinks were topped up, and Jennifer enjoyed the evening and the love of their guests. They were fed and watered, and from now on, they could fend for themselves and fill their own glasses—she'd done her bit. She could let her hair down and enjoy her party. It wasn't a special occasion like a birthday or an anniversary. It was just something they'd decided to do. Maybe it was an end of lockdown party, or just because they hadn't had one in ages. She didn't know, and it didn't matter at all. You don't need a reason to throw a good party, a messiba as it was called in Hebrew.

The idea for the party came from a casual comment Ilan threw out one evening. On a personal level, the idea had been born out of their newfound passion for one another. They had never been closer than these past months but hadn't sat down and discussed it until they were in the planning stage.

'We should invite some people over,' he'd said.

'Who?'

'Nurit, Reuben, and the kids, your friend Miriam, maybe, Talia, Saul and Rachel, Nathan and his husband. Then there's Uri and one or two others, several in fact, and their wives and girlfriends.'

'You mean for dinner? Ilan, that's a lot of people to cook for.'

'It is. But we could throw a party.'

Jennifer raised her eyebrows, surprised at his suggestion but she didn't think about it again. When she remembered and mentioned it to Nurit, the younger woman's enthusiasm had convinced her it was a great idea. It was definitely something to consider, and so it had grown.

Two hands grasped her shoulders from behind and made her jump, interrupting her thoughts and causing her to splash some wine over her knee. A kiss was planted on the top of her head.

'I don't know who you are, mister. But if you want to have your wicked way with me, we'll have to be very discrete. My husband is nearby, and he's the jealous type. He could kill you with his bare hands or with just a look. He's a spy, you know.'

'He told me he didn't mind and that I was welcome to you tonight.'

'Oh, did he now? Well, in that case, it's okay.' Jennifer turned sideways on the chair and tilted her head up as Ilan leaned forward. Their lips met, and his kiss was gentle.

'You're all alone? Are you okay?'

'I'm fine,' Jennifer smiled as she played with the condensation on her glass. 'I'm just taking a few minutes' break. Do you know this is only my second glass of wine this evening? I keep losing them and I haven't had a chance to sit down and drink one until now.'

'Come with me,' Ilan said as he pulled her to her feet.

He led her to the side of the house where there was less light, and nobody could see them. Still holding her hand, he spun her about to face him. His arms went around her, and he pulled her into his embrace.

They could hear the music playing on the patio, and Ilan nuzzled her ear as he held her.

'Dance with me,' he said as he caught her wrist and lifted it up to put it around his neck.

They swayed to the music, and she lost herself in his arms as they danced together.

When the music stopped, and another tune played, Ilan kissed her again. More passionately this time. Jennifer was still holding her wine, but she managed not to tip the contents out as she returned his kisses until she was breathless. She moaned against his mouth as she felt the familiar ache of arousal.

Ilan stopped and stepped back. He was grinning.

'I've wanted to do that all evening.'

'You do realise this is our house, and we don't have to sneak around, don't you?'

'I know. I just wanted some alone time with you.'

Jennifer laid her head on his chest as his arms went around her again. Someone had turned the music up loud, and Jennifer would have to turn it down before one of the few neighbours who weren't in her garden complained. They enjoyed a moment of calmness before they went back to join their guests.

Hand in hand, they walked back. Her chair had disappeared, but her shoes were lying on the ground where the chair had been. She gathered them up to take inside and stash them somewhere safe.

Nurit and Reuben were still on the dance floor, and they danced as if they were the only people there. His hands were all over her, and she was clinging to him with her arms around her neck. Ilan stopped, and Jennifer looked at him to see what halted him.

'Watch this,' Ilan said as he walked over to the dancing couple.

He sneaked up behind Reuben and tapped his son-in-law on the shoulder. 'You enjoy feeling up my daughter in public? Yes?'

Reuben spun around and let go of his wife as though she was burning him. He had the sense, or maybe a healthy enough fear of his father-in-law, to look shamefaced. Nurit blinked in confusion as she swayed, ready to fall over without Reuben to support her.

'No. I'm sorry. I didn't mean to,' he said, and Jennifer heard the respect in his voice.

'I'm kidding,' Ilan burst out laughing. 'I'm going to get another beer. Want one?'

Reuben swallowed and nodded as Ilan walked off.

'Your father is evil,' Reuben said to his wife.

'I know. And people tell me I'm just like him,' Nurit burst into giggles.

Jennifer was beside them, and she tried her best to keep a straight face, but Nurit's laughter was infectious. Soon, the two women were in each other's arms, holding one another up as Nurit hiccupped between giggles. Reuben was less inclined to join in with their laughter. He was annoyed with himself for falling for one of Ilan's jokes again.

'One of these days, he will be driving over the speed limit, and I'll be there, waiting for him,' Reuben muttered as he plotted his revenge.

The last of their guests had said goodbye and thanked them for a wonderful evening. Jennifer rubbed her eyes and yawned as she switched off the light and climbed into bed. Half asleep, Ilan turned to her and gathered her into his arms. He had steered her to the bedroom even as she protested that she had to tidy up. And they had made love.

'Leave it,' he'd growled. 'I want you now.'

Jennifer slipped out of her clothes, and they had the perfect end to a lovely evening.

Afterwards, she had dozed for a while but couldn't sleep properly. It would be morning soon, but although they were both tired, they discovered that neither of them was close to sleeping.

'The kitchen looks like a bomb has gone off,' Jennifer said. 'But I loaded the dishwasher, and everything else will keep until the morning.'

'Did you have a good time tonight?'

'Oh, I did. It was wonderful, and I enjoyed the evening so much. It was nice to get everyone together. I met three new neighbours, and we've been invited to their houses sometime.'

Ilan snuggled closer. 'I saw Miriam Melandri earlier. Was that her husband?'

'Yeah. It's the first time I've met him. He was stuck in the Antarctic for most of the pandemic, and Miriam was going nuts worrying about him. He's a lovely man, and it was obvious that she's relieved to have him home.'

'It was a shame Saul and Rachel left early,' she said after a pause. 'I saw him taking a phone call, and he took off after that.'

'Rachel was probably in pain from her arthritis. Saul told me it's getting worse every year. Did you know she was a Mossad officer?'

'Get the fuck out of here. That mousey little lady was an officer? Was she really?'

'She was very old-school and one of the best in the business. Her record is legendary. Saul met her when she was attached to the Paris station. I'm not sure, but I think they were both married to other people when they met. They fell in love, and their romance became known. It was a big scandal because office relationships weren't encouraged, especially where the parties were married.'

'Nathan looked nervous. I think he's shy. When I asked him, he said he hates large gatherings of people. I never considered him to be such an introvert.'

'I'm sorry. I can't sleep,' Ilan said as he sat up, punched the pillow behind him and reached for the television remote.

'Me, neither,' Jennifer replied. 'I think I'm too pumped after the party. I had such a great time, Ilan. It's a night I will remember forever. This one and all the nights we've shared recently.'

'It was good,' he said with a smile. 'They all are.'

Jennifer nodded in agreement.

'What do you want to do today? I know we talked about going to the beach but how would you like to go camping? While she was sober at the party, Nurit offered to collect the cats from the cattery and look after them, so we're free for a couple of days.'

'Camping? As in roughing it in a tent? Or did you mean glamping, like in a luxury chalet or something?'

'The first one.'

'No. No way, Ilan. I don't want to lie in a sleeping bag on hard ground, surrounded by creepie crawlies and snakes and whatever lurks in the darkness. I want to spend the morning tidying up the house, and then I'm going to relax, maybe catch up on my sleep this afternoon, and then catch up on the wine I didn't get to drink last night.'

Ilan nodded. 'That works too. We can go camping another time. Or glamping, if you prefer.'

It was still too early to get up, so Ilan switched on the television and found a news station. He muted the sound and slid down the bed to a comfortable position that let him relax but still see the television and read the breaking news scrolling across the bottom of the screen.

Jennifer's eyes were fixed on the screen as she read the words, and the colour drained from her face when she saw the photograph. It was an image of the man she had been dreaming about a few nights before—she recognised him as the British MP who was passing secrets to the Chinese. He had died in a tragic car accident.

Chapter 23

Jennifer wanted to say something, and it was on the tip of her tongue to blurt out what she knew. Or what she thought she knew. The British MP killed in a car accident near his home in Surrey was the same one she'd followed and watched passing information to the Chinese. And she wanted to say that it was more than a coincidence that he happened to die in an accident a couple of days after his secret was discovered. By her—and passed to Saul, who, in turn, forwarded the details to MI6.

Of course, Jennifer couldn't prove anything. She knew that. It could have been a tragic accident and a genuine coincidence. It was probably wise to keep her big mouth shut when she thought about it. Her job was to find out what people were up to, not hand out sentencing. If that's what it was.

And if he had been assassinated—maybe his car was tampered with, or he was poisoned or something—then the authorities would discover the truth during their investigation. If it wasn't covered up, of course.

Jennifer needed to stop thinking about it. She could spend all her time going over the what-ifs and the maybes and her theories—conspiracy theories—until she went crazy. She would still be none the wiser.

So, she said nothing. And Saul didn't mention it. He didn't say anything about his early departure from her party last weekend—or comment that it was the same night the man had been killed. Was that another coincidence? Maybe. Maybe not.

The frown on Saul's face and the downward turn of his mouth made her keep her thoughts to herself. Saul wasn't in a chatty mood—just in a mood. He wasn't all that conversational at the best of times, but there wasn't even any small talk. He didn't ask how she was or even mention her party—a thank you for their hospitality would have been nice. He nodded in acknowledgement of her presence, and as she sat down, he handed her a brief.

'I wonder what intriguing things I'll dream about tonight,' Jennifer said to lighten the sombre mood. She took the file, opened it and read.

'Oh, shit.'

'Not the words I would have used, but I understand the sentiment,' Saul replied.

'How? I thought their security was stepped up after the attempt to blackmail her father.'

'It had. And yesterday it failed. She hasn't been seen since. Laura decided going to a bar for the evening with friends was more fun. She gave her security detail the slip and attended several bars throughout the evening. She foolishly decided to make her own way home after the bars closed, and her friends didn't know anything about the danger going alone put her in. They split up and went their separate ways.'

'She could have gone off with someone. A boyfriend, maybe, or someone she met that night?' Jennifer said.

Saul looked shocked.

'Saul. She's a student. I know you disapprove, but it happens. They drink, and they like to have sex. Her inhibitions would have lowered considerably if she'd been drinking all night. She could have met someone, fancied them and gone off with them for the night.'

'I don't think she's that sort of young woman,' Saul replied.

'I know you don't.' Jennifer's voice was sympathetic. The young woman in question was a family member, and it made sense that Saul was concerned for her whereabouts. 'But what makes you think something bad has happened to her? Apart from the threat regarding her mother and the recent blackmail of her father? Do you think someone is still trying to get to the mother?'

'Yes.'

'Why?'

Saul considered his reply. 'I wasn't entirely honest with you regarding her mother's employment when I told you she was a liaison between the government and the military. That was her cover story, and her real work was on the highest need-to-know security level.'

'And I didn't need to know. I get it. Can you tell me this time?' Jennifer asked.

'Yes. Laura's mother is involved in Iron Dome.'

Jennifer let out a low whistle. This was big. If Laura had been kidnapped to pressure her mother, the country could be at risk. She thought back to what she'd read about it a year ago when the country, particularly Jerusalem, came under heavy and sustained rocket fire over several nights. All but a few of the rockets had been intercepted and destroyed. The few that got through caused slight damage and minor injuries to a couple of people.

Thanks to Ilan and the internet, she'd discovered that Iron Dome was a mobile all-weather air defence system designed to intercept and destroy short-range rockets and artillery shells fired into Israel from four to seventy kilometres away. It was launched in early 2011 and proved its effectiveness repeatedly.

Jennifer remembered it had three central components, radar tracking detection, battle management and weapon control, and a missile-firing unit deployed in a scattered pattern. Each launcher had twenty interceptors, and it was independently discharged and operated remotely via a secure wireless connection.

However, it was vulnerable to hacking. It was thought that, between 2011 and 2012, attackers from China hacked into the networks of three top Israeli tech companies. They stole large amounts of highly sensitive data. It was believed that the data taken by the hackers was related to Iron Dome intelligence.

Since then, data security was increased with the necessary patches inserted into the software to ensure firewall integrity.

Jennifer looked at the file. Sharon Varon, a computer expert, was a vital asset in the cyberwar that was waged every day. She was instrumental in protecting the system's security. Varon was one of the few people who knew the strengths and weaknesses of the program that kept everybody safe in their beds at night.

'Wow. Just wow,' Jennifer said.

'More wow than you might think. Mrs Varon is a renowned software engineer. She was instrumental in designing the new patch that is a hundred per cent infallible.'

'Nothing's infallible. Not completely.'

'That's what I would have said, but this is an AI patch. It's designed to react to any threat—or attempt to break through the firewall—and it counteracts the attempt. I don't know how, but it shapeshifts in layman's terms.'

Jennifer frowned. She had no idea what he was talking about.

'The AI in the patch can reconfigure and mutate to block any hacking attempt. It learns and grows with each attack, thus blocking the malware. Please don't ask me to get any more technical than that, Jennifer, because I'm an old man and have no idea. It's not within my remit.'

'Oh, believe me, I wasn't going to.'

'One other thing that concerns us. Suppose someone—some nation—obtains it. They can retro-engineer it to protect their own systems but what concerns us is that they could destroy our security from within.'

'Do you think they've kidnapped the daughter to force her mother to hand over the secrets to this thing?'

'Firewall patch.'

'Thanks, the firewall patch she's invented, engineered, whatever. But surely you have her under guard? How can she do it now? Even if they say they'll kill Laura, she's hardly in a position to give them what they want.'

'You're correct, Jennifer. But our immediate priority is for you to locate Laura so we can get her home to her family.'

Jennifer cast her eyes down to the file in her hands. She knew this was personal to Saul. The young woman was related to him and he wanted her safe for the family's sake, not just for the potential threat to national security. It was a lot more than that. If she couldn't be found, her mother would be detained. She wouldn't be given freedom until another software genius could upgrade or replace the patch protecting the Iron Dome from hackers. But finding her daughter without knowing who was holding her would make Jennifer's task more difficult. But not impossible.

She didn't know how to tell him what a long shot this would be, and she felt sorry for him.

'I know what you are going to say, Jennifer. You'll tell me it's impossible.'

Jennifer shifted in her seat. She didn't want to make promises she couldn't keep. It wasn't something she liked doing if she could help it. But she didn't want to give Saul the impression she could go into a dream, connect with the missing girl and find her. It wasn't as cut and dried as that.

There were times when it was easy getting into some-one's dream. She could log into their thoughts and emotions. But times like that could never be predicted. Her gift, although successful, could be hit and miss, and she reminded Saul that she couldn't make promises.

'It's not impossible. But it will be tricky if she isn't asleep. If that is the case, the remote viewing might work better, but I'll need more than what you've given me to get a trace.'

Jennifer paced the confines of the small office while she waited for Saul to speak. He didn't.

'To make this work if she isn't asleep, I need some-thing that connects to Laura. It has to be something that makes me feel I'd know her if I met her. Not just a phys-ical description, although that helps, but her personality. Her likes and dislikes and hopes for the future.' Jennifer winced at her choice of words because the girl might not have a future.

It was up to her to change that.

'Tell me more about Laura and her mum. Describe them to me. What do they look like? What sort of a relationship do they have? Give me all you've got, Saul.'

Saul thought before answering.

'Sharon is highly intelligent and a brilliant engineer. Though you wouldn't believe it to look at her. She has this hippie vibe—long, dark hair with blue streaks in it one day and then green or red ones the next time you see her. She dreams of living in the woods somewhere, going off-grid, as they say, and she wants to grow lentils. She wants to leave the rat race and build a cabin by a lake or in a forest. Maybe she will one day. Maybe she won't. But she does like to talk about it.'

Saul smiled. 'I remember many family gatherings where Sharon brought this up and told everyone that it was the ideal way to live and we should all be doing it. Then Nevan, that's her husband—Rachel's nephew—would laugh and say the forests would be awfully populous. And she would be bereft without her superfast broadband and proximity to her favourite shops and restaurants.'

Jennifer watched him as he lost himself in his memories.

'And Laura?'

'She is similar to her mother but also very different. A younger version in looks but poles apart in personality. Sharon is a party animal, whereas Laura is an introvert. She's only ever developed a few friendships that she's been close to since childhood. Laura is more in tune with animals than people, hence her dream of graduating from veterinary college and opening a rescue and treatment centre. She's planning to specialise in equine illnesses and injuries.' Saul smiled. 'Of the two, she'd be most likely to live in the wilderness.'

'What does Laura look like?'

'She is tall and slender. Similar in looks to her mother. She has long, wavy hair. Brown, but with some blonde bits.'

'Highlights?'

'Is that what they are called?'

'Yes.' Jennifer smiled.

'Well, if that's what they are, then, yes, she has blonde highlights in her hair. She's athletic. She swims, runs and plays soccer along with her horse-riding activities. Laura works part-time as a stable hand and in a teaching role, helping the young riders.'

'Anything else?'

'She has a small scar under her chin. It happened when she fell off her bicycle as a child and landed on her face.'

It wasn't much to go on, but it was better than nothing. 'Let me think about it for a while. It's good information, Saul, and I can work with it. However, if she isn't asleep or is heavily sedated, she can't go into REM sleep. I won't be able to reach her unless I try my other method. And well, you know it can be unreliable.'

'I know. Just try your best, Jennifer.'

A thought occurred to her, it was a long shot, but it might work. She suggested it to Saul, and he picked up the phone and barked orders for someone to go to his nephew's house. They were to ask the family for a stuffed toy called Fluffy Tail and bring it to his office.

'Just do as you're told.' He ordered.

The toy arrived thirty minutes later, and Jennifer suppressed a smirk when she caught the raised eyebrow of the man handing it to Saul. He gave the lad a curt thank you as if he asked for things like this all the time. Nothing out of the ordinary—nothing to see here.

Jennifer was expecting Fluffy Tail to be a teddy bear or a dog—battered with age but well-loved. She smiled as she turned the small toy squirrel over in her hand. It had been cute at one time. But, with age, it had lost most of its fur, and it only had one glass eye, and some of the tail hair was missing. Jennifer understood the appeal of a young girl who loved animals. She cradled it in her hand and sensed Laura from it.

'It was more than a favourite toy,' Saul said. 'She called it her good luck charm and took it everywhere. It went to school every day, tucked out of sight in her bag, and she couldn't sit an exam without it. She said she wouldn't have passed any of them without Fluffy Tail to help her. She's very intelligent, but she still believed in her toy squirrel.'

'Hello, Fluffy Tail.' Jennifer said.

Saul couldn't speak and sat down. He had risen through the ranks of the Mossad with hard work and a dogged determination to get the job done—but he had tears in his eyes. Jennifer realised that her boss—the manipulative, authoritarian, often devious man, was on the brink of breaking down in front of her.

'Right then. I'll get started.' Jennifer was determined to get out of the office before they found the embarrassment too much. It was natural for Saul to be upset—the girl was his niece. But she knew him well enough to know that he didn't wear his heart on his sleeve, and he'd hate to be seen as weak.

Maybe she could have said something and given him sympathy with a few kind words. But they didn't have that kind of relationship. Jennifer worked for him. There was nothing more to it. Besides, finding his missing niece would alleviate his suffering, not kind words.

Saul cleared his throat but didn't speak. He turned to the window, and Jennifer was dismissed.

She took the toy squirrel as she closed the door and went to the sleep room.

Chapter 24

'Hey. What are you doing with that? How did you get it?'

Jennifer jumped in fright at the sudden voice. She had opened the dilapidated barn door and stepped through.

The voice made her step back, and a horse snorted as he watched her from over the top of the stall door. For a fleeting second, she thought it was the horse that had spoken. She almost laughed at the notion of a horse talking to her, but she smiled as the girl stepped from behind the beautiful animal.

The young woman had a weapon in her hand.

'That's mine. Give it back to me,' she said as she raised the knife.

Jennifer could see it better now. It wasn't a knife. It was a hoof pick—like a screwdriver but bent at the top. It was used to clean debris out of a horse's hoof.

It wasn't a weapon by design, but it could cause serious injury if somebody was attacked with it. Jennifer kept her eyes on the young woman and wondered if she knew how dangerous a hoof pick could be.

However, the fact that the girl could see and speak to her was more concerning than the weapon in Laura's hand. Jennifer had never experienced this much interaction in a dream.

Usually, when she went into someone's dream, Jennifer could be there without them feeling her presence. Once or twice, someone would look at her, and it was obvious they could see her. Occasionally, the person would frown and glance around as though they'd experienced an uncomfortable sensation. As if they thought a ghost had walked over their grave. They didn't understand who she was. If they saw her, they didn't recognise her and didn't have enough control of their dream to interact with her.

It was different with Lucy. They'd been aware of each other over the nine days they spent in medically-induced comas. When they talked to one another through their dreams, they learned how to interact and even engineered a dream where they met to discuss their situation.

Twice Jennifer spoke to Ilan in her dream. Their interactions were stronger than with a stranger. They were more vivid, as though they were interacting in real life and not in a dream engineered by Jennifer. She had no control over what happened back then, but she had talked to Ilan and made contact with him. The happy dream had turned to terror when he threatened to kill her. It left her traumatised and almost destroyed her love for him. The second time they had dream contact was when she'd thought he was dead. He told her where he was going and made her memorise the coordinates of his pick-up point.

Ilan had no recollection of either encounter—he never remembered any of his dreams.

But to have this young woman standing in front of her, glaring at her, and wielding a weapon, was something Jennifer had never encountered. It was like there had been a shift in her abilities, and they'd evolved into something more. Something stronger. That, or Laura was a lucid dreamer.

The horse stamped his hoof on the concrete and straw-covered floor of the stable and forced Jennifer to ignore thoughts that were nothing more than speculation.

'I want that back now. It belongs to me, so give it back to me.' Laura spoke with steely determination as she pointed the hoof pick at the toy in Jennifer's hand.

Jennifer looked down. The toy squirrel was as scruffy as it looked in Saul's office, with half its fur missing. It was identical. Jennifer didn't understand.

This isn't possible. I had it beside me when I fell asleep. How can it be here?

She found her voice. 'Laura? I'm sorry. Your uncle Saul asked me to give it to you. He wants me to find you.'

'Find me? Who wants to find me? What are you talking about?'

'Your uncle. And your mum and dad. They're worried about you, and they sent me to bring you home. All you have to do is tell me where you are.'

'No.' Laura's long hair was tied in a ponytail, and it whipped in time to her movements. Jennifer noticed the dirty jeans and the old grey hoodie she was wearing. A pair of well-worn muck boots were on her feet—grimy and covered with dust and dried horse manure. She was here to clean out the stable and see to the horses.

'We need to know that you're okay and not under any threat, Laura. Can you tell me where you are so I can get someone to bring you home?'

'Bullshit, what threat? Who are you? I have no idea what you're talking about. I don't know you. And I want to know how you got my squirrel.'

'This?' Jennifer raised her hand. 'I know it's called Fluffy Tail, and you've had it since you were a child. And I know it's your good luck charm.'

'How do you know? Who are you?'

'My name is Jennifer, and I work for your uncle—Saul Mueller.'

A frown of confusion and maybe fear flitted across Laura's face.

'He's Mossad,' Jennifer whispered. 'And so am I. Your uncle gave me the toy because I needed something tangible of yours to find you. I could look at it and touch it to get a feel of you and your whereabouts when he asked me to find you.'

'I don't understand. I don't need to be found. I'm here. Working.' Laura waved her arm in a sweeping gesture around the stable, and her eyes fell on the horse, nosing his empty feed bag.

'He's beautiful,' Jennifer said. She realised that Laura believed she was in the stable. She had to calm her so she could help her to redirect the dream.

'He's not mine,' Laura said as she stroked his neck. 'But I wish he was.'

Jennifer saw the adoration in the young woman's eyes.

'If you tell me where you are, we can get to you, and you'll be okay. Then you can go and see him again,' Jennifer kept her voice gentle and placating. 'Just tell me what happened and where you are. I promise I will come and get you.'

Laura's face crumpled with fear, and she stepped away from Jennifer. 'No. It's dark there. I'm frightened, and I want to stay here. Go away and leave me alone. I won't go back. You can't make me go back there.'

Laura had backed herself into the corner of the stable and was pressed against the wall. Much to Jennifer's relief, she dropped the hoof pick and covered her face with her hands.

Jennifer took a cautious step toward her. She was concerned that the horse might react to the presence of a stranger in his stable, but he didn't seem to see her.

I guess he isn't dreaming about me. Do horses dream? Who knows?

She watched Laura hunker down as though trying to make herself small and invisible and wondered what the girl was going through.

'Laura?' Jennifer kept her voice soft as she stepped closer. 'I'm here to help you. But I need you to talk to me. You have to tell me where you are.'

Laura kept her face hidden as she began to cry. Her sobs were heart-wrenching, and Jennifer wanted to sit beside her and comfort her.

'Please leave me alone. I'm safe here. If I go back, they'll kill me. That's what they said. Please go away and leave me alone.'

Her tears spilled down her cheeks, and she tried to wipe them away, but it was an incessant stream.

'Tell me about the horse, Laura. What's his name? Is he friendly, or does he give you a nip on the backside now and then?' Jennifer was concerned that the distress Laura experienced would cause her to wake up, and the chance to find out where she was held would be gone.

Laura stopped crying and stared up at her. 'Who are you? And how did you get here?'

'I'm known as a lucid dreamer. Look, I'm fond of horses, but I'd rather not be at the kicking end. Would you mind if I sit down beside you for a while?'

Jennifer didn't know how much she should say to the young woman. Explaining that she was here to rescue Laura because her uncle wanted her back home, safe and well, might make her sound like a crazy woman. Laura didn't know she was dreaming. Until Jennifer burst in, Laura's mind had taken her to her safe place with the horses. This level of interaction was a new experience for Jennifer, too, and she had to learn how to handle it—fast.

Jennifer was worried that something had happened to Laura to make her dream so vividly. Head injuries had allowed her to connect with Lucy, and she was concerned for Laura's wellbeing. Laura might have received a blunt trauma when she'd been kidnapped. It made sense that if she'd been knocked out, her consciousness brought her here with a horse that reminded her of happier times. And now, a strange woman had popped into her realism escape asking questions. She had to tread carefully.

Jennifer noticed a change in the atmosphere, and Laura's shoulders and demeanour relaxed. Jennifer still had to go easy and not terrify Laura into waking from her dream, or all would be lost. She stood still and waited for Laura to make the next move.

Laura wiped her eyes with the sleeve of her hoodie. With a patting motion against the straw, she indicated for Jennifer to join her on the floor.

Jennifer wasn't comfortable being in proximity to the horse's rear legs. Even though it continued to ignore her, she gave it a wide berth as she inched her way around the confined space of the stall. She slid down until she was sitting on the straw, which smelled how straw should smell. Her hay fever hadn't materialised as it would have in reality. She was asleep in the Dream Catcher room, and her head rested on a quality hypoallergenic pillow.

The women sat beside each other until Laura leaned her head on Jennifer's shoulder.

'I don't want to go back,' she said.

'I know you don't, sweetheart,' Jennifer gave Laura her squirrel and took the girl's hand. 'But your parents are worried about you, and they want you home. I can help you, but you have to help me do that. Let's get you safe, eh?'

'No.' Laura pulled her hand out of Jennifer's. 'I'm safe here.'

'But you can't stay here, Laura. I can help you get home.'

'How?'

'I need you to tell me what happened. We know you met friends for a drink that evening. When you were still missing the next morning, your parents contacted your Uncle Saul.' Jennifer hesitated, then decided she had to be honest with Laura to gain her trust. 'They had a phone call from someone who said he had you. If your mother didn't do what he wanted, he would hurt you. Has he hurt you, Laura?'

Laura nodded and flinched, then she pulled her knees up to her chin and wrapped her arms around them. She lowered her face, and her shoulders shook with wracking sobs as she tried to make herself small and hide.

'What did they do, Laura?'

'They beat me.'

'Did they assault you? You know, sexually?'

Laura's eyes were wide, terrified at the thought of it.

'No. But they threatened to rape me. They caught me, dragged me by the hair, and slapped me. Then they kicked and punched me and said they would kill me if my mother didn't meet their demands. They called her horrible names.'

'Oh, sweetheart, I'm so sorry,' Jennifer slipped her arms around Laura and pulled her close. She gave her time to cry.

Jennifer didn't know how long they sat in the corner of the stall. Time had no relevance in the dreams. The black horse didn't seem to know either. He was doing that amazing thing horses do and fell asleep on his feet. Jennifer watched his ears flick forward as if he'd heard something, but it wasn't important enough to disturb his nap. His body would move as he shifted the weight from his legs.

Laura's tears had subsided, apart from the occasional gulping sob. She lay down with her head on Jennifer's leg and seemed to have fallen asleep while Jennifer stroked her hair. Jennifer didn't know if it was possible to sleep in a dream, but she supposed it was. She discovered anything could happen since taking on this amazing and sometimes frightening journey.

But they couldn't sit in the stables for much longer. Laura—or indeed, she—would wake up naturally, and she had to find out where Laura was held before that happened. She could try again, but that might be too late for Laura.

They were on borrowed time, and while it was nice for her to hide from the real world, Jennifer had to get Laura to talk. Laura had to reveal the circumstances of her kidnapping, and Jennifer might have to open communications. She debated telling the woman her story—and how she came to be a lucid dreamer working for the Mossad. It wasn't something she wanted to talk about, but she'd say anything if it got her to open up. And Laura would have no recollection of this when she woke up.

I'll tell her some of it, but only if I have to. Let's see how it goes.

As if she'd read Jennifer's thoughts, Laura opened her eyes and sat up. She pushed her hair away from her face and was ready to accept help.

'What do you need to know?' She gave Jennifer a small, hopeful smile.

Chapter 25

Jennifer tugged her jeans on and pulled her sweatshirt over her head. She wasted time searching for one of her flip-flops—it was under the bed. She splashed cold water on her face, brushed her teeth, and rushed to Saul's office. This case was so time-sensitive that she couldn't wait for her wake-up coffee.

Saul was at his desk waiting for her. When she opened the door and walked in, she saw hope in his eyes.

'I know where she is.'

'Is she okay?'

'Yes. She's been roughed up, and she's traumatised, but that's expected. She'll have cuts and bruises from when they beat her up—she told me she fought back, but there were three of them, so, you know. Don't worry, they didn't do anything else to her. It could have been a lot worse.'

Saul's shoulders relaxed as he breathed the tension away.

'Thank you, Jennifer, give me what you have.'

Jennifer went over the details of her dream efficiently. She left out the part about the horse. Every time Laura withdrew, Jennifer brought her back by steering the conversation to horses and Laura's plans for the future. Jennifer let Laura escape into her dream and go to a place where she was comfortable when she needed to. For a few minutes, she could escape the reality of her situation.

'So, this youth she met—the one who invited her to the party—did she know him before his invitation?'

'She knew him casually—to see rather than talk to. She found him attractive, although she didn't say that. Well, not in so many words,' Jennifer smiled. 'He was part of a group that hung around together at university. Laura is on the periphery of his group.'

'I see. Carry on.'

Jennifer was gasping for a coffee, but Saul didn't offer one or let her get one herself, so she plodded on.

'Laura was reluctant to go with him. It was late. She'd been drinking. But that's probably what persuaded her to throw caution to the wind. The young man was persistent—cajoling her and telling her that she'd have a good time. She was reluctant, but he smiled at her and swayed her decision. They talked, and he said they should go to the party together. And that's how he got her,' Jennifer said. 'She got in his car. Two others joined them, and they drove to a darkened area where they bundled her into a van and drove away.'

Saul tut-tutted.

'She should have known better,' he said. 'She's been warned from a young age that she had to be more careful about her personal security because of her mother's work. I don't understand how she let this happen.'

'Give her a break, Saul. I've learned she's a sensible and intelligent young lady. That doesn't mean she can't let her hair down and throw caution to the wind—young people do. Besides, peer pressure is a powerful incentive.'

'Yes, well, she should have been more careful.'

The youth in question didn't have the sense to give a false name, and he was picked up by the police and brought in for questioning. He confessed his part in Laura's abduction. He told them where she was being held without much persuasion—the phrase sang like a canary came to Jennifer's mind.

He knew where Laura's mother worked, but he had no idea what she did. He guessed it was something important and connected to defence.

He finished by saying he was sorry and that it was stupid.

Jennifer grabbed a coffee and hung around long enough to hear the outcome of the police raid on the house where Laura was held.

Laura was brought out, dazed—they had kept her tied up, blindfolded and locked in a darkened room. She fell into the arms of her tearful and relieved parents. The two young men, both students, were arrested for kidnapping. The third youth—Laura's potential boyfriend—was still in custody. They reckoned he'd get a lighter sentence because he was quick to confess.

All three were looking at a few years in prison, a criminal record that would be theirs to keep, and a lifetime of regret for their actions.

Neither Jennifer nor Saul mentioned that she had interacted with Laura in her dream. It was something she hoped he wouldn't bring up. Still, she had no doubt that he'd stored the interesting development for future reference—and would expect her to be able to do it every time.

Chapter 26

Although it was late summer, the sea was still warm, and Jennifer stayed in the water for an hour and a half. It felt wonderful. She would look like a wrinkled prune, but she didn't care.

Ilan had swum ahead, and he was back on the boat, drying himself off and reaching into the cooler for a beer. When she first met Ilan, Jennifer hadn't been keen on swimming. A quick dip in the ocean, then an afternoon sunbathing and reading, usually with a glass of wine, was enough for her. Ilan changed all that. He encouraged her out of her comfort zone and taught her to snorkel first. As she became more confident, he gave her scuba diving lessons and even taught her basic sailing. After years of sharing his passion for the ocean, it became hers too. She probably never would be as adept as he was. But that was okay. She could hold her own, and she loved spending her time in the warm waters of the Med, swimming among the small, brightly coloured fish that seemed to be as curious about her as she was of them.

A day's scuba diving had been her idea, and when she mentioned that she fancied it, Ilan had jumped at the opportunity to do it in style.

He chartered a boat for the day—one with a galley for cooking, a deck for relaxing and sunbathing on and his favourite part—a high-powered engine. Jennifer packed a picnic lunch that included beer and wine packed in ice. They stopped at the nearby scuba hire shop to pick up the gear they had booked in advance before setting off.

When she had suggested scuba diving, Ilan told her about two places he wanted to visit. When he explained why Jennifer frowned.

'Old wrecks, Ilan?' Jennifer sipped her coffee and picked the last piece of fruit on her plate. 'I don't think I'd like that. It sounds creepy, and so do the caves.'

He powered up his laptop, opened a website featuring the wrecks at Nahariya and hovered behind her as she read it.

'We can set off early—it's only a two-hour drive. We'll hire a boat and dive the wrecks before lunch. Then we can decide if you want to check out the caves. They're at Gordon Beach, and they are awesome.'

'Can't we just dive somewhere with lots of coloured fish?' Jennifer pleaded with a pout as she ran through her options of talking him out of exploring old ships.

'There'll be lots of fish at the caves, I promise. You'll even see octopus. But you'll love the wrecks, and there will be fish for you to swim around with there. The Nitzan is a new diving site. It's an old fishing boat that spent years at sea before reaching Israel in the nineteen-fifties.

The navy commandeered it for reconnaissance. It sailed around Africa for a while as a fishing boat off the coast of Eritrea before it was brought back and acquired by the diving association.'

'Will we be going on an organised dive with other people?' Jennifer asked.

'No. Because I'm a certified instructor and a member of the diving association, we can free dive by ourselves.'

'Does that mean we can have underwater sex?' Jennifer asked with a smirk.

'Sadly, no. This is the best time of the year for diving, and there will be lots of people around us.'

'Dammit. I was hoping to tick that off my bucket list.'

'Why do so many things on your bucket list involve sex in strange places?'

'It saves me making two lists.'

'Crazy, woman. But I love you,' Ilan shook his head. 'Anyway, we can do the Nitzan and this one on the same trip.'

'Two wrecks? I dunno, Ilan. Maybe one, and then we can go another day.'

'There are other sites we can visit but let's do these two because they are close. I think we'll keep the caves for another day.'

'Okay, what is the other one?'

Ilan pulled up the webpage. 'The Shira is an Italian submarine from the second world war. In nineteen-forty-two, it was set to destroy Haifa, but it was discovered by the British when it was nine kilometres off the coast. It was sunk by planes and coastal artillery and has been a popular diving site since it was discovered.'

Jennifer wasn't convinced. Especially the thought of exploring a WW11 submarine. The fishing boat she could live with, but the submarine sounded dark and claustrophobic.

'You could do the exploring while I sit on the deck, drink wine and read. Then you can tell me all about these fascinating old sunken ships over lunch.'

'I thought you said you wanted us to spend time together.'

'Yeah, I do, but isn't this more a man thing? You know, you and your old army buddies?'

'I can do that, but I want to be with you to share things I enjoy.'

'Well, okay. If you insist. But if I see an old skeleton smiling at me through a porthole, you are in big trouble.'

'Trust me, you'll love it. Maybe not the skeleton part, but you'll enjoy the rest of it.'

Jennifer took his assurance with a pinch of salt at the time, but she should have known that Ilan would be right. She was having the time of her life exploring the two wrecks. The old fishing boat was interesting because they could swim in and out of it and see the beautiful coral growing on it. But it didn't fascinate her as much as the submarine, and she spent ages swimming around it. She explored its length and as far as she could get down to the underside. She tried to imagine the sailors—were they called sailors? Or submariners?—in the oppressive tin can under the water. Did they get claustrophobic and panic, or had they been conditioned in training to live life underneath the waves? She couldn't imagine living like that, and it made her shudder.

Ilan tapped her arm and pointed to the shoals of fish swimming by, but she dismissed him with a wave of her hand as she explored the old sub in its watery grave.

As well as the fish swimming around, the wreck was covered with an abundance of sponges, mussels and shells.

Jennifer took her time and examined every one of them. She wished she'd brought an underwater camera. But it hadn't occurred to her, and she kicked herself for not thinking of it.

Despite his enthusiasm, Ilan was the one to get bored first. He indicated that he was going back to the boat with an upward signal. Jennifer gave him a thumbs up. She gestured that she was right behind him, but she wanted a couple more minutes.

After the last look, Jennifer had seen all she was going to see and ran her hand along the hull in farewell. She reluctantly pushed away from it and swam through the shoals of beautiful fish. She expected them to swim away, but they didn't. She supposed it was because she was in their world and was large and cumbersome to them.

They took the time to investigate her. She watched them watching her and swimming at a speed to match their agility.

Jennifer checked the dial attached to her weight belt that told her how much of her air supply was left. Her time underwater was almost up, and she had to say goodbye to the crystal-clear world she floated in.

She made her way to the surface, observing protocol and slowly ascending. Then she swam the short distance back to the boat. She saw Ilan on the deck, and he waved his beer bottle in the air to acknowledge her.

'That was amazing,' she said as she climbed out of the water, up the three steps onto the deck and turned around to let him help her off with her gear. 'Where are we going to dive tomorrow?'

'I've created a monster,' Ilan laughed.

'Seriously, though. That was amazing,' Jennifer said as she turned on the tap for the deck shower. The water came out in a steady but icy spray, and she jumped back with a high-pitched squeal at the shock from the cold water.

She rinsed the saltwater out of her hair. Shivering, despite the hot sun, she took the towel Ilan handed to her, stripped off her swimsuit and dried herself before changing into her bikini.

'Take a seat and relax for a while,' Ilan said as he handed her a bottle of water nestled among ice cubes in the cooler. Jennifer made herself comfortable on one of the two fixed loungers and took a grateful mouthful as she watched him pack away the diving equipment in one of the storage compartments.

With the heat of the sun and the gentle sea breeze, Jennifer felt her body warming. Ilan chucked the sunscreen at her with a word of warning to use it, and she caught it deftly and put it on the deck beside her.

'In a minute.' She rummaged in her bag for sunglasses and checked her phone for messages from Saul. Thankfully, there weren't any. He either didn't need her, or the phone signal was poor this far from the shore. This day was too perfect to be cut short.

'Anything?' Ilan asked.

'Nothing,' she replied with a grin. 'I mean, I would go if there was an emergency, but it's great that he doesn't need me tonight. I can relax with you.'

When the Dream Catcher Programme was up and running, Jennifer was happy to spend as much time as she could on it. She and Ilan could barely look at each other, let alone speak civilly. Things had soured between them when he came home from Syria, and she couldn't believe that she'd considered leaving him. She hadn't known what to do and spent as many nights away from him as she could. Work was a welcome escape route for her back then.

Things changed. Her anger dissipated, and she accepted that her fear of him was irrational. They were talking, and they learned how to be friends again. Their past problems seemed so trivial now. Jennifer had never stopped loving him, and once they got over the issues between them, she was reluctant to leave him in the evenings.

She stuck it out for another week and then asked Saul if she could be on a fixed schedule with regular nights off through the week.

Naturally, he had refused. Her work was essential to national security and the programme. And terrorism wasn't a nine-to-five business. Jennifer put her foot down and insisted that she would quit if she didn't get certain nights off through the week. Her marriage meant more to her than saving the world. And she told him she meant it.

Saul agreed but insisted she would be required in an emergency. It was a compromise that they agreed to and could work with.

She could plan her social life better with a set pattern of working two or three nights a week— more if needed. Sometimes, she wasn't required for a whole week, but the other side of the coin meant occasional emergencies when something came up that was live, as Saul put it. She had no choice but to drop everything and hit the road.

Ilan was happier with this arrangement. But he still brought up her quitting every now and then.

He got a look, and Jennifer knew before he spoke that he was about to bring it up again.

'You could quit. It's not like we need the money. You don't have to work.'

'It's not about the money, Ilan. It never was. I did it for you, but now it's something I have to do. Of all people, you must understand that.'

'You are quite the patriot, neshama.' Ilan smiled.

Jennifer shrugged. 'Yes and no. What I'm doing is fascinating. It's a new world to me, and I'm making a difference. You have to admit this ability I have is very cool. Sometimes, it's frightening, but I don't think it's dangerous, and I help catch the bad guys. I've stopped them from doing bad things. And I've saved lives. I'm the only person who can do what I do—how can I not?'

In the face of her argument, Ilan had no comeback because he agreed with her in principle, if not in spirit.

'I'm starving and thirsty,' she said. 'I need something to eat and another bottle of water.'

She opened the cool box and took out their lunch. A packed chicken salad she'd made up for Ilan, and she had chosen egg and onion sandwiches made with white bread and her not-so-secret ingredient, mayonnaise. As Ilan pointed out, when she unwrapped the sandwich and took a big bite, there was still some British in her.

'I can't help it,' Jennifer said between mouthfuls. 'I just love a good butty.'

With lunch over, their hunger abated, and they relaxed on deck for a while. Jennifer wanted to indulge herself with another swim before they had to return home. She allowed herself a glass of wine from a miniature bottle in company with Ilan, who made slow progress on his solitary beer.

They sat together. Ilan was in the corner on the padded benches surrounding the edge of the deck area, with his feet on the storage compartment that doubled as a table. Jennifer was stretched along a bench with her back against Ilan's chest. He draped his arm around her shoulder and stroked her upper arm. They rocked with the motion of the waves that lapped the boat's sides as they chatted. Mostly it was companionable small talk, but they delved into what was happening in the world.

Jennifer sipped her wine, relaxed and contented. She wouldn't have been surprised if Ilan didn't bring up the topic of her work again. But other than the brief conversation earlier when she checked her phone, he'd let the matter rest for their day out.

Ilan had brought the subject up a few times recently. He kept it casual, but he said she had more than fulfilled her obligation to Saul, and she could stop anytime she wanted to. But, somewhere along the line, Jennifer discovered she enjoyed it. He was surprised by her statement but didn't comment.

She didn't enjoy having to get up off the couch in the evening, kiss her husband goodbye and leave him but, apart from that, she liked her work.

'So, you enjoyed exploring the wrecks? Yes?' Ilan asked, interrupting her thoughts.

'I did. Very much. I thought they would be creepier. They were a bit, but they were fascinating when I really looked at them. Thank you so much for talking me into it.' She turned her face to his and kissed him on the cheek.

'So, next time we'll go camping? Yes?'

'Not a chance. No way. I don't want to sleep in a tent, or under the stars, with bugs and little creatures climbing all over me.' Jennifer feigned a dramatic shudder, although she was serious. 'Besides, it's my turn to choose our next outing.'

'And what are you thinking?'

'Nothing yet. I have a couple of ideas, but I haven't decided which one I like best. But it'll be something fun, for sure.'

'Promise me it doesn't involve shopping or art galleries. Or shopping in art galleries.'

Jennifer had just taken a mouthful of wine, and she snorted with laughter. She choked on the wine when it went down the wrong way and sat up, coughing.

'Don't say stuff like that when I'm drinking. Making me choke like that is a waste of good wine.'

'My apologies, neshama. Are you okay?'

'I'm fine, now. I'm going for one more swim before it gets too late.'

She dived off the boat's edge into the cool water.

Ilan watched her for a few minutes before joining her.

Chapter 27

Jennifer was determined to make the most of her time off before the summer ended. Saul hadn't needed her for over a week, and she wondered if other projects had taken prevalence over Dream Catcher.

She had told Ilan her thoughts, and he said it was unlikely that it was slowing down. From what Saul had told him, Dream Catcher had yielded good intelligence. The people who knew about it were more enthusiastic than when first Saul proposed it.

'Maybe they've found somebody else like me.'

Ilan smiled and kissed her forehead. 'There is only one like you.'

'I'm serious. What if they found another lucid dreamer? For all we know, they could have a whole lot of them? There could be a dozen rooms like the one I work in with other people hooked up to monitors, dreaming and spying on bad guys.'

Jennifer wondered if Laura could be working for Saul now. He might persuade her to work for him if he suspected she was a lucid dreamer. And if he could do that, he could find others with similar talents. The gift she sent as a thank you confirmed that she'd interacted with Jennifer.

Jennifer glanced at the ceramic squirrel figurine sitting on the shelf. It had been wrapped in soft tissue and presented in a gift box. There was no card or note to say who it was from, but Jennifer knew it came from Laura. She was surprised and delighted by it but curious why Saul hadn't said anything.

Is Laura capable of lucid dreaming?

It was a possibility. Saul knew Jennifer had interacted with people she was dreaming about on several occasions. It wasn't much. They just registered she was there, but Jennifer had an actual conversation with Laura. It might be enough to make Saul think she wasn't so unique.

Jennifer wanted to tell Ilan about it. But he would see this development as a breach of her personal security. He'd insist she quit, change her hair colour and move to Siberia to avoid detection. She hated the cold, so she kept quiet.

But right now, at her idea of Saul employing dozens of lucid dreamers to replace her, Ilan smiled at his wife. He pulled her into his arms.

'If that's the case. Then there's no need for you to keep working.'

And there it was again. This little thing was more irritating each time she heard it.

'Oh, not again, Ilan. Why do you keep bringing it up?'

'Because you don't have to work. Especially this kind of work.'

'I don't have to, you're right. But it's something I want to do, Ilan. At least for now. Do you know how worthwhile it makes me feel to know that I'm helping other people?' Jennifer stepped out of his embrace and went to the other side of the kitchen to put space between them. She shouldn't feel the need to do this.

'I could change my mind tomorrow or next year. But right now, I want to do it because I feel as though I'm making a difference. It might not be much, but what I'm doing is important, and I am aiding the fight against terrorism. And you should be proud of me for that.'

'I couldn't be more proud of you, but it's dangerous work. I get it. It's your choice. I just like having you at home with me.'

'Oh, for fuck's sake. I'm away overnight for two, some-times three, nights a week. That's all. And it's not like I buggered off to Syria for eight months and almost got myself killed in the process.'

'That's not the same.'

Ilan's jaw was clenched, and his lips tightened in disap-proval. Jennifer knew if they didn't put an end to this, it would escalate into a full-blown argument. And that was the last thing she wanted.

She didn't know how they got to where they were. One minute they were joking about Saul not wanting her. The next, they were sniping, and she was on the brink of calling him a control freak. He wasn't. He was the kindest, most loving man she had ever known, and she was determined not to have an argument with him if she could help it.

She turned to him, but he wasn't there. It was as though he'd vanished into thin air.

Then, just as suddenly, he reappeared.

Jennifer squeaked in surprise and took a step back.

'I dropped this,' he said as he held the bottle of e-juice as evidence. Jennifer watched him unscrew the cap and fill his vape pen.

'I'm sorry,' she said.

'For what?'

'For what I said about you going to Syria. I didn't mean it.'

'I know.' He took a long pull on the pen, inhaled and then let out a cloud of vapour around him that dissipated in an orange-scented haze.

'Do you forgive me?'

'Jennifer, there's nothing to forgive. I know how you felt about me going away, and I understand your feelings.'

She put her arms around his waist and pressed the side of her face against his chest.

'So, you'll stop going on about me quitting work?' Her voice was muffled against the fabric of his shirt.

Ilan caught her wrists and pulled them from around his waist. He clasped her hands together in front of him and kissed her fingertips.

'I'm not sure I can do that.'

'Why not?'

'Because I worry about you. Apart from going into the minds of some of the most dangerous people globally, we don't know how this ability could affect you long term. What if one of the bad guys wakes up and remembers his dream in detail—I know it doesn't happen, but what if it did? Or what if something's happening in your brain that we don't know about? Do you think the firm would give a toss about you if you stopped being useful? They'd drop you like yesterday's news. I'm scared for you. And sometimes I feel that you're being used, and I don't like that.'

'They check me over every month. I get a full medical workup that involves MRI scans. Nothing funny has ever shown up.'

'Not yet.'

'Do you think something will show up?'

'I don't know. I guess it's just a feeling. I'm concerned about it, that's all. Sometimes, when you come home, you look tired. Tired isn't even enough. You look exhausted. And worse, sometimes you even seem frightened. As if you've seen things that disturb you too much.'

'That's because I have, Ilan. I've seen how crooked and evil people can be. I've been right there in their minds, and believe me, some are just pure evil. Some are sad, and others are frightened or coerced, but many bad people are out there. And helping stop them is why I do this.'

'It's not just the way you come home, Jennifer. What about the migraines you get?'

'Sweetheart, I've had migraines all my life. They're not connected to this. Please believe me. There is no risk. Now, go. Get outside and fill the paddling pool, Nurit is bringing the kids over this afternoon, and I'm making chocolate biscuits for them.'

Ilan didn't mention his concerns again. He didn't get the opportunity because he spent most of the day splashing about in their inflatable pool with his grandchildren while Jennifer and Nurit caught up on their gossip as they watched them.

As soon as they went home, Ilan crashed in front of the television with a well-earned glass of whiskey.

As soon as she finished clearing up, Jennifer joined him on the couch. The three-child tornado they had been caught up in had passed, and calm had returned to the house. They were content, watching a movie and enjoying the peace.

The argument they almost had that morning was forgotten.

At least Jennifer hoped it was and would stay that way.

Chapter 28

'This is outside of your normal remit, Jennifer,' Saul remarked as he handed the thin file to her.

'Oh. Sounds interesting. What is it?'

Jennifer took a seat and opened the folder. There was only one sheet of paper inside. Her eyes scanned the page and looked at the printed photograph. A male in his late twenties—early thirties at a push. He was dark-haired and good-looking in an intense way. His height and date of birth were listed, with the bare bones of his scholastic and employment history. There was no driving licence number or passport number. And that was it. She turned it over, but nothing was typed on the other side.

'Who is—Amir Souad, and what did he do?' Jennifer asked as she handed the file back to Saul.

'So far, he hasn't done anything. It is what he's going to do that interests us.' Saul took off his glasses and wiped the lenses with a soft cloth from his drawer.

It wasn't like Saul to be so mysterious. He usually told her the facts and then left her to get on with it.

'Okay.' She drew the word out. 'What am I supposed to be looking for?'

'Amir Souad is an Israeli Arab. He was born and raised in Israel. At least, that's what he claims. A few days ago, he approached a young Mossad officer and said he wanted to work for the Mossad.'

'How did he know the guy was in the service?'

'He didn't. They are acquaintances and have been for a year or so. He mentioned it in a general conversation when they met up and discussed their respective jobs' pros and cons, although our guy was talking about his cover employment. Souad is a used-car salesman, and he's disenchanted with it.'

'So, he wants to go from being a car dealer to a Mossad operative? Yeah, I can see why you would have reason to doubt his intentions,' Jennifer said with a grin. 'He could think he's more important than he is—with delusions of grandeur, maybe. As my dad would call him, a legend in his own lunchtime.'

'Care to explain?'

'Is it possible he's a daydreamer? Watches too many James Bond and Jason Bourne movies and fancies himself as some sort of spy superhero? He sounds like a fantasist to me.'

'That is a possibility. Or, he could be someone employed by a foreign service to infiltrate us. A double agent. When people shout their mouths off about things like this, we have an obligation to take it seriously and investigate them. A seasoned operative would never discuss their work—we have people whose own families don't know what they do. Either way, it's your job to find out what this guy's about. It's possible that he's onto our employee and sounded him out. He could be hoping to groom him for information.'

'So I find out what his game is. Yeah, I thought so.'

'It might take several sessions, Jennifer. Are you okay with that?

Jennifer nodded.

'We need to know what he's dreaming about. Your brief is to find out who and what he is.'

Jennifer closed the bedroom door and gave Amir Souad some privacy while he dreamed about an evening with the woman of his dreams. And that's all she was. Jennifer discovered this fact very quickly when she realised the dark-haired beauty Amir was dreaming about was the weather girl on one of the television channels. He was also having a fling with the blonde that read the morning news, a female sports commentator, and two soap actresses.

Jennifer wondered if he ever had a dream, or maybe a nightmare, where they all met and discussed him.

Now that would be fun to watch.

She yawned, climbed out of bed and went through her usual morning routine.

Nothing yet. Maybe more luck tonight.

Ten minutes later, she was driving through the gates and was on her way to meet Miriam for breakfast at their favourite café. Over the last months, the security guys had come to recognise her. They waved as they opened the barriers to let her leave the complex.

Miriam's car was parked opposite the café. There were no available spaces, so she drove past and continued along the street until she spotted a car pulling away. She dived into the space before it was taken by someone else.

The morning air was pleasant. It was almost but not quite autumnal, and Jennifer smiled as she walked to the café. Her stomach rumbled at the thought of a hearty breakfast and a good cup of coffee.

The aroma of freshly baked bread and rich, roasted coffee hit her and made her stomach growl again. She made her way to the table near the window where Miriam was waiting.

Miriam had a newspaper spread on the table. She was so engrossed in it she didn't look up until Jennifer sat down and coughed to get her attention.

Miriam smiled when she looked up and saw her friend.

'Boker Tov, Jennifer. Ma Nishma?'

'Oh, nothing much. I'm just finished work, and that's about it,' Jennifer said with a self-deprecating shrug.

'How are things at work?' Miriam asked.

'Are you asking as my friend or as my psychiatrist?'

Miriam laughed as she folded up the newspaper and signalled to the waiter to bring two menus.

'Maybe a little of both. But mostly as a friend. One who loves to catch up on all the gossip.'

Jennifer told her what she had been doing. Miriam had full disclosure clearance as her therapist and as an employee of the firm. They could talk freely about cases—but still had to be aware that walls had ears. It was serious stuff, and any security breach could be tried as treason. She paused as the waiter appeared to take their order and waited until he was out of hearing distance before continuing.

'I've been in his dreams for three nights and found nothing other than he seriously needs to get a girl-friend—a real one. I'm bored with his fantasy television dates. But Saul wants me to continue with him.'

While Jennifer was bored with her current case, she noticed Miriam was not.

'You find this dream stuff fascinating, don't you?'

Their breakfast arrived, and they stopped talking as they tucked in. Jennifer loved this place. The food never let her down, and she came as often as she could. She had breakfast and lunch there with Miriam many times. Then she'd introduced Ilan to it, and he loved it. She sometimes called in on her own for a coffee and a snack, usually on her way home from work. The staff knew her and appreciated the generous tips she always left.

Their hunger was sated, and they picked up the conversation.

'Yes. I find it fascinating,' Miriam said between sips of black coffee. 'Until Saul brought me in when Ilan was missing, I'd never heard of anything like this. There's no one like you, Jennifer.'

It was on the tip of Jennifer's tongue to say that she didn't believe she was that unique, but she decided not to. If she told Miriam that people could see her in their dreams, her therapist would be obligated to relay that it was accelerating back to Saul. It could open a can of worms that Jennifer didn't want to open. If Saul didn't already know the full extent, he was damned suspicious. Jennifer had held back on some of the details, but he'd had it confirmed when Laura sent the ornament for her. And then there was Ilan, if he ever found out, there'd be trouble.

'Does it bother you?' Miriam asked.

'In what way?'

'The things you see in their dreams? I've read the reports as it's part of my job, and there have been a few incidents where you've seen some gruesome stuff. Does that affect you?'

Jennifer looked at her friend. She had got to know Miriam so well over the past year that she was familiar with her inquisitive nature, so it could be that. However, she wondered if Miriam's intrusive questions were a fishing expedition. Had Saul asked Miriam to access her?

'Sometimes it's shocking, and it can be bloody awful at the time. But I see it in a detached way. It's as if I'm watching it on the television. And then, when I wake up, it genuinely feels like something I've dreamed of. Maybe that sounds cold and clinical, but I'm there as an observer, not a participant. It took a while and a lot of sleepless

238

nights, but I'm learning not to take my work home with me. You have to.'

'So, it's just remote viewing then? Nothing more?'

'Yeah, I think so. Mind you, I know less about that than you do. All I know is the stuff I've read on the internet.' Jennifer grinned, but her suspicion was raised with the last question.

Miriam smiled back, but Jennifer could see the cogs turning. It was time to shut this conversation down.

'So, what have you been up to since I saw you?'

'Not much. Arguing with my mother, mostly.'

'About what?'

'Grandchildren, or more specifically, the lack of them. She keeps reminding me that I'm into my thirties, and I need to hurry up and produce some for her. For her, she said. Not for me.'

Jennifer laughed. 'So, I take it you don't want kids?'

'No. Not really. I remind her that my husband spends six months of the year on a research station, and if I had children, I'd be bringing them up on my own. Do you know what her response was?'

'No. But I can probably guess.'

'My darling mother told me to tell him to quit. Then she told me if he wouldn't quit, I should find a man who stays at home. Can you believe it?'

'Ouch. That's a terrible thing to say.'

'Oh, I'm used to it. It doesn't bother me. But she's nothing if not persistent. Do you want another coffee?'

'Yes, please.' Jennifer smiled, but she was trying to shake the ghost of the probing questions.

When the coffee arrived, Jennifer was contemplating her plans for the evening. Ilan would want to stay in as they'd been out a lot over the past few weeks. He'd taken her to concerts, the cinema, and for meals at their favourite restaurants. They'd tried some new ones they talked about visiting but never got around to until now. Jennifer had even dressed up to go to the theatre a few times. He commented the day before that it would be nice to stay home and crash in front of the television for a change.

In a similar vein, their days were spent out and about. They went hiking, swimming, and diving. It wasn't her favourite thing, but Ilan had taken her fishing. Twice.

Visiting the markets, the long drives to stop somewhere for lunch and her newfound love of exploring historical sites made for busy days. It meant they'd spent little time around the house, so Ilan had decided to redecorate, leaving her to do some essential maintenance on the garden.

Despite her reservations, he was doing a wonderful job, and she was happy to let him carry on—with a few diplomatically suggested tips on colour coordination.

But tonight, for one night only, she wanted to do something for herself and away from Ilan.

'Mir? Do you fancy hitting some bars tonight? Nurit should be up for it, and we can get a few others—a girl's night out. Lots of booze and giggles?'

'Oh, yes. Definitely yes, with knobs on.' Miriam smiled, and Jennifer's eyes lit up at the thought of an evening spent in good company.

Jennifer burst out laughing, almost choking on her coffee.

'I hope I didn't hurt you when I twisted your arm,' she said.

'I'll heal,' Miriam replied with a grin as she took out her phone and texted some friends to invite them along.

Jennifer did the same. She smiled. A fun night out would be great.

Jennifer opened her eyes and glanced at the clock on the bedside cabinet. It was late in the morning, and unlike her to sleep so long. She sat up and rubbed her eyes and groaned as her head throbbed. Although her memories of the night before were foggy, her nauseous stomach reminded her how foolish she'd been to have so much alcohol.

The bedroom door opened, and Ilan's smiling face appeared around it. He was holding a bottle of water which he handed to her.

'Would you like me to make you some coffee?'

'What do you think?' Jennifer replied as she took the bottle from him. She didn't stop drinking until she'd downed half the contents to quench her raging thirst. A few drops of water dribbled down her chin onto her breasts, and she realised she was naked.

'I can't remember much of last night. What did we get up to?'

She slid over to the middle of the bed as Ilan sat. He wiped away the droplet of water suspended above her right breast.

'I didn't get up to anything. I sat in front of the television, then read for an hour, and I drank coffee and waited for your text message telling me to pick you up. But, from what you were able to tell me when I poured you into the car at two in the morning, you did okay. You and your notorious gang of not-so-impeccably-behaved ladies spent the evening bar-hopping and drinking everything put in front of you. Oh, and you went bar-hopping instead of staying in one place because you were thrown out of several of them.'

'Bloody hell.' Jennifer closed her eyes and groaned as she put her hands over her face. 'I can't remember anything.'

'It was nothing too serious. Although the police were called and your court appearance is scheduled for next Monday. Just appear very contrite and be very apologetic. I'm sure you'll get off with a fine or community service, perhaps.'

Jennifer's mouth hung open as she stared at her husband. 'Are you serious?'

'I'm afraid so. But don't worry. This is your first offence. You'll be fine.' Ilan patted her hand. He tried to look solemn and serious, but the sides of his mouth couldn't help turning up in the shape of a smirk. 'It is your first offence, yes?'

242

Jennifer caught the smirk and the gleam of laughter in his eyes.

'Oh, you evil bastard. You had me convinced I'd been arrested,' she said as she slapped him on the arm and then threw herself prone on the bed again. She pulled the bedcovers over her head to hide from the agony of her hangover and the blinding brightness of the morning.

'Where's the coffee you promised me?'

'I will go and make it for you,' Ilan said. 'Do you want to shower before breakfast or afterwards?'

'I doubt I could eat anything. Let's see how I manage with the coffee.'

A shower, two mugs of coffee and two painkillers later, Jennifer still wasn't confident in her ability to keep her breakfast down. Ilan steered her onto the patio, set her on one of the seats and disappeared into the house. He returned with a bowl of delicious-looking shakshuka with a side plate piled with warm bread, and her stomach rumbled.

'Aren't you having some?'

'I ate earlier.'

'Thank you,' Jennifer smiled and ate her meal, tentatively at first, as she wasn't sure she could manage it, but after a couple of mouthfuls, she enjoyed it. The spicy food was the cure she needed.

Ilan broke off some bread and dipped it into the sauce, and they shared the meal until she was finished. She felt much better, although she was still tired and thirsty. She went into the kitchen and poured another glass of water to rehydrate.

She cleared the plates, rinsed them and stacked them in the dishwasher. Then she joined Ilan on the patio again.

'So, tell me the truth this time. What state was I in when you picked me up, and what did I do in the bars you claimed I was thrown out of?'

Ilan bit his lips to keep from laughing. 'You really don't remember?'

'Bits and pieces are coming back to me. The first place we went to was as dead as it gets, so we had one drink each and left. The second bar was packed to the gills, and we gave it a miss. The third one, this is sounding a bit like the three bears fairy-tale, was just right, and in we went. Nurit started on beer, then switched to whiskey. Miriam's friend, Simone, was drinking mojitos. She was very quiet but livened up when she had a few. Tamar, Nurit's cousin, was drinking wine. Talia was the sensible one and only had two or three before going home. I know she doesn't really like to drink, so I wasn't surprised, and then we—what did we do? That's where it gets hazy. Oh, someone mentioned another place, and we decided to go there. This one was class. There was a band playing. I wish I didn't remember this part.'

Jennifer stopped talking and covered her face in shame.

'There was a band?'

'Yeah. I remember that part. They were all lads, and they were cute. We got a bit loud, and there were a few whoops and hollers and shouts of 'Get 'em off.' And I don't mean off the stage, although everyone seemed to think we did. That's when we were asked to leave.'

'Go on.' Ilan kept his serious face on. Just about.

'Well, the next place was the one with all the country music, and we enjoyed singing along with everyone. Not sure if they enjoyed it, though. After that, it gets cloudy, and I'm not sure what happened then.'

'What were you drinking?' Ilan asked.

'Me? I was drinking tequila.'

'That's why you were so drunk and singing country and western songs when I collected you.'

'I was not.'

'I'm sorry, my darling, but you were. You were very drunk and singing at the top of your voice. It was some cowboy song, I believe. It always happens when you drink tequila. Then, on the way home, you mentioned a book you'd read and that you wanted to try something kinky, or dead sexy as you called it, involving pineapple rings because it was in the book. Then I had to stop the car because you needed to vomit.'

Jennifer had the good grace to blush and shake her head in remorse. 'I don't think I want to remember any more, thank you.'

'But I'm only joking about you getting thrown out of the bars. You had a plan to try three or four different ones, which you did, apparently. Oh, and everyone made it home safely. Including Nurit, who probably won't be seen for a day or two because she is very ill.'

Jennifer cringed. 'Yeah, I think I remember teaching her the words to some songs.'

'All in all,' Ilan said as he put his feet on the table. 'I think you had a great evening, and you deserved to let your hair down. You've been working a lot lately.'

Jennifer kissed his knuckles. 'Thank you for looking after me, and I apologise for ruining your evening. I love you.'

'Bevakasha. I love you too. And I have read the book you mentioned, so we'll discuss the pineapple rings later. But today, I think we should relax and enjoy the sun and do nothing. Until later, when you're feeling better.'

'Sound like a plan.'

Jennifer sighed. Life didn't get much better than this, and despite her hangover, she had never been as happy and contented as she was now.

Chapter 29

Jennifer smiled as she manoeuvred the car into her assigned parking space to wait for Saul. He had messaged her three days ago to say that her current project had been suspended and she wasn't required for a few days. He didn't give her a reason. It wasn't uncommon for something outside Dream Catcher to claim his attention, and she grasped the opportunity to enjoy her time off.

And enjoy it, she did.

Maybe it was a residual effect of the Covid pandemic, the terrible number of deaths and the subsequent lockdowns, but Jennifer and Ilan wanted to spend their spare time outdoors. They weren't the only ones with this mindset. They passed dozens of people out walking everywhere they went—beaches, hiking trails, parks.

Normally, Jennifer would have preferred to spend the day on the beach alone or with Ilan. Or walk the length of a hiking trail without meeting another soul. But that was in the past. After so long in isolation, with most human interaction via a screen, it was nice to meet friends and even strangers in the flesh.

Jennifer would stop and chat to strangers about the beautiful scenery, the dog with them, or even the weather. It was a pleasant substitute for the polite greeting she usually gave them. The introvert had turned into an extrovert.

Ilan was content to take a step back and smile at her animated chatter until she was ready to carry on with their walk.

Whatever troubles their marriage had faced when he returned from Syria had disappeared like an early morning mist, leaving sunshine and laughter in its place. Most of her smiles and lively conversation were for him. She had grown young again and was so full of life. She told him she loved him every day. And at night, she would make love to him with a passion that matched his.

They both felt it and marvelled at it.

They almost lost it two days ago when he told her to wear a pair of good walking boots and comfortable clothes. She was to pack her toothbrush in her backpack because he was taking her on a surprise trip.

It had started so well. He had hidden everything they needed in the back of his car, and Jennifer was none the wiser. She had squealed in delight when they pulled into the dusty driveway at the riding centre. Then he gave her the cowboy hat he had bought for her.

'Yee-Haw.' She had shouted as she put it on—it was a perfect fit—and Ilan laughed and said that her grin was the widest he had ever seen.

He wasn't crazy about horses, and she was thrilled that he was making this sacrifice for her.

'No. I'm not keen on them because they bite and kick and are very uncomfortable,' he told her when she suggested riding. Now here he was, prepared to take part in something she knew he disliked. And he was doing it for her.

Jennifer tilted her hat back on her head, threw her arms around her husband and kissed him like there was no tomorrow.

'Thank you.' Her words were interspersed with kisses.

Jennifer gave Ilan another kiss and then turned to her horse. He was a beautiful bay, and she had been told by the handler that his name was Bandit. She stroked his neck and tickled his muzzle. He curled his lips in response, and she laughed. She whispered hello in his ear, then gripped the reins in her left hand and turned the stirrup towards her to step into it.

She faltered, doubting her confidence and even her ability. It had been over twenty-five years since she had ridden a horse, and suddenly, she wasn't so sure she would be able to ride one now.

Bollocks. It's like riding a bike. Once you learn, you never forget.

She took a deep breath, placed her booted toes in the stirrup and with a bouncing step, she propelled her right leg up and over Bandit's rump. Her leg found the other stirrup, and she settled comfortably in the western saddle. She was pleased with herself that, at her age, she was still supple enough to throw her leg over a horse.

I'm not that old. But all this hiking and swimming is worth it.

The bay took a step backwards before settling down, and Jennifer glanced around to see Ilan already on Blaze, the big chestnut gelding. He held his phone and was snapping photos of her.

Jennifer grinned and stuck her tongue out at him.

As soon as the rest of their group—seven in total—had saddled up and were ready to move out, their guide informed them that this would be a three-hour hack, mostly walking, but it included a few open areas where they could canter. Then they would stop for lunch before going on to their destination. The hack leader motioned to everyone that it was time to go.

Jennifer knew her whole body, her backside and thighs, in particular, would be aching tomorrow. Ilan would be the same, and he would grumble about it for ages, but she didn't care because she was on a horse again.

With a happy heart and not caring where they were going, she took the reins loosely, clicked her tongue and lightly pressed her calf into the horse's flanks.

Her horse thought about it for a few seconds before putting his best hoof forward and setting off at a steady, comfortable pace. Jennifer relaxed her body and allowed it to sway in time to the horse's gait.

Ilan was more hesitant and lagged a few metres behind her, but it didn't take him long to gain some confidence and catch up with her.

The horses' path was wide enough to walk two abreast, and Jennifer turned sideways in the saddle to glance at Ilan.

In his white T-shirt and jeans, coupled with the three-day stubble on his face and the black Stetson he bought for himself, he made a very sexy cowboy. His relaxed and happy demeanour made him look as though he had been accustomed to riding a horse. He was heart-stopping in a tuxedo, but this was a whole new look for him, and Jennifer couldn't help biting her lip as she stared at him and then pulled her phone out of her pocket. She filed the image away in her mind—it was definitely one to keep—but she also needed a photo.

While waiting for Saul to arrive, Jennifer took her phone out of her bag and scrolled through the photos of the two days they had enjoyed. She had taken dozens. Some were good, some mediocre, and one or two were so lovely they were worthy of printing to have them framed.

Her favourite was the one of Ilan, his face in serious concentration, as his horse side-stepped and almost stumbled over loose rock. A small dust cloud kicked up by the horse's hooves swirled around him, presenting Ilan and his horse in front of a beautiful backdrop. She was proud of that one even though it had been a lucky shot rather than a skilled one. The next—several of them—were funny, but one or two of them were blurred, to her disappointment.

Jennifer remembered how the group had arrived at the open area. They were told they were allowed to canter across it. Along with the three most experienced riders, she took off. They raced to the far side, where the terrain was rocky and the trails narrowed. Ilan and the other three had been held back by their guide and told they could cross it at their own pace and canter only if they wished to. Jennifer suspected Ilan was happy enough to keep the steady pace he had become accustomed to, but his horse had other ideas.

He did try just walking, but Blaze seemed pissed off at the thought of a casual walk over the ground that was meant to be cantered across. With ears flattened, the chestnut gelding took off. And it wasn't content with cantering across the open land. This had to be a gallop because Ilan's horse had decided this was his big moment. The chance to race for glory. Maybe some primal memory stirred in his soul. A pride of lionesses could have been chasing him. A prehistoric clan of men with sticks could have been trying to capture him. Or his best friend was waiting on the other side of the open ground.

Whatever the reason, Ilan's beautiful chestnut horse, with the lovely white flash down his face, flaxen mane and tail, decided to take off like a bat out of hell into a full-blown gallop.

To his credit, Ilan managed to stay in the saddle. But it was not graceful, by any stretch of the imagination. His legs were sticking out. He was clinging on to the mane and the reins with one hand and holding his hat with the other, and it seemed to Jennifer that he was more concerned with keeping his hat than keeping himself on the horse. She couldn't tell from the distance, but she imagined she could see the panic on his face.

Oh. I have got to get a photo of this.

She whipped out her phone, opened the camera app, and began snapping. One photo after the other. Trying to keep her hands steady as she did so.

As Ilan and his lightning steed drew closer, she concentrated the phone's camera on his face, hoping to get at least one shot of him, grimacing in fear and panic. She wanted one amazing photo they could laugh at when they viewed it. And one she would keep so that, when he was reminding her how adept he was at just about everything, she could whip it out and remind him he wasn't quite as perfect as he thought.

'Except horse riding,' she would tell him and show him the photos to prove it.

The camera on her phone didn't have a speed setting, and Jennifer kicked herself for not taking her digital SLR camera. With all the bells and whistles she needed to take a decent photograph, her real camera included a speed setting. But one photo was perfect. It was a head-on shot as he came racing towards her, and she could see the mixture of fear and grim determination in Ilan's scowl compared to the sheer joy of the gallop evident in Blaze's eyes. It was a shame the rest of this set was blurred, but this one was a winner, and Jennifer reckoned it would look great printed onto canvas.

Maybe she could sharpen the others up with one of the online photo-editing apps. She decided to have a look when she got home.

Ilan managed to get his horse to stop or, more likely, it had reached its destination and had no reason to gallop anymore. It stopped beside her, throwing up a cloud of dust. Ilan was still in the saddle. He was grinning from ear to ear, took it as a win, and said so as he pulled up close to her.

'That was so cool.'

Jennifer nodded.

'No, seriously. It was very cool.'

'You barely managed to hang on. I thought you were going to end yourself.'

'But I did hang on.'

'Yeah, okay. I'll give you that. Well done, cowboy.'

They stopped for an hour for a lunch of delicious sandwiches, washed down with flasks of coffee, and then mounted up and continued with their hack. They rode over the rocky ground with occasional flat areas where the horses could walk or canter. They knew where they were going. Which was a lot more than Jennifer could say.

An hour later, they reached their destination.

They had rounded a small hilly area. Jennifer could see a large barn and a corral and something very suspicious in the background. She turned a quizzical face to Ilan, but he shrugged and concentrated on keeping his horse from taking off again.

'A campsite. It's a fucking campsite.'

Jennifer remembered how she swore a couple times as she glared at him and told him that she would never fucking go fucking camping.

A tap on the driver's side window of her car interrupted her reminiscing. She opened the door.

'My apologies for being late, Jennifer,' Saul said. 'My meeting ran on longer than I expected.'

'No problem. I didn't mind waiting.' She shut her phone. It would have been nice to continue scrolling through her photos. It was an experience she wanted to relive. But duty called.

She slung her bag over her shoulder and followed Saul into the building.

'This is a criminal case the police have asked us to look into,' Saul said as he handed her the file.

'They know about Dream Catcher?' Jennifer asked as she took the file from him.

'No. They are aware that we have had some good results, and without asking us too many questions about what we do and how we do it, they have asked us to assist them.'

'It sounds interesting.'

She read the brief.

'On the other hand, maybe not.'

She felt sickened by what she read. A man had raped and killed three women in the past three months. The police were closing in on him when he gave them the slip and had gone to ground. The families of the dead women were baying for justice, and the police wanted him caught and behind bars before he struck again.

Going into this man's dreams would make Jennifer feel sick, but what he did to those women made her determined to do what she could to stop him. Even if it meant seeing what terrible things lurked in his mind. She shuddered.

'You don't have to do this, Jennifer. I would understand if you declined this one,' Saul said when he caught her expression of distaste.

'Shush. It wouldn't take too many words to talk me out of this. Let's get it over with. Hopefully, it will only take one session.'

Luck was on her side because it wasn't long before she walked through the door when she located him. But that was when Jennifer's luck ran out.

With a smile bordering on gleeful, he opened the door—the same one Jennifer had walked through when she went to sleep. The woman was lying on the stained mattress. She was battered and bruised and looked barely alive as he stepped over to her and poked her thigh with his foot to see if she would respond. A faint moan escaped her lips, and he grinned and repeated the action. She regained consciousness and whimpered as she moved

256

away from the object touching her. He crouched down beside her and took her jaw in his hand, forcing her head towards him. Her eyes flew open, and she cried out as he leaned over her again.

Jennifer wanted to stop him. Scream at him. Grab him and pull him off this poor woman whose life he was about to end, but her body was frozen. She could only stand there with her back pressed against the wall and watch the horror unfold before her eyes.

He took his time, toying with his victim as he prolonged her suffering to increase his own pleasure. Tears streamed down Jennifer's face as she was forced to watch it all.

Why can't I move? I could stop him and save her.

When he finished, he stood up and walked to the window. As he looked out of it, Jennifer could see the street below and the intersection with the street name on a wall. It was as though he was giving her his location.

Does he want to be caught?

As though he heard her thoughts, the killer turned around, threw back his head and laughed. Jennifer screamed because the look on his face told her she was next.

She was still screaming when her body was hers again, and she could fling open the door and rush through it, back into her own world.

She was alone in the sleep room, but only for a moment. The female medic on duty heard her screams and rushed in to see Jennifer suddenly sit up in bed. The scream died on her lips as their eyes met.

The medic, whose name Jennifer remembered was Romi, rushed to her side and asked her if she was okay.

'Yes. No. I'll be okay in a minute.' As Romi held her hand and gently rubbed her shoulders, Jennifer's voice was ragged.

'Bad dreams, eh?' Jennifer gave a wry smile as she took comfort from the woman standing beside her.

'Are you sure you're okay? I can page a doctor.'

'I'm good. Todah. It was a bad one, but I'm okay. Now.'

The medic was reluctant to leave her side, but Jennifer shooed her away, insisting that she was fine. However, the horror was still with her, on her skin and in her eyes. She had an overwhelming urge to call Ilan and hear his voice, if only to remind her that most men were good. She reached for the phone by her bed, muted so as to not disturb her.

But it was still early, and she resisted the urge to talk to him and reluctantly put the phone down. Ilan would be waiting for her when she got home. Right now, her most pressing concern was to get her information to Saul so he could forward it to the police and get this piece of scum arrested. He'd spend the rest of his evil life behind bars when he was found guilty. She grimaced at him spending even another day as a free man.

Jennifer shut the thoughts and images out of her mind as she dressed. Although it was early, Saul might be in his office. If he wasn't, she'd phone him as she had no intention of hanging around on this one. She wanted to get out of there to hurry home and curl up in her husband's arms. It was there that she was safe from the evil in the world.

The house was in darkness. No lights were on, and there was no sign of movement when Jennifer unlocked the front door. She set her bag down and fed the cats before taking a peek into the bedroom. Ilan was sprawled across the bed with his head on her pillow and his feet and legs on his own side. He was naked, and the duvet had been kicked off. He was snoring.

Leaving him to sleep, Jennifer went into the bathroom, where she stripped and threw all her clothes into the laundry basket. She turned on the shower, waited until the water ran hot, and turned it hotter before stepping in.

The water did little to dispel how dirty she felt. She shampooed her hair, but as she closed her eyes against the lather, the images came back as though they were imprinted on the insides of her eyelids.

I can't even wash him off me.

She pressed her hands against the tiled wall and lowered her head as the water washed away the suds from her hair, but she couldn't get rid of the images she had captured in her dream.

259

The scenes were so horrific Jennifer wanted to scream. She clamped a hand over her mouth and did it silently into her palm, letting only an agonised moan escape her lips. She began to cry. Her tears spilled and mixed with the water on her face as it washed them away. She was crying for the women whose lives that monster had taken and the agony they suffered at his hands. She had witnessed their fear and pain and the knowledge that their lives were over when they still had so much to live for.

The noise of the shower door sliding open startled her.

'Jennifer?' Ilan frowned, and his unbuttoned jeans threatened to fall to the floor. She pushed away from the wall, stood up straight, and wiped the tears and water from her face.

'I didn't hear you come home,' he said. 'What's wrong?'

'Oh, Ilan. It was terrible,' she said as she grabbed him and pulled him into the shower, without caring that his jeans were getting soaked. 'Hold me, please.'

'Not in the shower, Jennifer.' Ilan pulled back. He managed to get her out despite her resistance. He pulled a towel off the rail, wrapped it around her, leaned in, and turned off the shower.

Buried in the warmth and softness of the towel, Jennifer's tears began again. More roughly than he intended, Ilan pulled her close and wrapped his arms around her, and as she pressed her cheek against his chest, she sensed his concern and confusion.

'Please tell me what's happened. Has somebody upset you at work? Did something go wrong?'

'No.'

'Then what is it? Jennifer, you have to tell me.'

'Take me to bed, Ilan. I need you to hold me and lie in your arms where I feel safe. I'll tell you later. Is that okay?' She looked at him through her tears, begging him to do what she asked without any more questions.

Ilan nodded. He walked her into the bedroom, and she was thankful for his strength because she doubted that she could have made it on her own.

She stood in the bedroom and didn't know what to do next—something about her hair, but she couldn't think what and let him take charge. Ilan pulled the towel away and used it to dry her hair. He rubbed until most of the moisture was out. He got one of the vest tops Jennifer wore in bed out of the drawer.

'No,' she said. 'Can I wear one of yours? I mean, your T-shirt? The one you were wearing last night? I need your smell on me.'

Ilan looked around for it. He was too warm through the night, so he'd pulled it off, and it was lying around somewhere. He found it under the bedsheet and handed it to Jennifer. But all she could do was stare at it.

Ilan pulled it over her head and lifted her arms into the sleeves. She climbed into bed, pulled the duvet over her and said nothing as she turned away from him.

She wanted to sleep, but her eyes refused to close. The thought of what she'd see if she did terrified her, and all she could do was lie there, staring at nothing.

Ilan was hovering, and despite everything, he was a welcome distraction. Jennifer beckoned him to join her in bed.

'I want you to lie down beside me and hold me, Ilan.'

He stripped off his jeans, still splashed from the shower, and climbed in beside her. Jennifer threw her arms around him and moulded her body against his as she laid her head on his chest. Ilan tightened his arms around her as he planted a comforting kiss on the top of her head. Jennifer let out a drawn-out sigh. She could close her eyes. She was safe.

Chapter 30

According to her phone, it was eleven o'clock, and Jennifer slipped into her dressing gown, bleary-eyed and yawning. She padded barefoot into the living room, looking for Ilan. The smell of brewing coffee distracted her, and she turned to the kitchen, took a mug from the cupboard, filled it with coffee, and added a splash of milk.

He was on the patio, buried in the book he was reading. He looked up when he heard the door opening.

'Hi,' he said.

'Hi yourself.' She smiled sheepishly. 'Do you want a coffee? I can get you one.'

'I'm good. Come and sit beside me.' He put his book down and patted the two-seater couch.

Jennifer knew what was coming, and she was tempted to bolt back indoors and hide in the bathroom for an hour. But that was crazy. She had a good idea what his reaction would be, and it wouldn't aid her argument for staying at work, but Ilan needed answers, and she was prepared to tell him the truth in all its heinous depravity.

She glanced at the title of Ilan's book. It was in French. *Show off.*

'I'm sorry about this morning, Ilan. I can explain.'

'I know that, neshama.'

The caffeine was taking effect, and she was wide awake, but she was annoyed for sleeping so late. She was an early riser and considered a lie-in a wasted day, even though she had gone to bed and hid under the covers because she was frightened, not because she was tired. And if she was honest, it had done her good. Everything she'd experienced in her dream state was more like what it was—a dream. It was in perspective, and her emotions were that of someone who had suffered a nightmare, not a witness to events through the eyes of a killer.

But, still, Jennifer shuddered as the memories came back. They would return to haunt her for a long time.

Ilan was waiting for her explanation.

'I don't know if you've been told this, but sometimes Saul has me working for the police.'

At Ilan's sharp intake of breath, Jennifer held up her hand in a warning. 'Let me just tell it, please.'

He nodded, but his face darkened in anger.

'Last night was one of those briefs. They needed help to catch a serial killer. He was more than just a killer—he tortured, raped and murdered three women. Maybe more. They knew who he was, and they were closing in on him when he slipped the net a couple of days ago. His whereabouts were unknown, and their biggest fear was that he would attack another woman before he was captured.'

Jennifer paused and took another sip of coffee. It was only a little after eleven in the morning, but she would have killed for a glass of wine or a whiskey.

'Saul told me I didn't have to do it if I didn't want to, but when he showed me the reports and I read what the bastard had done to those women, I had no choice.'

Jennifer leaned forward, her head lowered, and her arms rested on her knees with her hands clasped together. She stared at the ground, fascinated by a beetle crawling across the ground. It seemed lost—like her. She moved her foot out of its path. Ilan's hand rested on her back, and she felt its heat. It comforted her, and she caught herself smiling for the first time—since.

'It was easy to get into his head. He was an open book. It was as though his mind was reliving what he'd had done on a continuous, glorious loop. I read something about serial killers. They keep doing it until they get bored with the same mental movie playing in their heads, and they go out and kill again to stock up on new footage. It keeps the excitement and lust thrilling in their minds. Then it gets stale, and that's why they always kill again. I need to read more about it.'

'No, you don't,' Ilan said, and his voice was quiet.

'No. You're right. I don't.' Jennifer laughed, but there was no humour.

'Screw it. I know it's early, but I need a drink.'

'Pour one for me,' Ilan said.

When she walked back into the house, Jennifer realised she was still in her dressing gown and was wearing nothing underneath.

There's no way I'm going to sit on the patio drinking at this time of the morning when I'm not even dressed yet.

Jennifer went to the bedroom and took some clean underwear from her cabinet drawer. She slipped on her panties and a matching bra and then looked in the closet for a top. She chose a sleeveless, figure-hugging black V-neck top, a clean pair of jeans, and her favourite flip-flops. She brushed her teeth and slapped some moisturiser onto her face.

Her hair needed attention, but she couldn't be bothered.

That'll do for now.

And she went back to the inquisition that wasn't really an inquisition. But it could become one.

With a glass of whiskey over ice in one hand and a gin and tonic—light on the gin and heavy on the tonic—in her other, Jennifer had to slide the door open using her elbow. The ice rattled on the sides of the glasses, and she tried to keep her hands steady.

She handed Ilan his whiskey.

'We ought to be ashamed of ourselves,' she said. 'Drinking at eleven-thirty in the morning. Luckily the neighbours can't see us from here.'

Ilan had taken a mouthful of whiskey and almost choked at her words. He swallowed the burning liquid and coughed. As soon as the spasm went, his shoulders shook with laughter.

'We drank all day, every day, through the first lockdown. And we did a fair bit of drinking through the other ones, too.'

'That was different. It was acceptable then. We're not in lockdown now.'

'Well, pretend that we are,' Ilan said and took another drink. He swallowed it more carefully this time.

'I haven't even had my breakfast,' Jennifer told him. 'I'll be plastered by lunchtime.'

'Jennifer, this was your idea.' Ilan raised his glass and jiggled it at her. 'And it's because you need it rather than want it.'

'Yeah, that's true.'

'So, now that you have a big glass of Dutch courage, will you tell me?'

'About what happened last night?'

'No, Jennifer. About Snow White and the Seven Dwarfs. Yes, what happened to you last night that sent you home in such a state?'

Ilan held her hand, and she felt safe and loved.

If he asks me to quit work, and I think he will, I'll have to say yes.

Jennifer circled the rim of the glass with her fingertip. She tried to make that humming sound, but it didn't work. Maybe because it was a tumbler or a cheap supermarket glass. She didn't know.

'Talk to me, neshama.'

'I don't know how to explain it,' Jennifer replied as she concentrated on making her glass sing, but it refused, despite her best efforts.

'You need to wet your finger.'

'Huh?'

'Dip your fingertip in the gin and then run it around the edge of the glass. It works if you do that.'

Jennifer tried, and almost immediately, the glass hummed. She felt her victory.

'Now, tell me what happened last night. Start at the beginning.'

Her face darkened like a cloud across the sun, and she surveyed the garden. 'Some of the flowers are almost over. I need to cut off the dead heads.'

'Stop it.'

There was a lot to do, but summer hadn't gone away yet, and there was still plenty of colour to love.

And at some point, they'd have to drain the water and deflate the above-ground pool before putting it away for the winter. It was a shame, really, as they'd spent some good times in it these past months. Nurit's three children were attracted to it like metal to magnets every time their mother brought them over for a visit. But they had spent many evenings in it as well—sometimes romantic and sometimes just to relax.

'I'll miss the pool. We should get a hot tub installed. A proper one with jets and Bluetooth speakers.'

'I was thinking the same. I even printed some brochures for us to look at.'

Jennifer smiled as she remembered a long-ago trip to British Columbia when she sat in a hot tub, drinking hot whiskies. The ground around her was covered by a foot of snow. It was beautiful. And now it was a good memory to cling on to.

'Saul told me this was a different case,' she said. 'The police had asked him to help.'

'The police know about you?' Ilan looked terrified.

'No. They don't know about it, or me, specifically. But there's some gossip, I suppose you could say. Someone must have asked Saul to help them out. There may have been more someones in the chain. Or there could have been less.' Her voice trailed off, and she took another gulp of gin. The humming game with her glass was forgotten like tiddlywinks on a deserted pavement.

'Jennifer. Stop beating around the bushes.'

'I'm not. I'm just explaining how I came to deal with this particular case.' She was tempted to tell him that the correct saying was beating around the bush, not bushes—but she held her tongue. It didn't make any difference how you said it. It meant the same thing, whether a peony rose or Kew bloody Gardens.

'I'm sorry, love. Continue, please.'

Jennifer's flow was broken before it even trickled. She stared at the garden and concentrated on the colourful flowers—the roses, geraniums, her beautiful lilies. And all the others she had selected for their delicate fragrances. She had spent many hours with Saul's wife, Rachel. They had poured over gardening books and visited garden centres together. She had been a keen student as Rachel gave her numerous lessons. The woman was a wealth of tips on how to get the most from the flowers, bulbs and shrubs she bought.

Jennifer was proud of her achievements, though she always gave credit to Rachel because she couldn't have done it without her.

They could spend their time gazing over the abundance of colour, listening to the sounds of buzzing insects, and watching the butterflies that the flowers attracted. And all the birds, she couldn't forget the birds. And even though the beautiful garden was a serial killer free-zone, she couldn't forget him either.

She tried to superimpose good images over the ones she had seen the night before. As soon as she told Ilan what she saw, they would all come back to haunt her.

Focus on the flowers. Focus on the bees.

'He's a serial killer. He has raped and murdered at least three young women. And they only identified him last week. I don't know how, DNA evidence, probably. Or maybe someone, a family member, suspected him. If he has any family,' Jennifer shrugged her shoulders. 'It doesn't matter. They found out who he was, and they were about to arrest him when he disappeared, and then they called Saul.'

'Did he disappear because they were onto him? How did he know?'

'I don't know. Saul only gives me basic details. He did a runner the day before the police finalised the arrest warrant. They had a planned raid, but he was gone when they got there. And Saul handed it to me last night.'

Jennifer lowered her head as the images came racing back. Her hopes that the garden would prevent that happening were dashed.

'Do you want another one?'

She looked up. Ilan was on his feet and pointing to her empty glass. She hadn't realised she'd finished her drink.

'Please. But don't make it too strong.'

While she waited for him, Jennifer stared at the garden again, but all she could see was—

No! Don't look there. Concentrate on the flowers. Don't see the blood on her wrists where she fought against the rope he tied around them. Turn away from the bruises and the blood on her lips where he hit her, and the blood on her thighs where he destroyed her. Look at the flowers and that little bird. Is it a sparrow? It seems to be very hungry the way it's tackling the bird feeder. I must remember to order more for them. Don't look at the terror on her face and the fear in her eyes, the pain and the humiliation. Don't look at it. Is that another weed coming up near the rosebush?

Ilan handed her the glass of gin and tonic. She took a large gulp and grimaced. It was a lot stronger than she expected. She glared at Ilan, who merely smiled and took a mouthful of his drink.

He's in a boozy mood today. What is he up to?

'You are using this to loosen my tongue, aren't you?' She held up the glass of gin. 'A cunning plan to make me talk about something I might not want to?'

'Of course, I am.'

'I understand why you became a spy,' she said. 'You'd make a rubbish detective.'

Ilan pretended to look insulted. 'You are cruel? Why would you say such a terrible thing?'

271

'Because a good detective wouldn't need to ply his suspect with alcohol to get them to talk.'

'I have never had to ply you with alcohol. You manage that quite well on your own. And what makes you think you're a suspect and not a witness?'

'Ah-ha! Caught you. A good detective would know the difference between a suspect and a witness and would know which one I am.'

Ilan lowered his head and covered his eyes with his hand. He shook his head. He pretended to look exasperated, but Jennifer saw the humour in his grin.

'Drink up, darling. It could be a long afternoon.'

'Ilan, I don't want to get pissed. Besides, what if Saul wants me in tonight?'

'He doesn't. I called him and told him you're ill.'

'Oh.'

'Now, will you tell me what happened last night that made me lie to your boss?'

'He's your boss, too.'

'No, he isn't.'

'Yeah, right. I bet if he called you tomorrow and said he needed you, you'd be there in a flash.'

'Jennifer.' His voice was stern. 'This conversation is about you. Not me.'

The playfulness in his voice had disappeared, and Jennifer knew it was time. He would always be there for her. She could talk to him about anything, and he would always listen and give her support and advice when needed. Or sometimes, he'd just put his arms around her. He loved her more than life itself, and there was nothing she could say to make him stop loving her.

Jennifer took a mouthful of gin, swallowed it, and took another one. She could feel the buzz now, and she was glad he'd put extra gin in it. It was what she needed to get through this again.

'When I went through the door, I did tell you how I do it, didn't I?'

Ilan nodded.

'Okay. I was in his dreams straight away when I went through the door. Oh, Ilan, it was awful. I could see what he did, and I sensed how much he enjoyed it. He was gleeful about it. And he was all-powerful. He felt in control. And I think that's what it was about.'

Jennifer tried to block the images that flew around in her mind. But they were relentless, and she was bombarded with them. She saw the victims with terrified eyes filled with tears. There was so much blood and bruising. The humiliation and the silent screams tormented her. All of it was there as a running film. And when he'd finished and cast the poor woman away like a used dish-cloth, he smiled. He knew she was there in his mind. He had known all along that she was watching him.

She shook her head like a wet dog shaking off water, and Ilan's fingertips brushed her arm gently.

'Are you okay?'

She wanted to scream and tell him she wasn't okay. She'd never be okay, and she would never be able to unsee what she saw last night.

273

But instead, Jennifer nodded her head and took another sip of her drink.

'Yeah. I'm fine.' She couldn't tell him that the killer had known she was there in his dreams. What she had been asked to do was bad, in his opinion, but if Ilan found out that she had interacted with such a monster, it would sound the death knell to her work on Dream Catcher. She filed that part away where he couldn't reach it.

She was lying, and Ilan knew she was lying. She was surprised by his behaviour. Instead of talking to her and telling her everything would be okay and that she should try not to think about it too much, he was just sitting beside her. He sipped his drink and said nothing.

Instead of feeding her trauma, he played it down. It was considered and deliberate. Instead of hugging her and kissing her and telling her everything would be okay, he sat there, sipping his drink and allowing her to tell him about it. And this allowed her to process it. And then she realised that he let her process it in her own way by drip-spilling it at her own speed.

It was probably something he'd been trained to do over the years. How best to deal with something hard to talk about.

Her realisation lifted her spirits, and although it was still terrible, it was less acute. She found it easier to think about. The images were still there, but she could accept them and move on while she wasn't hardened to them.

Ilan had come through for her again. He was her strength and anchor, and she loved him more for it.

Jennifer caught his hand in hers and smiled.

'I get you. Thank you,' she said. 'And I love you so much.'

'You are only getting me now, neshama?' Ilan laughed, but it was gentle and kind.

'In this respect, yes.' Jennifer let go of Ilan's hand and leaned forward. She placed her elbow on the table and rested her chin, staring into the distance over the fence and the rooftops of the houses beyond.

'When I dreamed about you in Syria, you told me about your friend, Eitan, and how you killed him. You said you shot him to put him out of his misery. I was horrified. I couldn't imagine anyone doing that. But now I do.'

Ilan frowned, and Jennifer figured he wondered what the relevance to her situation was.

'These women were going to die. Actually, they are already dead. But, in his dream and memory, they were still alive, and he kept them like that until they'd served their purpose. I begged for him to kill them. Get it over with and end their suffering. I wanted them to die—not him. That part was just disposal to him. I felt awful for thinking it, but I just wanted their suffering to stop.'

She gulped back a sob as her eyes filled with tears.

'And then he did. And he smirked and wiped his hands. The bastard. And luckily for me, as soon as he finished, his dream turned to his location. I could see outside the building through the window, and that's when I knew where he was holed up. I told Saul, and I assumed the police would have him by now. I hope.'

'They did. The killer was caught this morning and is in custody. He won't ever see the light of day again. When I sent Saul the text to say you wouldn't be in tonight, he replied that it was fine, and then he told me and said to thank you.'

The relief Jennifer felt was unbelievable. It was as if her body had been on high alert. Her shoulders relaxed, her breathing was slow and steady, and she felt a terrible weight lifting from her shoulders and her soul.

'Oh, thank God. The thought of that monster still being out there would be unbearable.' Jennifer shuddered and laid her head on his shoulder, thankful that this man would always be by her side.

'You know, you could have told me sooner, Ilan.'

'I could have. But you needed to process the whole thing first, and by relating it to me, you could do that. If I'd told you he had been captured and was now under arrest, you would have drawn a line under the whole thing. You would have considered it done and dusted and something you didn't need to think about ever again.'

'Well, yeah. Of course, I would.'

'A few weeks or a few months from now—maybe a newspaper article or the announcement of the trial—something would remind you of what you've seen and experienced in this bastard's head. It would hit you like a wrecking ball. You would be curled up on the bathroom floor, reliving it all again.'

Jennifer stared at the flowers. She concentrated on the beautiful mixture of colours and told herself that when winter came along, and they were all dead, she could relive them as she saw them now.

'This way,' Ilan continued, 'you relive it now in controlled circumstances and at your own pace. It's out there, Jennifer. You've dealt with it, and now you can move on. Do you understand me?'

Jennifer nodded.

Ilan stared into his glass. He swirled the remains of the ice cubes around.

'This is why I want you to quit working for Dream Catcher.'

Jennifer sighed. She wasn't surprised. Although he'd stopped dropping it into their conversations, she knew it was still on his mind. His next words were a shock, though.

'This is also why I don't want you to quit Dream Catcher.'

Chapter 31

After a day spent relaxing in the garden and around the house, Jennifer was back to her normal self, and the experience of being in a serial killer's mind had been dealt with. She had tucked it away in the back of a cupboard where she didn't have to look at it again, and she felt fine. It was horrible, but Ilan had walked her through dealing with it, and she'd moved on. She had also hidden the booze, despite Ilan's half-hearted protests.

'No,' she told him. 'We spent lockdown like it was the world's biggest virtual booze-up, and when we were able to go out again, we still drank. I'm not quitting, but I am cutting way back, and you should do the same.'

They had spent the remainder of the day tidying up the garden. The hot tub was ordered. Ilan was going to drain the pool, but Jennifer told him they would still use it, and it could wait for a few weeks.

It had been another fiercely hot day, and all the gardening had Jennifer sweaty and overheated. She had been thinking about a cool shower and maybe a long, cold glass of water when a spray of icy water hit her on the back, and she spun around to see where it had come from. That was a mistake, for she was hit with a second spray and hoots of laughter from Ilan. She yelped and dashed away from him, but he was relentless, and his aim was perfect as he chased after her, spraying her with the hose.

She ducked and ran, this way and that, but there was no escaping him, so she gave up and stood still. She was drenched from head to toe, and there was no way she would win this battle, so she surrendered and spoiled his fun.

'Oh, I needed that,' Jennifer said with a smirk. 'Thank you for cooling me down, darling.'

Jennifer laughed as he turned the hose on himself, and it wasn't long before the two of them were completely drenched and giggling like teenagers.

The rest of the day had been like that. Lots of laughter and fun, interspersed with kisses and smiles. That night Jennifer lay in bed with Ilan's arms around her, keeping her safe from the world outside.

Now here she was the next morning, cooking breakfast and wondering what they would do today. She had planned on taking Beni to the beach for an early morning walk, something she did as often as possible, usually when she came home from work in the mornings. She would collect Ilan, and they would go together. Beni was content to go with other volunteers, but she was still his favourite dog walker.

She had phoned Talia yesterday to let her know she would call and pick him up, but Talia told her the old retriever was feeling poorly and had developed a sudden limp. It was nothing to worry about. The vet said he'd pulled a shoulder muscle and should rest it for a few days.

'What do you want to do today?' Ilan asked as he appeared in the kitchen. He had forsaken the shorts and the old, torn T-shirt from yesterday for a clean, white one and a pair of tan-coloured canvas jeans.

'I was just wondering about that.'

'Day trip somewhere?'

'Yes, please.'

Ilan put his arms around her waist and kissed the back of her neck.

'How are you feeling?' he asked.

'I'm stiff and sore from all that gardening, but I know that's not what you mean. I'm fine, Ilan. Honestly.'

'Would you like to take a trip to the Dead Sea after breakfast? A spa treatment would help with your aching muscles.'

'Screw breakfast. Let's go.'

Jennifer closed her eyes as the hands of the massage therapist worked their magic on her back and thigh muscles. She allowed herself to be rubbed and pummelled and kneaded like she was bread dough. It was manna from heaven, infused with lavender and rose, and she was so relaxed she almost slipped into a coma. A good one that wasn't medically induced this time.

Ilan had declined the massage, opting instead for the nearby sauna, but this was what Jennifer preferred. A sauna was nice, but a massage ironed out the creases in her body and left her feeling great for days afterwards.

They had gone for a swim at Eim Bokek beach on the southern basin. It was over four hundred metres below sea level and ten per cent saltier than the oceans, making it impossible to sink in the turquoise water. They held hands and floated on their backs for ages, staring at the cloudless sky.

Jennifer had already enjoyed the black-mud body scrub, what she called an all-over mud facial.

She sat on the beach until it dried on her skin. The mud absorbed toxins, dead skin cells, and excess oils as it dried. She rinsed it off, and her skin felt healthier, softer and completely purified. Not to mention nourished by all the minerals found in the rich water as she floated beside Ilan.

But this is a million times better than floating on top of the salty water or covering myself in mud. This is proper relaxation.

The treatment included fifteen minutes alone to relax or sleep if that was what she chose. Jennifer didn't think it was a choice as she could hardly keep awake and felt as though she was going to melt and spill onto the floor in a puddle of contented goo.

She gave herself five minutes, then got off the table, picked up her clothes, and dressed.

Ilan was waiting for her when she came out of the treatment room. He looked relaxed and happy as he smiled and waved her over.

'That was wonderful. Thank you,' Jennifer whispered against his lips as she kissed him.

Hand in hand, they took a walk along the path that split the resort from the beach proper and walked until they stopped at a seafood restaurant where they had a light dinner before going home.

'Much better fun than gardening, don't you think?' Jennifer asked as they made the two-hour drive home to Tel Aviv.

Ilan smiled and nodded in agreement.

Chapter 32

Jennifer yawned as she felt her eyes closing, and sleep took her to where she wanted to go. Being as sleepy as this was a good thing. It meant she could slip through the door easily and go where she needed to be in her dreams. In this instance, it was the young man Saul wanted her to check before his application to Mossad was approved. They had put this on hold while she was dream-catching the serial killer.

Jennifer was relieved to be back on a mundane assignment. Mundane was good. She could cope with that.

Before she went back to work, they'd spent a couple more days working in the garden, tidying up and cutting back dead plants and shrubs. They'd composted the debris in the organic recycling bins until they were full and stored the rest in a pile for the next bin cycle. Ilan had changed his mind and emptied the pool for the winter, and Jennifer watched the water flowing into the pipe to the storm drain on the street. They'd enjoyed it all summer, and she was sad to see it empty and folded up until next year. She and Ilan had appreciated it as much as the kids.

But the hot tub was coming soon, and they were looking forward to it. Ilan loved the idea. He loved water and enjoyed having an outdoor shower. He hated it when there was too little rain, which had been the case for a few years, and water restrictions came into force every summer. Ever since she mentioned the tub that day—when she drank gin in the morning and talked about the worst case she'd had since joining Dream Catcher—it was all they could think about.

At least in the winter, they could use it without worrying about the lack of water.

Jennifer couldn't wait, she was as much a water baby as Ilan, and the thought of romantic evenings in the tub appealed to her.

Nurit's eyes lit up when Jennifer told her they were getting one.

'Cool. We'll book a babysitter and join you.'

Jennifer yawned as she pulled the covers back and lifted the leads from the hook beside the bed. She attached one of the adhesive pads to each temple and another one to her chest over her heart. The laptop on the desk was open and running. The app recorded everything, and she selected record on the dropdown menu. It monitored her heartbeat, breathing, and brainwaves and alerted them if she was in distress.

She settled down in the bed and sighed as she pulled the light duvet over her body and let her head sink onto the pillow.

Here's to another fun-filled night in Dream town.

Her eyelids grew heavy, and she gave up the struggle to stay awake. Closing her eyes, she stepped through the door.

Chapter 33

Jennifer frowned when she saw how different Mr Squeaky Clean, aka Amir Souad, was compared to her other mental interactions with him. She nicknamed him Squeaky Clean, or Squeak because he'd never put a foot wrong in all his dreams. She knew his application to join the Mossad was almost processed, and it looked like he was on the verge of being appointed to the service as a trainee agent. Agents were trained to work on instinct, and something about this guy didn't ring true. Saul, always cautious, was doubtful, and he'd asked her to check him out again.

Right now, in his dream, he was sitting at an out of the way café. A small espresso cup and a glass of water were on the table. The cup was empty, yet he sat on.

Who are you waiting for, Mr Squeaky Clean?

One of the main differences was his appearance. He was wearing a suit and tie, and the suit looked expensive. That seemed odd because Jennifer had only ever seen him wearing casual clothes—usually jeans and a T-shirt with a light jacket. His dark curly hair was always unruly, and his thick moustache looked old-fashioned and out of place against his fine-boned facial features. Despite the casual clothes she was used to seeing him in, Jennifer had the impression he lived a life of comfort. If that was the case, his employment status as a used-car salesman in a downtown back-lot was a lie. Or, if not a lie, then a good cover story.

It was his movement and mannerisms that sparked Jennifer's interest. Whatever he was dreaming about made him nervous. His eyes shifted around, and his body was tense with nervous energy—his left leg jiggled as he tried to sit still.

He smiled and stood up, and Jennifer realised he wasn't nervous. He was excited, and he could barely contain it.

What are you up to? Why are you so pleased with yourself?

The scene shifted, and Jennifer was in an office with Squeaky and another man, with a smile that struck Jennifer as smarmy and false. This man was dressed in a suit, but it wasn't as well-cut as Squeaky's. He was Middle Eastern, and his hair was swept away from his face. He appeared to be in his late thirties, and he greeted Squeaky with a handshake, then embraced him like a long-lost friend.

'Nasir, my old friend. It is good to see you,' Squeaky said.

'And you, Tariq.'

Tariq? I thought his name was Amir Souad. Maybe Saul was right to be suspicious.

Squeaky's real name appeared to be Tariq—good information. He turned from the other man and took a seat behind an oak writing desk, and to Jennifer's trained eye, it was an expensive piece of furniture. A closed laptop and a phone were the only items on the desk, and Squeaky, now Tariq, showed no interest in either of them.

'Well?' Tariq asked.

'We believe at least two Israeli agents infiltrated the camp in Syria,' Nasir replied.

At his words, Jennifer turned her focus from the man sitting behind the desk to the man standing in front of it. Concern flitted through her mind, and she felt the fear settle in her heart.

Who is he talking about? Please don't let it be Ilan.

'At least two?' Tariq said.

'Two confirmed. The one we captured and one more. The one who was close to Sayeed and killed the captured Israeli himself. We cannot confirm if there were more, but it is possible.'

Tariq's face darkened with anger. His lips thinned into a grimace as he considered the consequences of the audacious infiltration.

'How has this been confirmed?' he asked.

'The sole survivor confirmed it. Before he died from his injuries, he gave us a detailed eye-witness account of what transpired, including the events leading up to the destruction of your cousin's camp.'

Cousin? Oh, shit.

'How was he able to identify the second Israeli?'

'As I said, this Israeli was close to Sayeed—he was known as Jamal, and your cousin was working with him. The survivor gave a detailed description of this Jamal to a sketch artist. I compared it with CCTV footage around Sayeed's home in Damascus. We also checked out areas he frequented before they left for the compound. This man showed up on camera many times with Sayeed. They appeared to be good friends.'

'Yes. Go on.'

'I could hack into the Israeli facial recognition database and use the sketch artist's impression. It threw up several dozen possibilities, narrowing it down to five. But one of the five stood out, and we believe he is the Mossad operative. He is a wealthy businessman who uses his legitimate interests as a cover for his work as a spy, or at least he did. He worked out of Cyprus for many years until a cartel of Russian criminals he crossed put a contract out on him. He fled back to Israel with his English wife. He remained under the radar for approximately three years until he surfaced again in Damascus. And in the company of your cousin.'

'What?' Tariq frowned.

Yeah. I'm wondering that as well.

'You may also have to consider two scenarios, my brother.' His voice was full of hesitation and fear.

'And these scenarios are?'

'That Sayeed was fooled by this Israeli.' He stopped, clearly uncomfortable about going on.

'Or?' Tariq barked.

'Or that Sayeed was working with the Israeli Intelligence forces.'

Tariq glowered in a red mist of rage. He tapped his fingertips on the surface of his desk as he considered his next move.

'What is the name of this Israeli spy?'

Jennifer gasped when she heard her husband's name, and her heart thumped in her chest as she debated what to do next. She couldn't wake up now. She had to control her panic. Otherwise, the alarm would sound, and she'd be woken by one of the medics.

Tariq, in his expensive suit, seemed frozen as he sat there. His eyes were menacing, and she felt the cold fury from him.

He put his elbows on the desk, and his solid gold cufflinks peeked out from the sleeves of his tailored suit as his hands arched together and his fingertips, with manicured nails, tapped against his lips.

Jennifer inched a few steps closer, thankful to be an invisible presence in the room. And in this man's dream.

'Who else knows his identity?'

'Only me, my brother,' he replied, and Jennifer detected a tremor in his voice.

'Do you know where he lives?'

'I haven't been able to ascertain that.'

Jennifer felt she could breathe again.

'When did the eye-witness die?'

'Yesterday evening.'

'And he talked to no one else? Is that correct?'

'Yes. When he was found, he was in much pain from his injuries. He was incoherent, and then he collapsed into unconsciousness and was taken to a hospital for treatment. He remained that way until yesterday evening when he awakened in my presence and told me his tale. I procured the services of a local sketch artist and obtained from the man the description of the Israeli.'

'How much does the artist know?'

'Nothing. He believes the patient was set upon by thugs who set him alight when he tried to stop them from stealing his money.'

'And the sketch itself?'

'I took it upon myself to destroy it. I hope that is okay. As has my search record in the facial-recognition database. It cannot be discovered and traced back to me.'

Jennifer could tell by his tone that he was frightened, and she wondered why. She turned back to the man she was supposed to be watching. Saul wanted her to investigate him to see if his eagerness to work for Israel was genuine—and now she knew his motives.

He seemed irritated about the source, and she assumed he was debating his options. He was as cold as ice. He opened the desk drawer and pulled out a pistol.

Without a word or even changing his demeanour, he fired the gun at the man standing in front of him.

It happened in seconds. The gun fired with less noise than she expected, and the man clutched his chest as he fell to the floor.

Jennifer screamed in shock and stepped backwards. Her hand reached behind her for the door handle. She couldn't find it and a moment of panic set in as she groped for it. Then her fingertips touched the cold metal. She pulled the door open and stepped back, but not before her eyes met those of the man behind the desk. And in his calm look, she saw awareness.

Chapter 34

Jennifer didn't wait for Saul, and she ran. She was beside herself with panic and had driven home on auto-pilot, checking her mirror every three seconds to see that she hadn't been followed. Ilan wasn't in. There was a note from him on the kitchen counter where she wouldn't miss it. She read it, and her blood turned to ice. He'd gone fishing with friends, but he'd be back around lunchtime. She knew his phone had no signal when he was out on a boat. Would he be safe until then—would she? The problem with dreams was that they had no timescale. They could have minutes or days before this man came for them. She calmed herself to think. She ran around the house, locking doors and windows.

Maybe it was good that Ilan wasn't home. She needed time, without distractions, to sort out what had happened in her dream—and more importantly, to work out what was real and how much of it was just that—a dream.

Before leaving to go home, she'd tried to reach Saul, but he wasn't answering. She left a message for him to contact her urgently. Jennifer left her report on his desk and said he was correct to doubt the man's motives for wanting to join the Mossad. 'It could be nothing, or this could be huge, Saul. I have information about him, but I need more time to be sure. Call me,' she wrote.

She deliberately didn't tell Saul that this man was after Ilan, and it crossed her mind that she was crazy not to. But the thought of the two of them being packed up and shipped off somewhere into hiding kept her from rational thought. She couldn't do it all again.

He didn't know their address. Not yet. All she had to do was keep calm and stay alert until she could confirm everything and have him stopped.

Keep calm and carry on, as the saying goes. Yeah, easier said than done.

As she thought about the target, she assessed him and everything she knew about him up until that morning.

He knew Ilan's name but not where he lived. That took the immediate danger away. He knew about the Syrian Mission because Sayeed Qahtani was his cousin. He'd seen her but only for a second in his dream. He couldn't know she was married to the Israeli spy who infiltrated them and scuppered their plans to unleash a bioweapon on the world. He'd started out as a man, keen to do a job that most people would shy away from. As an Israeli Arab working for the Mossad, the risks to his life were massive.

That was what she had been tasked to find out.

And boy, did I find out.

More questions popped into Jennifer's mind as she continued her mental deliberations.

Is he just someone else in his dreams? In real life, he's a scruffy or, at best, a casual dresser, but, in his dreams, he wears an elegant suit with his unruly hair styled and slicked back. Which is the real one? He had their information—that data didn't appear in his dream by accident. Would Saul put her and Ilan in a safe house until he was taken in for questioning? Does he know Ilan in real life from somewhere? Was that how he got their names? That could make it a dream—just a stupid dream. Maybe it was a scenario he fantasises about with no intention of doing anything about it. But how did he know about Syria? Is the elegant, rich man him, or is he just another persona? One thing was for sure, he knew things he had no right knowing.

Jennifer recalled a conversation with Miriam on the psychology of how people are younger, slimmer, more intelligent and wittier in their fantasies. They are loved and wanted by every woman or man they meet. They are the hero who saves the day, defuses the nuclear bomb, rescues the drowning puppy, and wins the girl before lunch.

'We are all legends in our own minds,' Miriam had told her.

But this was a dream, not a fantasy. There was a big difference between the two. You could be whatever and whoever you wanted to be in a fantasy. In a dream, no matter how mixed up it seemed, it was caused by the brain compartmentalising what it knew. He didn't dream up the facts.

The dream last night belonged to a man who knew who he was and what he was doing.

He wasn't Amir Souad or Squeaky Clean. His name was Tariq Qahtani. At least Jennifer assumed he'd have the same last name as Sayeed Qahtani—the terrorist Ilan had gone undercover to befriend.

And now, he wanted revenge for the foiled plot to kill thousands of people and for his cousin's betrayal and death. And he knew who the man called Jamal was. He was Ilan. Her husband and the love of her life. And this man, Qahtani's cousin, wanted to kill Ilan and take away everything she held dear.

How the hell didn't the Mossad find this out?

And taking that thought a step forward.

They're going to kill Ilan.

It began at work with a tightness in her chest. At first, Jennifer thought she was having a heart attack. Then she was trembling, and her hands were shaking. She moaned and covered her mouth with her hands as if she was keeping her fear a secret.

Her mind raced at a speed that matched her heartbeat, but her thoughts were insane.

What should I do? They're going to murder Ilan. How did Saul not know? Did he know? They could kidnap Ilan and torture him. They might know me. They could kidnap me and torture me to torture him. I have to stop them. I don't want to move from here. I love this house, but Saul will make us move. He'll put us in witness protection—or the Mossad equivalent for our own safety. We'll have new identities. We'll even have to change our appearance and leave Israel and move to God knows where, and we'll never see our families again. I can't go through that again.

I might have to do this alone. Do what, though? I don't know. Find him and kill him before everyone finds out. Maybe, but I don't know how to. And then, I'll be a murderer. So what? Ilan will be safe. But I don't know how to kill someone. I'll have to figure it out. That makes it pre-meditated. Jennifer Ben-Levi, premeditated murderer. I'll go to prison for the rest of my life. But Ilan will be safe. Ilan will be alive and safe. And he'll come and visit me, and he'll be proud that I did this for him. Then he'll find someone else, and I'll never see him again, and I'll rot in prison. No. He wouldn't do that.

She unlocked the patio doors and recklessly stepped outside before she suffocated. The cool breeze felt good on her skin, and she took a few deep breaths. Her heart rate slowed.

Tears filled her eyes as she gazed over her garden. It looked so good and was still filled with an abundance of colourful flowers and shrubs. It was worth all the back-breaking work to make it the garden they wanted.

Not again. Please, not again. I did it once, but I can't start over again. We're too old to have to leave everything we've worked for. We can't. It's not fair. We can't leave our friends and family.

Her thoughts raced back in time to the house in Cyprus. It felt like so many years ago. They'd met and fallen in love in Cyprus and made that house their home. They had so many happy times, and there was so much love in that house. Until they had to abandon it and run for their lives.

And then we crashed, and I was in a coma and met Lucy in my dreams. And the Mossad talked me into working for them to save Ilan. And now I have to save him all over again.

She didn't even get a chance to properly say goodbye to their home in Cyprus. Their belongings had been packed up by someone else and shipped to them in Israel. The cats had been rehomed, and the house, emptied of everything that had made it their home, was sold and the money sent to their new bank account in Israel. Minus all the fees, of course.

It was prime real estate, and it sold before she was discharged from the hospital. She never got to say goodbye.

Jennifer sat on the top step and drew her knees up to her chest. She lowered her head onto her arms and sobbed.

She cried until there were no tears left. And when her tears dried, her heart hardened.

Jennifer sat on the steps leading to her beautiful garden and promised herself that she would not let the rug be pulled from under her again. She would fight to keep what was hers, but she would fight for Ilan more than that. And if it meant losing her freedom, she didn't care, as long as he was safe.

I just need to figure out how.

She changed into her jogging clothes, grabbed a small water bottle from the fridge and set off.

As she pounded along, she ignored the anger that had overtaken her earlier and allowed her mind to relax before concentrating her thoughts on a plan.

As she ran, her idea took form. She didn't know if it would work—it had never been tried before, to her knowledge—but she couldn't think of a reason for it to not work.

She hoped that Saul, and everyone else, would never find out what she'd done to protect her husband. If her involvement was ever discovered, the repercussions would be horrendous. She knew that, and if necessary, she was prepared to accept responsibility for her actions.

If it works.

Her jogging route took her up an incline, and Jennifer covered it fast. The purpose of her run was to give her a cover for checking the vicinity for any strange vehicles lurking in the neighbourhood.

Stop it. They don't know our address. Yet.

She felt the stress building as she crossed the quiet road and turned onto the street leading to her home.

Chapter 35

'Saul sent me a text earlier—something else has come up, so I don't have to work tonight. But I have to go in tomorrow,' Jennifer said as she carried the plates and cutlery outside. 'So, let's make tonight special.' She tried to make her voice sound normal.

Her hand shook, and one of the knives almost fell off the plate. She stood still to steady her nerves.

Stay calm, Jennifer. You've got this.

Ilan was grilling the fish he'd brought home, and he turned to her with a smile.

'Every night with you is special, neshama. You know that.'

'I do know. But after dinner, we could stay outside for a while this evening? It's still warm enough. Maybe even turn off the lights and have dinner by candlelight. Then we can just sit and enjoy the rest of the evening. Then later we can enjoy each other.' Jennifer gave him a seductive smile.

'Have I forgotten any important date?'

Jennifer put her arms around his neck. 'You haven't forgotten anything. I'm just in the mood for romance.'

'Romance, you say?' Ilan turned the grill down, and his hands rested on her waist as he pulled her close to him.

'Well, not hearts and flowers. You know that I hate all that mushy stuff. But a nice meal in the candlelight. Some soft music and maybe a dance. And then us.'

'And then us?' Ilan's hand caressed her lower back.

'I thought you and me could slip under the covers later on.'

'And?' Ilan's fingers ran underneath the loose top she was wearing and found her bra strap.

'And that fish will be ruined if you don't cook it now.'

Jennifer smiled as she touched his cheek and looked into his eyes. She wanted him so badly. A promise passed between them of love and pleasure in the evening light.

'Screw dinner. I want you now.' Ilan growled as he looked at his wife. But, with a rueful smile, Jennifer slipped out of his embrace.

'Later, my love. I promise. But for now, I want the foreplay of good food, candlelight and the best person in the world sharing it with me.'

'Then I should give him a call for you. And make sure he's available at such short notice.'

'Oh, that would be awesome. Thank you so much.'

The dinner—grilled fish with tossed salad, was delicious. Afterwards, Jennifer kicked off her sandals and put her feet up. She closed her eyes, relaxed in the warm evening air, and tried to keep thoughts of the bad things she would do to keep them safe out of her mind so as not to spoil the beautiful evening.

'This is nice,' she murmured as she leaned her head against Ilan's shoulder.

Ilan's arms tightened around her as he planted a kiss on her head. Jennifer got a whiff of the sandalwood and bergamot shower gel he used, and that familiar feeling surfaced in her. She turned her face to his and kissed him gently, then firmly, as her senses told her brain and heart what she wanted.

Ilan returned the kiss. His tongue probed and searched, and his hands caressed her. She threw her arms around him and softened her body against him.

They kissed like teenagers. His hand cupped her breast and squeezed as his thumb caressed her nipple through her bra.

She wasn't a submissive partner in this lovers' dance. Her hands were pressed against his chest, under his loose shirt, and she revelled in the warmth and strength. She felt his heart, the heart beating for her. Her fingers travelled downwards, across his stomach to his jeans. They moved over the belt buckle and his zip to the bulge straining underneath. She rubbed it with her fingertips. Aching to hold it and feel it inside her.

She went to unbuckle the belt, but Ilan stopped her.

'Not yet. I just want to kiss you for the next hour or so.'

'I can't wait that long.'

'You'll have to. You wanted this evening to be special, and special it will be.'

'You're cruel.'

'Yes. I am,' he told her.

He stopped further protests with his mouth and hands. Jennifer melted in his arms, and they kissed like there was no tomorrow.

Then he stopped. In the candlelight, Jennifer saw the gleam in his eyes. Love, lust and the humour that was always present combined into a moment that she never wanted to lose.

'We should tidy up and load the dishwasher,' he said as his fingers rubbed against her sensitive nipple. 'We can keep having fun while we do it.'

'What's a dishwasher?'

'Okay. You win,' he said.

He gathered her up in his arms and carried her to their bedroom, where he set her down on the bed.

The lovely meal was forgotten as they got caught up in the passion they felt. Ilan was undressed in a heartbeat while Jennifer struggled in her excitement as her fingers unhooked her bra and slipped out of her jeans.

After fumbling with the hooks, she got there, and naked, she reached for him. He was poised above her. His mouth touched hers, and she opened her legs, inviting him into her. He tracked kisses down her neck until he got to her breast. He took her nipple in his mouth and sucked, and it seemed that every nerve in her body was super-charged to the point of exploding. She shivered, but not from the cold.

Soft kisses. He laced his fingers with hers and gently kissed each knuckle, her wrist, and her lips again. Slow and easy, each touch of his lips lit a soft, warm fire in her soul.

He reached between her legs and slipped two fingers into her wetness.

Jennifer's breath caught in her throat as she felt his touch. Her muscles tightened around his finger as he probed and caressed. He was driving her crazy, and she loved it.

Ilan turned his attention to her clitoris. He circled the small bud as Jennifer writhed beneath him. She felt her need for him pulsating, and she was more than ready for him.

She took matters into her own hand, reaching down to grip him. She circled him with her fingers and massaged his shaft, enjoying how rigid it was. She loved how his breath caught with every movement. Her pace quickened, and she was in charge when he pulled away from her and hooked one knee over his arm to raise her hips.

He plunged into her.

Jennifer arched her hips up to meet his gentle thrusts, and they found the rhythm they had never lost. His lips were against her lips, and his tongue matched the rhythm as Jennifer climbed towards her orgasm.

There had been enough wham-bam-thank-you-ma'am recently, and she turned down the pace. Ilan responded to her unspoken directions, and he took her slowly. Each movement was an act of love, and it was more powerful, more intense than anything she had felt before.

They reached the top together, and Jennifer gasped as she felt his hot semen filling her. Her own orgasm exploded, and she held her breath as every muscle, every sinew, and nerve ending in her body sparked and burned with a white-hot, searing flame.

On the way down, Jennifer thought she was going to faint. Her heart was pounding in her chest, and she couldn't breathe. For a moment, she thought she really was going to faint.

Her breathing eased, and her heart slowed to its normal pace. She opened her eyes.

Ilan was slumped on top of her, with his head resting on her shoulder. His eyes were closed. He was either asleep or dead, she reckoned. Until she heard his ragged breath.

He lifted his head and rested it on his arm.

'That was fun,' he said.

'Wasn't it just?' Jennifer replied with a satisfied smile as she pushed his weight off her, grabbed his wrist and pulled his arm around her. She snuggled close to him and committed the evening to memory—the meal and the happiness.

Just in case.

It was now or never. One of those don't-try-this-at-home moments as she lay in the darkness with drowsiness closing in. Jennifer wondered if she was crazy to try it here

305

instead of in the safe and controlled confines of the Sleep Room.

As she counted back from ten, the door appeared in front of her. She opened it and slipped into Tariq Qahtani's dream.

In the darkness, Jennifer looked at the clock beside her. The illuminated numbers told her it was after four in the morning. Ilan was snoring beside her, his arm draped over her hip and his breath tickling her bare shoulder. She wriggled over and turned onto her back. Ilan stirred at her movement but settled down again.

Well, that was a waste of time.

Although, when she considered it, Jennifer realised it hadn't been a complete waste of time. She only managed to stay in Qahtani's dream for a few seconds before she was forcefully thrown somewhere else—into her own dream, she suspected. She had learned that her ability didn't work at home. Maybe because Ilan was lying beside her, moving, breathing deeply, and even muttering something intelligible in his sleep. Because her sleep patterns were attuned to his, she couldn't lucid dream at home in her own bed.

It was a theory and something Jennifer had often wondered about but had never tried. Until now. And her question had been well and truly answered.

The annoying part was that she hadn't put her plan into action. She wanted to do it away from the Dream Catcher Programme and the observant eyes of Saul Mueller. But she realised that she'd have to tell Saul at least some of it. She's already broken protocol by going renegade.

Ilan stirred. He rolled onto his back and opened his eyes.

'What time is it?'

'Almost four-thirty.'

'Why aren't you asleep?'

'I don't know, Ilan. I woke up and couldn't get back to sleep.'

He put his hand on her inner thigh, just above her knee.

Jennifer parted her legs in an invitation that he readily accepted.

Chapter 36

'Saul? Hi. There's a problem, and we need to talk about it,' Jennifer said as she slipped into the office.

'What is wrong, Jennifer?'

'Have you read my report? The potential recruit you've had me looking into? I think he's connected to the leader of the terrorist group Ilan infiltrated in Syria.'

'Yes, I've read the report. It's damming stuff, but your evidence is sketchy at best, and there's nowhere near enough to make an arrest on. We need to keep this on the lowdown, proceed with caution, and gather more intel.'

'Right, for a start, Saul, this guy is not who he says he is. He's rich. He is also known by another name—Tariq Qahtani—and I overheard someone talking to him.'

'Did you say Qahtani?' Saul frowned.

'Yes. I think that's his name. I didn't put it in the report because I don't know for sure that he has the same name as his family member. I wanted to talk to you first before making it official and signing my name to it. But it certainly looks that way. And I heard another man talking about his—Tariq's—cousin's death. He mentioned the Syria connection and capturing an Israeli spy. Then he talked about a survivor who has since died from his injuries. And before he died, he identified a second Israeli. That's Ilan, isn't it?'

'Go on.' Saul didn't answer her question.

'Well, there wasn't much else because our guy pulled out a gun and shot the man who told him.'

'You are completely sure of this? Yes?'

Jennifer chewed the inside of her cheek. Of course, she was bloody sure, but she had no intention of telling Saul her plans. However, she had to convince him to give her another session.

'Not a hundred per cent. No,' she lied.

'Can you do it again tonight?'

'I think so. Yes.'

'Let's go.'

Jennifer followed Saul out of the office with a smile. He'd taken the bait.

Jennifer wondered which persona she would find her target inhabiting as she fell asleep. He could be the eager young man in the tatty jeans and sweatshirt or the man in the expensive suit committed to exacting revenge on those responsible for his cousin's execution.

She was scared for the first time since she began this journey into the dreams of people she had never met. She didn't want to meet these awful people, and Jennifer felt a small frisson of fear as she reached for the door handle. This one was close to home and what she was going to do was so very wrong in every sense of the word.

This could be the last time I ever do this.

She turned the handle and opened the door.

Then let's make it the most successful one ever. It's certainly the most important.

She stepped into the crowded restaurant and cast her eyes around the people. They were a varied bunch. Couples, friends who probably met up every week, and a lot of businessmen and women. The men were in suits, and the women were power-dressed in dark skirts and jackets. Corporate types, every one of them.

She saw him. Dressed in his expensive suit, with his hair slicked back. He was huddled at a corner table with two similarly-dressed men. They were eating a meal, and they appeared relaxed as they enjoyed their food.

Jennifer lifted a silver tray that was sitting on a nearby table. A napkin draped over it, and she knew what was underneath it without even looking.

She squared her shoulders, took a deep breath and walked toward the man who wanted her husband dead. She carried the tray, still covered by the napkin, in her left hand.

When she was a few feet away from him, Jennifer stopped. She pulled the gun from underneath the napkin and threw the tray to the ground. The noise caused everyone to turn and look in her direction as she raised the gun. Qahtani saw it and rose to his feet, knocking the table with his leg. A glass of water toppled, and its contents spilled over the table. He held his hand up, and Jennifer could see the fear, and the anger, in his eyes.

She raised the gun and fired. The bullet struck Qahtani on his left shoulder. He stopped with his eyes wide open in surprise as he stared at her—this woman who had dared shoot him. He took a step towards her, his hand outstretched and with an expression of puzzled confusion. Why? He seemed to be asking. Her finger was still on the trigger. Jennifer closed one eye, concentrated and fired another bullet into him. The sessions she had at the gun club with Ilan were unnecessary as she was close enough to him that she couldn't miss. Her aim was true, and the second one struck him on the forehead. This one was fatal as the bullet tore through his flesh, shattering his skull and ripping into his brain. His eyes dulled, and he hovered before falling on the floor.

Jennifer was frozen to the spot. The gun was in her shaking hands as the shock of killing another human being seeped into her soul. But, at the same time, she felt relief. He could never hurt Ilan. He couldn't come after him in revenge for his cousin. She had saved her husband's life for the second time. But at what cost to her?

Qahtani's dinner companions sprang into action and rushed towards her.

Jennifer turned and made a run for it. Towards the door and safety. But before she could grab the handle, open the door and wake up, a hand slammed the door shut again.

Jennifer was about to turn around to see who had closed her door that would take her back into her own world. With it closed, she couldn't exit the dream that had turned into a nightmare, and she was trapped here.

Dreams are a different world that we visit when we sleep.

Are they?

She couldn't remember where she'd read that quote, or even if it was real, but she realised she could be caught up in this dream forever. She felt as if she'd been trapped in a snow globe. One good shake and her world would collapse in an avalanche of other people's making. But that wasn't right. She'd done this to herself and only had herself to blame.

She reached for the handle again. Something heavy struck her on the back of the head, and everything went dark. She fell to the ground, her hand still stretching for the door and her life beyond it.

The alarms sounded. Saul dropped the paperback he was reading and hit the response button.

'What's happening?' he shouted into the intercom.

'It's Jennifer. She is seizing, and I can't wake her up.'

'Call the medics, and contact Nathan Cohen. Tell him what's happened. I'll be there immediately.'

By the time he made it to the fourth floor and into the Dream Catcher team's room, someone had shut off the alarms. Jennifer was still thrashing on the bed, and someone he didn't recognise had inserted an IV line into Jennifer's arm and was about to push a syringe full of an unknown liquid into it.

'Stop. What are you giving her?' Saul demanded.

'Anti-seizure meds. Diazepam.' The medic held up the bottle.

Saul nodded for him to carry on.

As the drugs hit her system, Jennifer's body reacted. The seizure eased, and gradually, she sank onto the bed and seemed to be fast asleep.

And that was the problem. She was fast asleep.

'Check her vitals.' Saul stood out of the way and ran his hand through his hair.

'Pulse and oxygen saturation normal. Brain activity isn't great. It's minimal.'

'What does that mean?'

'It means just that. Minimal. There's hardly any brain activity. It's enough to keep her body functioning, but that's all. She's in a deep coma.'

'What caused it?'

'I have no idea, sir.'

'How do we fix it? Her?'

The medic was silent.

'I need an answer.'

'I don't have one.'

'Then find someone who does.'

Saul slammed the door shut behind him and went back to his office, where he'd left his phone. He had a call to make, and he wasn't looking forward to it.

Ilan opened his eyes and blinked a few times in the darkness. Something, a noise outside perhaps, had woken him. Disorientated, he fumbled for his phone on the nightstand beside him and checked the time. It was almost four-forty in the morning. His phone was muted, so any notifications—text messages or news updates—wouldn't disturb his sleep. He yawned as he checked them, but there was nothing of importance.

He was still, his ears searching for the noise if that's what it was.

There was nothing.

An uneasy feeling crept over him. Something wasn't right, but he couldn't pinpoint the source of his foreboding.

He switched the light on. He moved slowly, not wanting to wake Jennifer beside him. He looked at her and saw the empty side of the bed.

Of course, she's at work with Saul.

In his half-asleep state, he'd forgotten.

The feeling that something was wrong still nagged him, and he got up and dressed in the jeans and T-shirt he'd dropped on the floor. He checked the house.

The doors and the windows were all locked, as they should be. He checked them every night before turning in. Both cats were asleep. Nobody was hiding in the garage, and nothing had fallen over anywhere. He opened the door, stepped outside and ignored the damp grass against his bare feet as he checked the garden, and then walked around the property. He found nothing. Everything was quiet and still.

Still uneasy, Ilan went back inside. He was wide awake now and couldn't go back to bed, so he fed the cats, who had woken up when they heard him moving around the house. He rattled their food box, and they came running to him.

At five o'clock, his phone lit up and performed a slow, circular dance as it vibrated on the table. Ilan snatched it up.

'Ken?'

'Something has happened to Jennifer. Get over here right now.'

Saul's voice sounded urgent, terrified even, but he disconnected the line before Ilan could ask what was wrong.

Clutching his phone, Ilan grabbed his keys, remembered he had nothing on his feet and wasted time hunting for a pair of socks. He put them on, stepped into his shoes and rushed out. He reversed onto the street and spun the car around in a single, fluid manoeuvre. His tyres squealed in protest as he floored the accelerator and didn't care how many neighbours he disturbed. And he didn't take their usual route, opting for the back road that would be quicker at this time in the morning.

Something has happened to Jennifer. Happened. To Jennifer. Something? What?

Saul's words repeated in his head. It was a continuous and frightening loop in his mind.

What?

He had no idea. It could be anything. She could have fallen down the stairs or choked on a sweet. But the most likely scenario was that something happened while she was asleep. She could have seen something in a dream that terrified her. Or maybe she died in someone's dream. He didn't trust the Dream Catcher Programme. There's a myth that you don't wake up in real life if you die in a dream. He didn't know. It could be a story, it could be real. He just didn't know enough about it to understand what could happen. Nobody did, and that was why he considered it dangerous.

He rounded a corner and was faced with a parked garbage truck. He yanked the steering wheel, accelerated hard, and swerved out of its path at the last second.

'Chara. Shit.'

He swore aloud, first in Hebrew and then English. His breath caught in his throat, and his heart thudded in his chest. His knuckles were white as he gripped the steering wheel, and his eyes scanned the road for any hazards, including police cars. Getting stopped and explaining his identity would waste vital minutes. Being stopped by traffic cops didn't feature in his plans. They could try, but he knew he was a better driver than most. He would outdrive them easily.

Twenty minutes and three flashing speed cameras later, Ilan abandoned the car half in somebody's designated parking space. He lost precious time when the guard at the gate, who didn't know him, insisted on checking his credentials. He pitied the guard, who would have to face Saul's wrath at some point later that day. This was the downside to not being an active part of the organisation, and it took a phone call to Saul to allow him entry.

The elevator to the Dream Catcher room took forever, and Ilan regretted not taking the stairs.

Ilan ran along the corridor to the room they used. He barged through the door, almost knocking it off its hinges, and slamming it against the wall, so hard that it left an indent.

'What happened to her?' he demanded.

Saul caught him by the arm and pulled him back. Angrily, Ilan turned on the older man.

'What happened?' His voice was low and mean.

'We don't know. She had a seizure that we got under control with diazepam, but she hasn't come around yet.'

'Is she in a coma? Like when we crashed in Cyprus?'

'I don't know, Ilan. That's all I can tell you right now. We don't want to try and wake her in case it causes more damage. Nathan Cohen is on his way. He'll know what to do.' Saul tried to sound hopeful.

As if on cue, Nathan arrived. Everyone looked at him as though he was an avenging angel and held all the answers.

'What happened?' he asked.

As Saul brought Nathan up to speed, Ilan went to Jennifer's bedside. He took her hand and stared at his wife. Her face was pale against the white pillow, but everything looked normal except for the pallor. She looked like she always did when she was asleep, as though all he needed to do to wake her up was nudge her, tickle her ribs, or waft a cup of coffee in her direction. There were no obvious signs of distress to sully her features, and she appeared to be sleeping peacefully. Maybe too calm and peaceful, he thought, because she wasn't making any of the usual movements a person makes to indicate natural sleep.

They shouldn't have left her alone. Wasn't someone supposed to be with her at all times?

Ilan kept his anger under control. There would be time for accusations later. Right now, getting his wife back was all that mattered to him.

He overheard part of a hushed conversation between Nathan and Saul. Nathan explained that she may have seen something in a dream that shocked her, and the seizure was the physical manifestation of her fear.

'Then why didn't she wake up afterwards?' Saul asked.

'She has to walk through the doorway. That's the awakening process, and something in her dream may have stopped her getting to it,' Nathan explained.

'Or someone,' Ilan said. 'Jennifer told me a few people are aware of her. Not just her target but people in the target's dream, too. She was worried they might wake from their dreams and remember her. They could even recognise her somewhere. But then she said that it had only happened a couple of times, and she wasn't too concerned about it.'

'When was this?' Nathan asked.

'Within the last week.' Ilan struggled to remember. 'She only mentioned it in passing, and I wasn't paying much attention because we watched Formula 1 on television. It was last Sunday. That's when she brought it up.'

'Did she mention anyone specifically?' Saul asked.

'No. Look, is this relevant? Shouldn't you be figuring out a way to wake her up, not asking me about her dream encounters?'

'Yes. You're right,' Nathan rubbed his hand across his face as he tried to figure out the best course of action. The one with the best outcome.

'We could try what we did last time,' he said to Saul.

'Last time, Saul?' Ilan's voice rose. 'Are you telling me this has happened before?'

'I thought you knew. When you were in Syria, she thought you'd been shot. She was so distressed she forgot to use the door to wake up.' Nathan used air commas, and Ilan was tempted to punch him. People who did that were pretentious and annoyed him.

'She wouldn't wake up, so we got Nurit to sit with her and talk. Her job was to persuade Jennifer to open the door and walk through. It worked, and I think it might work again.'

'What are we waiting for?' Ilan asked.

Nathan looked to Saul for permission.

'Do it,' Saul nodded.

Chapter 37

Jennifer opened her eyes. She was lying on a dirty mattress on a hard floor. And she was in total darkness.

Or I'm blind.

That thought didn't do much to allay the terror she was feeling. And it didn't explain how she was lying on a filthy mattress in the dark. And with a headache as well.

Hangover? What the hell was I drinking?

No. Not a hangover. This was an external pain, an aching, throbbing pain that hurt more when she touched the back of her head. There was no sensation of anything wet and sticky on her fingers, so whatever caused the blow, it hadn't broken the skin, and she wasn't bleeding.

She had to find out where she was, and there must be a way out of this dump. She couldn't stay here in the darkness with smells that made her think she was in a musty cellar, or it could be a cell.

No. It's a cellar. Keep thinking that. You need to stay positive. At least try not to panic.

Which was easier said than done as she couldn't turn into a terror-stricken, screaming maiden just because the lights went out. She didn't like not being able to see where she was.

And on that thought, all the horror movies she'd watched over the years, with vampires, werewolves and zombies, came rushing back to haunt her. Lions and tigers and bears. Oh my. Creatures created by someone's imagination came alive in her head as they flew and leapt and shuffled towards her.

Her thoughts, combined with the darkness and the rankness of her surroundings, made her shiver in fear. The smell was bad. It wasn't just musty dampness, it reeked of death and decay, and she had to get out of this room.

And mice. Please don't let there be mice in here or rats. No, don't even think about rats. Never mind the vampires and zombies—even the serial killers—mice were the worst.

The thought of a mouse anywhere in her house would have Jennifer sitting in the locked car, yelling instructions at Ilan on how best to catch it.

'Use the flame thrower. I don't care if the house burns down. Nuke the fucker,' she'd scream.

And as for a rat, if she ever saw one, she'd put the house up for sale and move out.

They got the occasional fieldmouse indoors. It was usually in autumn because they'd left the door open, but thankfully she'd never had to run screaming from a house with a rat in it.

She breathed in through her mouth to avoid the stink and pushed herself onto her hands and knees. She still felt groggy, and it crossed her mind that she might have been drugged and struck over the head.

But who? And why?

She had no idea. But it was the least of her concerns. Getting out was the main thing.

Before they come back for me. Oh, stop it. Stop thinking stuff like that. No one is coming for you, either killing you or saving you. You're on your own, and it's up to you to get off your arse and find the door.

The door. Of course. She was still in a dream. She was lying on a bed in the Dream Catcher room at Mossad Headquarters, and to wake up and get back, all she had to do was open the door.

But where was it? It was pitch dark, and she couldn't see anything.

Jennifer stood up and spun around in the darkness. She did a full turn as her eyes searched for a sliver of light that would guide her.

'Okay, Ilan,' Nathan picked up a chair. 'Sit here, take her hand and talk to her.'

'What do I say?'

'You need to convince her to open the door and walk through it. Cajole her. Plead with her. Offer her the moon, the stars, and everything in between if she walks through that door. Try anything, but it'll help if what you say is pertinent to your lives at present.'

'Nurit talked a lot about the cats,' Nathan said. 'I don't know if that will work again, though. The main thing is to let her hear your voice and know it's you.'

Ilan talked as he let the memories flood back. He went to the time after the accident in Cyprus when she was injured and in a medically-induced coma. He sat by her bedside while she hovered between life and death during those nine terrible days. He told her, then and now, that he was as absent as she was, knowing that his life would end if she died.

Here she was, again hovering between life and death, and he was the only one that could bring her back. It wasn't down to the skill of a surgeon like last time. Even her strong will and love of life couldn't guide her home. It fell on him now. And all he had to do the job was his love for her.

'Jennifer?' Ilan called her name again. His voice was hoarse with emotion, and he coughed to clear his throat. 'Jennifer? Can you hear me? It's me, Ilan. I'm on the other side of the door, but I can't open it, darling. I need you to open it. Can you do that, Jennifer?'

In the darkness, Jennifer stood in what she hoped was the middle of the room. She searched for anything that indicated the way out.

Then she stopped as a voice called her name.

It was Ilan. He'd found her and was coming to get her out of this terrible place. He was somewhere close.

'Ilan? Oh, thank God. I'm trapped here in the dark. I don't know how to get out. Can you hear me? I need you to help me.'

She stood in the darkness, her ears straining, as she listened for his voice again.

'Ilan. Where are you? I can't see you. I can't see anything, and I don't know where I am. Please come and get me. Please.'

But the voice didn't reply, and Jennifer wondered if she had heard him or if it was just her imagination.

Ilan looked to Nathan, who encouraged him with a thumbs-up.

'Keep going. But keep mentioning the door,' Nathan said.

Everyone in the room felt a sense of déjà vu as they remembered Nathan using similar words of encouragement to Ilan's daughter. They must have wondered what Jennifer had seen in her dreams this time.

Nurit saved the day last time with pleas and entice-ments. She succeeded in connecting with her stepmoth-er, and Jennifer had woken up. The physical and emo-tional link between Ilan and Jennifer, as husband and wife, was stronger. If Nurit could do it, there was no reason Ilan would fail.

'You have to emphasise the door and tell her to walk through it. Offer her anything. Play on what she likes, anything that makes her happy. Give her a reason to come back.'

Ilan's lips touched Jennifer's ear. He blew on it. He knew it tickled her. Sometimes it annoyed her, but it never failed to get her attention.

'Jennifer. Open the door and come home. I'm lonely on my own, baby.' Ilan paused and thought about what to say. 'I need you home with me. We can take the car and go for a drive up the coast. We'll stop at all our favourite places, maybe call in somewhere and have lunch.'

'No,' Nathan interrupted him. 'Don't go into a long, elaborate speech. It's important to keep it short, staccato sentences. Be specific about the door.'

Ilan nodded and scratched at his beard as he searched for the words to bring her back to him. But he knew how stubborn Jennifer could be when she wanted. If she was determined to do something, no amount of cajoling could change her mind. But this had to be different. She wanted to come back to him, but she was trapped. He knew that as sure as he knew how to breathe. Something that happened in her dream prevented her from opening her eyes and smiling at him, happy to be back.

Something tickled Jennifer's ear. A cobweb or a disturbance in the air? She waved it away as she stood still and listened. She was surrounded by darkness and was suffering from sensory deprivation. There was nothing to touch, see, hear or taste. There was only the smell. The musty, rank smell of death and decay. And she wasn't about to rely on her sense of taste by licking the rank walls. She held her breath and strained to listen, but there was only silence. What she thought she had heard—Ilan's voice—was her imagination. She covered her face and fought back the tears filling her eyes.

Ilan held Jennifer's hand, and he never wanted to let go of her.

'Neshama, I'm here. I'm on the other side of the door. You have to open it. I can't get in because there's no handle on my side. You have to turn the handle, open the door, and walk through it. I'm here waiting for you. On the other side of the door. Just open the door and come

326

through it. Please, Jennifer. All these years we've been together mean so much to us. And we have plenty more years ahead. I love you with all my heart, and I know you love me. Please, open the door and step through it. That's all you have to do. Do it for me, for us. Step through the door, Jennifer.'

Jennifer wheeled around. That wasn't her imagination. It was Ilan, and he was calling her, telling her to open the door.

What door?

'I can't see anything. I can't find the door, Ilan. Where is it? Where are you?'

There was no answer.

'There's no change,' Nathan whispered softly. 'Take a break, Ilan.'

'Shouldn't I keep talking to her?'

Saul had been standing behind them. 'Nathan is correct, Ilan. If it was going to work, it would have by now. Let's make her comfortable and see what happens.'

'What about medical intervention? If we transfer her to a hospital, will that help?'

'Out of the question. It would compromise the Programme. We have state of the art medical facilities here. Now, come away and let's give it twenty minutes and see if she wakes up independently.'

'And if she doesn't?'

'Let's cross that bridge when we come to it.'

Jennifer focused her mind and refused to let her fears overcome her.

I'm in a pitch-black room. There's no other explanation for it. How I got here isn't my biggest concern. Getting out is. It's a room, and rooms have doors. So all I have to do is find the door and get out. Yeah, but how? Just like this. Watch.

She held her arms out with her palms facing outward and took a step. And then another one. After five steps, her hands touched a wall. She slid her hands across it. It was definitely a wall.

Now I just need to find the door and get out of here.

She kept her palms flat against the brick and moved to her left, a step or two at a time, until she came to a right angle. A corner. She continued past a second corner until she found what she was looking for.

Jennifer traced her hand down the wood until she found the handle. She turned it and pulled. Nothing happened. The door was locked. This had never happened before.

Chapter 38

'Let me try again,' Ilan pleaded with his ex-boss after Saul insisted they leave the room to let the resident medical staff check on Jennifer. They were in Saul's office, where he'd produced a bottle of whiskey and two glasses. Saul blew the dust out of the glasses and put them on his desk. Ilan needed to calm down. He'd kicked up a fuss, and it took a lot to persuade him to leave Jennifer, even for a few minutes.

'I can get through to her. I'll convince her to wake up,' Ilan said.

'She's stable at the moment, and her vitals are good. Let's wait. We'll try again when the medics have checked her over.'

'Isn't it a bit early in the morning for that?' Ilan said with a raised eyebrow.

'We might be here all day, and you could use a nip. I know I need one.' Saul poured a small tot into each glass and reached one across the desk to Ilan.

'L'Chaim,' he said as he raised his glass.

'Not this time, Saul. I'll drink to Jennifer's life instead,' Ilan said as he downed the liquid in one mouthful, then reached for the bottle and poured another measure. He offered it to Saul, who declined.

'I am going to try talking to her again. Nobody will stop me.'

'I expect nothing less of you, Ilan,' Saul replied.

He lifted some papers, shuffled them together and stacked them in a pile before looking at Ilan.

'Jennifer is an amazing woman, Ilan. Thanks to her, the Dream Catcher Programme is a resounding success.'

Dream Investigation Initiative was the name he had come up with and the one he wanted to use. He stumbled over the word as, even now, it stuck in his throat. It was never his preferred choice. Then Jennifer, with an obvious smirk of competitiveness, said they should use Dream Catcher because they were using dreams to catch the bad guys.

Everyone started saying it aloud as though they were trying it on for size. It must have fit, as they kept it. Even the Prime Minister, who was present when the team were assembled, smiled at Jennifer and agreed Dream Catcher was the perfect name.

'The other one, Dream Investigation blah, blah, is too stuffy,' he said, and a ripple of laughter went around the room.

Saul reckoned he was fishing for votes in the next election, but he couldn't quibble with the Prime Minister over such a minor matter. He held his tongue, and the name was officially recorded as a top-secret Mossad operation.

'You and Jennifer fit well together,' Saul said after a pause. 'In some ways, you remind me of how Rachel and I were back in the day. Because Jennifer brings out the best in you.'

Ilan took another sip. He swirled the liquid around in his mouth before swallowing it. 'Are you testing her eulogy on me, Saul?'

'No, of course not,' Saul seemed shocked and embarrassed by Ilan's comment. 'I was telling you that I'll do everything I can for her.'

'Yes. You will,' Ilan said, and Saul ignored the menace in Ilan's voice.

The desk phone buzzed, startling them even though they were waiting for the call. Saul grabbed it and nodded as the caller spoke to him and then hung up.

'They just want to run some final tests, but they said we can go upstairs.'

Ilan was out of the door before Saul had stood up.

Ilan was first through the door, with Saul a few steps behind him. He stopped and took in the scene. It was a different setting, a different room, but it might have been the same as the one four years ago. It was filled with medical staff and equipment. The fluorescent lighting made him want to shield his eyes, and sensations of apprehension vied for domination.

They told him to sit on a chair against the wall and that they would be ready to let him speak to her in five minutes.

His eyes were drawn to the bed where she lay. She had been his best friend and partner for so many years.

Ilan's mind sped back to the moment he first saw her in Cyprus. He noticed her immediately when he walked in and went to the bar. He was happy to stand there, propping up the bar while watching the Chelsea versus Liverpool match. He'd only nipped in for one drink, but he had nothing else to do that night.

But then, the beautiful woman with the short, spiky blonde hair and big, blue eyes kept stealing his attention. He lost interest in the football match. Liverpool was winning, he remembered. He had a cousin who lived in London near Stamford Bridge and had been to a few games when he visited the UK and spent some time with Yosef—or Joey as he was known to his British friends. So, while he didn't dislike Liverpool, he wanted Chelsea to win.

He sipped his whiskey and watched her reflection in the mirrored glass behind the bar. She was beautiful, but she was also nervous and glanced around. He realised she was waiting for someone, as she looked at her watch.

And he was aware of how disappointing this realisation was to him.

I would never keep her waiting.

Ilan let his thoughts take him someplace where she was with him. Not his real world, that was too dangerous, but one where he really was the businessman his cover claimed. It was fun to imagine that he lived in this world and she was his lover.

He wondered what her name was.

And then she was on her feet, her bag slung over her shoulder, ready to leave.

Disappointment mingled with relief that her date had stood her up. Disappointment because she was leaving and relief because she wasn't going to leave with a boyfriend, who would later become her husband. They might live happily ever after. And he would never see her again.

Whoever she was and wherever she came from, she was amazing, beautiful, and without a date.

He turned back to the match on the television. The game was a draw. Chelsea had equalised in the closing seconds of extra time. But Liverpool had a commanding lead at the top of the league, and an away draw didn't dent it.

He would order another drink and then go back to the place he was renting. He felt a presence beside him. It was her.

'Hey. Can I get another drink? Please,' she said to the bar staff and raised her arm to get their attention. They didn't notice her.

'Please. Let me buy you one. What are you having?' Ilan said.

'Oh. Okay, I'll have a vodka and tonic, please. Thank you so much,' she had replied with a smile that lit up his world. 'But only if you join me at a table. If we can find one. Mine has been taken already.'

Their eyes met, and Ilan suddenly realised that he wanted to spend the rest of his life with this beautiful, sexy young woman.

'Okay, Ilan. We have an update.' Someone spoke and interrupted his too-brief trip down memory lane. Had it been like that? Their first meeting? As far as he could remember, it was. He made a mental note to ask Jennifer when she woke up because her memory was impressive, especially during their early days. They sailed by in a happy blur for him, but she remembered every detail as though she had stored them away for safekeeping.

'Sorry. What?' He slipped back into the here and now.

'We have run extensive tests on your wife, and she's fine. She is, however, in an extremely deep sleep, and we are currently unable to wake her from it.'

'She isn't in a coma?' Ilan asked, and the sense of relief brought him to his knees.

'No. Not a coma as we know it. Her brain activity is reading off the charts now, and she's in REM sleep. You know what that is, yes?'

'Yes. She's dreaming,'

Just like before. When she was in a coma after her surgery. She's not in a coma, but she won't wake up. This is different, but she's still in the same state. Why?

'We think something happened in her last dream that triggered an extreme fear response, which prevented her from using the door method that Mr Cohen taught her to exit her dream state and wake up.'

'So, she's caught up in a nightmare and can't wake from it?'

'Most likely,' the doctor replied.

'So, what can I do to help?'

'What you were doing earlier. What Cohen recommends. Talk to her and tell her to open the door and come through it.'

'That's all? Can't you give her a stimulant or something?'

'No. That would wrench her out of whatever dream she's in and could cause lasting psychological damage. Talking to her increases the chances of her wakening naturally.'

Ilan pulled the chair over to his wife's bedside and sat down. He studied her as she lay asleep like a princess in a fairy-tale. She was beautiful as always. The features he was so familiar with hadn't changed, the fine line of her jaw and how she jutted her chin out when she was thinking. The love that shone in her eyes and the smile only for him was still there—just hidden beneath closed eyelids. The sparkle of laughter in her eyes was hidden now, and her frown that easily changed to laughter was nowhere to be seen on her smooth brow.

Her face was relaxed as though in normal sleep. Only her eyes underneath the lids moved, almost in time to her chest's steady rise as she breathed. With the back of his fingers, he stroked her cheek and thought he detected a movement towards his hand. The memory of the last time he brought her back tugged at his heart.

And the thought of doing it again almost broke him.

He'd imagined her responding to his voice during those nine days and nights four years ago but knew it was only his imagination.

He knew his girl. She was healthy and strong, and this time she hadn't been injured in an overturned car. She'd recovered from that, and she'd recover from this. Whatever this was.

Besides, she loved him. That was enough for her to wake up and come back to him.

This time he could help her by speeding the process up. He'd remind her that he was here, waiting for her.

'Jennifer. I need you to open the door. I can't reach it from here. The handle is on your side. Just turn it and open the door. Open the door, please.'

Jennifer could hear him in the dark, and she did what he said. But the door was locked.

'I can't, Ilan. It won't open. I'm stuck here, and I can't get to you. I'm sorry.'

It was useless, and she slid down to the floor and covered her face with her hands as she sobbed.

'Just open the door, Jennifer.'

'I can't. It won't open.'

'I love you. Just try and come through the door to me.'

Ilan lowered his head and felt despair wash over him. And along with it came waves of guilt and anger. It was his fault. He caused this by his actions, and his wife was trapped in a nightmare and couldn't get out because of him.

'Please wake up, neshama. Please,' he pleaded.

Hearing his voice again sent a surge of strength through Jennifer, and she resolved to keep trying until her fingers bled. She reached for the door handle again. She turned it, but instead of pulling, she pushed against it this time. She'd pushed and pulled and heaved against it a dozen times already, but this time was different. It opened, and she almost fell out of the darkened room.

Chapter 39

After complete blackness, the daylight was blinding. It was too much, and Jennifer shut her eyes to shield them against the brightness.

But a reminder of the darkness she'd escaped was worse, and Jennifer opened them again. This time she held her hand in front of her face to give her eyes a chance to adjust.

In the glaring sunlight, Jennifer walked into a street and looked around. She didn't know where she was in the world, but she could see houses and bungalows on both sides. There were manicured lawns surrounded on three sides with shade-giving shrubs. The driveways were tidy, and the footpaths were clean, unfettered by litter or leaves. The buildings were uniform, and the place gave her a modern-day chocolate-box impression.

But something was wrong. There was an element of the real world missing. There was nobody around, not so much as a bird signing. There should be. It looked like a peaceful Sunday afternoon, but nobody washed cars or mowed the grass. No kids played with footballs, and no mums were chatting over fences.

Jennifer frowned. While it looked pretty and normal, it wasn't. It was too perfect. The houses and gardens were picture-perfection, and the daylight was too bright to be genuine. It was like watching a movie in HD that the lighting department had over-saturated.

She stepped forward and noticed she wasn't wearing shoes. She looked at her feet, and horror flooded her senses. She was naked. Not a stitch of clothing covered her.

With a squeal, she looked around for her clothes. She had to go back through the door into the dark room and get them. The door was gone.

She wasn't ashamed of her body and loved to flaunt it with low-cut tops and short shorts or tight jeans, and she liked to sunbathe topless. But being naked in public was the bad dream everyone probably had. It was frightening and embarrassing. Jennifer tried to cover herself with her hands as she looked around for something she could use to protect her modesty.

The street was too tidy, with not even an old newspaper lying around, and none of the shrubs had leaves big enough to use. There wasn't a fig leaf to be had, and there were no washing lines, let alone clothing pegged to them. She couldn't knock on somebody's door like this. Her only option was to sneak into one of the houses and steal some clothes. There had to be one with an unlocked door.

Jennifer dashed across the road to the small porch of the nearest house. She tried the door without any luck, and the windows were locked. She ran around the back and through a wooden gate that was so perfect it looked as if it had been hung that day.

The back door opened. What if there were people in the house? No, this was what she was meant to do. This door would take her back. But she didn't wake up in the sleep room. She stepped into a large room. A bay window looked onto the street. There were no curtains, and the floorboards were bare. No furniture filled the room apart from the farmhouse-style chair that Lucy was sitting on.

Jennifer stopped in her tracks, her eyes widened with shock, and she let out a surprised yelp.

'Hello, Jennifer. It's good to see you again,' Lucy said with a cheery smile.

Jennifer frowned at the sight of the dead woman. Her legs were demurely crossed at the ankles, and she was wearing a flowery, calf-length summer dress—in blues and whites—and a pair of tan-coloured strappy sandals. She held a nail file in one hand, scrutinising the work on her nails. She blew on them, in no rush to engage, and glanced up at Jennifer.

'What the fuck?' Jennifer said. Her shock had turned to angry surprise as she took in Lucy, attending to her fingernails and dressed like she was going to a garden party. Jennifer wouldn't have been surprised to see a cocktail next to her.

'Oh, I should have thought of that. A vodka martini or a mojito would have been perfect for this,' Lucy said.

'Perfect for what?' Jennifer was aghast at the thought that Lucy could read her mind.

'Well, I dunno. Isn't this your dream? You're not in a coma again, are you? That would be so boring—been there, done that.'

'No. I was in a dream, in someone else's dream, and I found something out. It was bad. And I woke up in the dark. I heard Ilan calling me, but I couldn't find him. Then I opened the door, and I was here, like this.' Jennifer looked at herself. She was fully clothed. 'I was naked, and I ran across the street to find some clothes. I opened this door.'

Lucy seemed to consider what Jennifer told her. 'I think there's more to this than you're telling me, J.'

'Don't call me J like we're besties or something. My name is Jennifer.'

'Sorry, J—I mean, Jennifer—but this is mind-blowing. Really crazy, out-of-this-world stuff.'

'It's not really. I'm just stuck in a shitty dream.'

'But why are you stuck in a dream? That's never happened before. Not even when we had our last chat at my house. Oh, of course. How could I forget? You got stuck when you thought Ilan had been killed—habit forming here, methinks. Did someone get killed this time, Jennifer?' Lucy looked at Jennifer with suspicion.

'No. That's ridiculous. I dreamed that someone hit me over the head,' Jennifer said.

Lucy laughed at her.

'What?' Jennifer asked as she tried not to squirm.

'You have to ask yourself, why did you dream that someone hit you over the head?'

'I don't know.'

Did Lucy know what she had done?

'I think I saw something I shouldn't have, and they knew, then I got hit. Someone must have crept up behind me.'

'Okay. If you say so. So, we have to get you back. But first, take a look behind you.'

Jennifer turned around. It wouldn't surprise her if Lucy was playing a prank on her. After all, she blamed Jennifer for taking her life. Her sense of humour was obvious even when she was alive, and Jennifer wondered if her mischievous nature was the same as a ghost in her dream.

The part of the room behind Jennifer wasn't bathed in bright sunlight now. Several candles cast a dim glow, and shadows danced on the walls in their flickering light. There was a bed in the centre of the candlelight, and two people were on it, entwined in a lover's embrace.

Jennifer was curious and stepped forward despite not wanting to intrude on their love-making. Why was she seeing them?

Lucy was beside Jennifer. The women watched the couple making love.

When the male lifted himself on his arms, Jennifer saw his face and the woman underneath him. It was her and Ilan.

'You two look good together,' Lucy said in a hushed whisper.

'Why am I seeing this?'

'You're in your own dream now, Jennifer. You dream about a happy life with the man you love when you're not dreaming for the Mossad.'

Ilan was making love to her. Jennifer watched as he lowered his head and kissed her. Her arms pulled him closer, and she lifted her legs to wrap them around him.

The bedsheet slipped off, and shadows danced across his back. A light sheen of sweat glistened across Ilan's shoulder as he entered her. Jennifer moaned, but she couldn't tell if it was from the woman on the bed or if it came from her as she watched.

Seeing herself making love was beautiful and very erotic, and Jennifer felt the heat of her arousal as she watched them. Their movements, and the sounds they made, were more intense with every moment.

Ilan climaxed with a groan and fell on top of Jennifer, who cried out in satisfaction as they lay entwined.

Ilan lifted his head. As their eyes met, he smiled.

He can see me.

The frightening part was that she could see the despair and grief on his face. Jennifer shuddered to see him so distraught.

'You don't have much time, and you should probably go back now before it's too late,' Lucy said.

'Too late for what?'

'You're going to die, Jennifer. If you don't wake up in the next few minutes, you'll never return. You'll be stuck here with me—forever. Now while I can see the appeal in that, I think you'd prefer to have a real life.'

'I don't know how.'

344

'I have to take you to the door and open it for you. Come with me. Tick-tock, time's running out, girl.' Lucy took Jennifer's hand and led her away from the scene on the bed.

Lucy put one hand on the doorknob, paused, and turned to Jennifer.

'You know, I never signed up for this guardian angel shit,' she said as she opened the door. 'But I saw you shoot that terrorist bastard. So, I'll give you one piece of advice about what happened.'

'What is it? And how did you know?' Jennifer was horrified that someone else knew what she'd done. Even if it was a long-dead woman who popped up in her dreams.

'It doesn't matter how I know, just that I do, and you need to understand that some lines are not meant to be crossed. There could be a price to pay if you do cross them. You've gotten away with it this time, but you must never do it again. Never. Do you understand me, Jennifer?'

Terrified now, all Jennifer could do was nod before stepping through the door.

Chapter 40

Ilan stood by the window, talking to Saul about the danger he'd subjected her to. Saul counter-argued by saying that this wasn't a normal situation. Jennifer usually woke from her work refreshed and with a great feeling of achievement. 'As anyone would after a good night's sleep,' Saul finished.

'She hasn't woken up refreshed this time?'

'She will. I'm confident that she will.'

'You have no idea what this is doing to her health and brain. You're winging it by the seat of your pants. There's no precedence for what you're putting her through, so you can't be confident that she'll wake. And if she does, she won't be doing this again.'

'Is that a threat, Ilan?'

But before Ilan could tell him that it was indeed a threat, the doctor called them over.

'Her eyes fluttered. I think she's waking up.'

Ilan was at Jennifer's side, almost knocking the doctor over in his haste.

Jennifer's eyes fluttered a few times, then blinked open. She glanced at the faces surrounding the bed as she tried to sit up. All of them were familiar to her, but she was surprised to see Ilan's face among them.

'What are you doing here?' she said, and a frown crossed her face. 'Did something happen?'

'You couldn't wake up, and you've been out for hours.'

The doctor found a space at the bedside. 'How do you feel?'

'Fine, I think. I've got a headache, but other than that, I feel normal.'

'That's excellent news. No harm done. However, we'd like to run some tests to find out what happened.'

'No.' Jennifer shook her head. 'I'm fine. I just want to go home.'

'But it's better if we check you over. It won't take long.'

'You heard my wife. She said she's fine. I'm taking her home,' Ilan said.

The doctor looked to Saul for guidance, and he shrugged his shoulders. Jennifer was awake, and there was no reason to suggest anything was wrong with her. Ilan resented the fact that if Jennifer left, it absolved him of any guilt. And, if she dropped dead outside their perimeter gates, that was her problem.

'She just needs to file a report about what occurred in her dream, and then she can leave,' Saul said.

Ilan was about to launch a verbal attack, but Jennifer put her hand on his arm and gave it a placating squeeze to still him.

'It's okay, love. Five minutes, and we're outta here and on our way home.'

Their eyes met, and Jennifer gave him a nod to say, 'I got this.'

She unhooked herself from the monitors and swung her legs off the bed. She felt a bit dizzy and nauseous, but she refused to let them see that. Ilan was nearby to catch her if she stumbled. She had no doubt of that.

'I don't have anything to report, Saul. My dreams were all over the place, and I only saw Lucy. I didn't dream anything about Qahtani.'

Saul looked surprised, but Ilan swore as his eyes darted from his wife to his ex-boss.

'What the fuck is going on, Saul? And why are you making Jennifer dream about Sayeed Qahtani? Never mind why. How? The dead can't dream. Can they?'

Jennifer's guilt was unbearable, and she wished she had never got involved. Chasing bank robbers and traitorous spies was one thing but this? It was too much for her to bear. She wanted to curl up somewhere quiet, close her eyes, and sleep. She never wanted to dream again.

If he felt any guilt, Saul was a master at hiding it. His face betrayed none of his thoughts or feelings.

Ilan looked ready to explode. She didn't think she had ever seen him so angry. If she didn't get him out, he'd kill someone and trash the place.

She told him to calm down. It hadn't worked, and they could go home and not think about it anymore. Once she got him out of the building and into the car, he'd calm down enough to get him home. He might rant for a while,

348

probably for most of the day, but at least he'd be less inclined to kill someone, especially Saul.

'Everyone except Jennifer and Ilan out. Now.'

Saul gave the order, and although they were surprised, his underlings knew better than to question him. They shuffled out, and Nathan was the last to leave. He gave Jennifer a quiet nod of support before he left, closing the door behind him.

'Not Sayeed, Ilan. His cousin. Tariq—the banker. They were as close as brothers from childhood, and he wants revenge for Sayeed's death.'

Ilan was speechless. Jennifer knew he was fuming, and she had a vision of him charging at Saul, the forward momentum taking them flying out of the window and plummeting to their deaths. And she considered whether Ilan would get a punch in on the way down.

She put the image aside because she had to diffuse the situation before something bad happened and Ilan got into serious trouble. It wouldn't be good if he punched Saul, with or without falling out of the window in the process.

'Ilan, stop. Wait. It was my idea. Not Saul's

'Seriously?'

'Yes. I overheard something a few days ago in another dream. Two men talked about the attack in Syria and how they were close to identifying the second Israeli spy. And I assumed they meant you.'

'Jennifer was working on something else, Ilan.' Saul jumped in. 'We had a young man claiming to be an Israeli Arab apply to join us—he wanted to join the Mossad.

His background checks came back clear—too clear, and I had a nagging feeling that something wasn't right with this guy. I wanted Jennifer to take a look at him. It was Jennifer who discovered his identity. He had learned your identity from a survivor who had since died from the injuries he received when we bombed Sayeed's compound. He planned to assassinate you, and we needed to organise protection for you and Jennifer. I can have that done before you leave. But I wanted Jennifer to confirm it before we took any action. And that's what she was doing last night.'

Jennifer turned to her husband and put her hand on his arm.

'It was exactly what Saul said, Ilan. I didn't know the name, but I suspected he meant you, so I mentioned it to Saul, and he confirmed it was Qahtani. Then he asked me to get more information, and I agreed to try.' Jennifer took a deep breath, and she prayed that the men would believe her. 'That's what I was trying to do, but I couldn't. I ended up chatting with Lucy Wilson. Maybe my mind was too afraid because of the threat to you, but I wasn't in her dream—she's dead. She was in mine.'

'Jennifer. We're getting out of here. Before I kill some bastard.'

'Yes. Definitely. Let's go home.' Jennifer gave Saul a pointed look to say this was for the best.

Saul's phone buzzed with an incoming message. Ilan's did the same. Although he wasn't on active service for the Mossad, he was still part of the organisation. His security clearance level was high. They opened the messages.

Both men were silent as they read what it said on their screens. And they remained silent while they digested the shit-storm coming.

'It would seem Tariq Qahtani is no longer a person of interest to us.' Saul said.

Saul glanced at Jennifer, and she saw suspicion there. And then his look changed, and it might have been her imagination, but she saw gleeful hunger in his eyes. He was like someone who got the precious gemstone they had coveted for years. A shiver ran down her spine at the thought.

'I don't understand. Why isn't he?' Jennifer said.

Ilan showed her his phone. Her clearance wasn't high enough for the information, but it didn't matter in this instance.

She had no idea who sent it, but it was genuine. Her face was as white as a sheet when she read it, and she had to lean against the bed to stop herself from collapsing.

Chapter 41

'I fucking told you this was dangerous. You almost died,' Ilan said as he opened the door and stepped back to let Jennifer into the house. The cats rushed to greet them.

'I know,' She was on autopilot, opened the cat food cupboard and dished some into their bowls. Jennifer knelt and stroked them as they fed, refusing to let her tears fall.

They had driven home in silence. At least Jennifer was silent. Ilan was as angry as fuck. His driving was erratic and impatient as he swore and sounded the horn at every vehicle in his path.

He also swore at his wife a fair amount.

Jennifer let him rant. He had to get it out of his system, and it was better to do it now before they got home.

He was still swearing when they pulled into the drive and parked the car.

Possum and Holly weaved between her ankles, thanking her for their meal, as Jennifer stood in the kitchen.

'You should have told me.' Ilan said when he had all the swearing and threats to kill Saul out of his system.

He opened a cupboard door and then slammed it when he didn't find what he wanted. He tried another one and grabbed the bottle of Jameson whiskey.

Jennifer selected two tumblers, inexpensive ones. She didn't care if Ilan threw one against the wall.

'I know,' she said.

He glared at her as he unscrewed the cap and poured whiskey into one of the tumblers. Some of it splashed onto the counter, and Jennifer resisted the urge to get something to wipe it up. He didn't pour any for her.

With a snort of annoyance, Jennifer took the bottle from him and poured a generous measure.

'So, tell me now,' he said.

She took a large mouthful of whiskey. It burned on the way down and brought tears to her eyes. She didn't want it and gagged. She wanted toast and coffee, but she had to make a point. If Ilan could stand there with a glass in his hand looking all angry and moody, then so could she.

'There's nothing to tell.'

'The hell there isn't. I don't believe you.'

'You heard me tell Saul what happened. That's what happened, and I don't get why you're so angry with me.'

'I'm not angry with you, Jennifer. I'm madder than hell about what Saul's making you do. I've said right from the beginning that I didn't like this. It's dangerous, and you won't be continuing with it.'

'Oh, you're telling me what I can do now.' Jennifer downed another mouthful of the whiskey.

Ilan ran his fingers through his hair in frustration. He set the glass down on the table. He hadn't even touched his.

He reached across the table and asked for her hand in a conciliatory gesture.

'I'm not telling you what to do. I am asking you, please, do not take any further part in this. If something happened and I lost you, I couldn't live without you, Jennifer. I don't want to be without you. I don't trust Saul because I know him. He'll always push you for more than you have to give. And I don't want you to take any more risks.'

When he got the notification that Qahtani was dead, the look Saul had given her chilled her. Ilan's words regarding Saul cut through her. He'd protect her and ensure she wasn't up for murder if he suspected her. He'd keep her safe from the authorities. But in return, she'd be his—forevermore, she'd be his unpaid assassin. He'd blackmail her and make her go into people's dreams to kill them. Jennifer had stopped being an observer—now she was a Lucid-Assassin. Jennifer realised she had handed Saul Mueller the keys to the kingdom. Or, in this instance, the armoury. And she was his nuclear weapon.

He would present his case as admirable, justified, even. He'd make it sound good and her moral duty as a human being. And with what he had on her—she couldn't refuse. That's if he had something on her.

'We are only stopping the bad guys, Jennifer,' he'd say. 'The terrorists, the criminals, the murderers and the rapists. Think of the crime we could stop and the people we could save. You must see the positive in that.'

The trouble was, she could. But only up to a point.

She wasn't a killer. What she did horrified her, and she never wanted to experience it again. But she did it to save Ilan. And she would—she'd do it again in a heartbeat.

Would I? For Ilan, yes. But as Saul's hired killer? No, never.

But could she refuse Saul? If she told him no, he could make life very difficult for her and Ilan.

Jennifer only had one option.

'Are you listening to me?'

'I'm sorry. What?' Jennifer looked at her husband.

'I have some things to do. Do you want to come with me? We can get lunch while we're out.'

She shook her head.

'I'd love to, Ilan. But I'm not feeling great. I think the whiskey on an empty stomach has gone to my head. Would you mind if I stayed here to lie down for a while? I'll make it up to you later.'

Ilan looked surprised but shrugged his shoulders and gave Jennifer a kiss on the cheek.

'Sure. No problem. I won't be long, and if Saul calls, ignore him. I'll text him and tell him you're sick and won't be in. And then we can figure out what you want to do.'

'Thank you, sweetheart.'

'Promise me you'll eat something? Yes?'

Jennifer nodded as he gave her another kiss, lifted his car keys and phone off the table and disappeared out the door.

When she was sure Ilan had gone, she opened her laptop and put the first phase of her plan into action.

Chapter 42

According to a website Jennifer read, fight or flight was the automatic physiological reaction to something perceived as dangerous or frightening. Apparently, the perception of a threat activated the nervous system, triggering an acute stress response that made the body want to fight what was threatening it or run away.

These responses are evolutionary adaptions designed to increase the chances of survival in a threatening situation.

Jennifer decided she didn't need a Google search to know what it meant. In her case, the flight was her best chance of survival.

And that was why she was sitting in seat number 45F on a flight bound for Brisbane, Australia.

A week earlier, when Ilan left the house, Jennifer had applied for a tourist visa. It was granted yesterday, and Jennifer was surprised it came through so quickly.

Seeing it broke her heart.

Saul was told she was suffering the effects of her experience, and she was taking some leave. He agreed that she should have a week or two off but said he wanted to see her when she returned to discuss what had happened.

I bet you do.

That was a conversation Jennifer planned to avoid. But the more she thought about it, the more afraid she was, and she had no choice other than to run away.

She felt like the criminal she was, sneaking off into the night. Ilan told her he was going out with friends for the day. Jennifer had booked the next available flight as the door shut behind him.

She had left a note for him beside the coffee machine. She wrote that she loved him with all her heart and she asked him to remember that and try and forgive her. Then she kissed the cats, told them she loved them and looked around her home before leaving with her suitcase through the front door.

On the way to the airport, she refused to let the tears fall and repeated the mantra that she was doing the right thing on a loop.

It was a long flight. They were five hours into a twenty-three-hour journey with one stop in Abu Dhabi, and Jennifer wished she had a couple of sleeping tablets in her bag. She had the row to herself as the flight was only half full, and if she had a couple of pills, she could swallow them and then spend the rest of the flight stretched out along the three seats, dead to the world. She hoped wine would have a similar effect.

The cabin crew could see Jennifer's call light was on but seemed to be ignoring it. Jennifer saw the look on the woman's face when she'd ordered four bottles of wine and a cup of ice.

The drinks trolly was eight rows ahead and going in the wrong direction. Jennifer looked over her shoulder to see if they were serving the food. She could get more wine with dinner, but it was still too many rows behind her.

Make it last. Can't. Need more.

There was an hour's delay at the airport, and Jennifer spent it avoiding as many security cameras as possible. She knew her face would be recorded by any that caught her. She could live with one or two, but the real problem was the security personnel. They concerned her more than the cameras. If they stopped her, Jennifer knew that guilt would be written all over her face, and they were trained to spot anybody looking suspicious. She'd shine a suspicious-person light to them like a beacon. Even if Saul hadn't put the word out, they'd know she'd done something wrong.

They'd take her to one side, maybe into a holding office, and start with a few casual questions. 'How are you? Are you going somewhere nice? Are you travelling on your own?' Softening her up, they'd relax her to let her guard down.

Then they'd invite her to come along with them if they hadn't already. 'Just to clear a few things up,' they would say as they took her by the arm—encouraging her with smiles and kindly eyes. Bang, they'd take her to a nearby interview room where Saul would be waiting for her.

Compliance was her downfall. But resistance would have the same effect. Whichever way she looked at it, if security stopped her, she was doomed.

Her hands shook, and her heart pounded, and they'd be that way until her flight was called and she was safely in the air.

Do not draw any more attention to yourself.

She knew her demeanour was a nervous woman, and she couldn't risk leaving her seat.

Soon she had no choice and went to one of the female toilets situated around the departures area. Jennifer locked herself in a cubicle for as long as she could without arousing even more suspicion.

She spent the longest hour of her life creeping about the airport, keeping her head down and avoiding everyone. She pretended to be interested in the items displayed in the gift shops and bookstalls. That was the normal thing to do. The cover and title of a book caught her eye, and she lifted it down to read the blurb. It sounded like a fun, light-hearted read that would take her mind off things.

No. Don't go there. Don't think about what you've done.

She paid for the book with cash, put it into her bag, and breathed a sigh of relief when she heard the 'Now boarding' announcement for her flight.

She went through controls, boarded the plane and took off without drama. Now let them stop her. She was a little way through her long flight. Although her fear had eased once she boarded and the plane took off, she was too agitated to read. The wine hadn't helped, and she thought about the possibility of being stopped by security at Brisbane airport. She could be arrested and deported back to Israel.

As the cabin crew interacted with every passenger except her, Jennifer focused on the stern email she would send to the airline's customer service department. She composed it in her mind for something to do, and each version was more indignant as she took tiny sips of her last glass of wine.

'Dear Sirs,

I would like to draw your attention to your shitty in-flight experience and your even-shittier flight staff. They are a pack of ignorant twats.'

Five minutes later, and before the trolly bearing food and more wine reached her row, Jennifer fell fast asleep.

With years of experience on long-haul flights under her belt, the cabin crew knew that a sleeping passenger was preferable to a drunk—and a demanding one at that. They decided to let Jennifer sleep undisturbed.

Ilan was late getting home. With reluctance, he'd agreed to go for dinner with his friends, and it was after midnight when he got home. The house was in darkness, and he was surprised that Jennifer wasn't waiting up for him.

Although her car was parked in the driveway, she wasn't in the house. Terrified for her safety, he was about to call her friends when he saw the note she'd left him.

He read what she'd written and flew through the house in a frenzy. He discovered that Jennifer's passport was missing, and he realised she'd left the country. Maybe there was still time. She could be at the airport in the process of leaving the country. He used the *Find my Phone* app to locate her phone's last known whereabouts. They confirmed she was at the airport over twelve hours ago. He swore.

It was unlikely that she was still there, but he decided to try anyway.

He pulled his jacket on, left a voicemail for Nurit to nip over in the morning to feed the cats, and in less than five minutes, he was in the car and on his way.

Jennifer opened her eyes and stretched. Her neck was stiff from the awkward position when she fell asleep, and she rolled her head in a futile attempt to ease the discomfort. Her mouth was dry. She needed water and reached above her head to hit the call button, then changed her mind as she figured they would ignore her anyway.

Instead, she took the opportunity to get up and stretch her legs. She'd go to the toilet and maybe apologise to

361

the cabin crew. Then, if she was really nice and polite, perhaps she could score a couple more bottles of wine along with some water.

And something to eat. I'm bloody starving.

Jennifer used the lavatory first and splashed cold water on her face to appear sober before she approached the cabin crew member who was keeping an eye on her.

'Hi,' Jennifer said with a cheery smile. 'I'm really thirsty. And hungry. Would it be possible to get a couple of bottles of water and maybe a sandwich, please?'

'Of course, madam,' The woman smiled, opened one of the galley cupboards and handed Jennifer a sandwich. She opened a different cupboard and took out two half-litre bottles of water.

'I hope you like still water. We're almost out of sparkling.'

'Still is fine, thank you.' Jennifer said with another cheery smile and pointed to the miniature bottles of alcohol on a shelf beside the water. 'Oh, and I'll take three of those if you don't mind. They'll help me fall asleep again.'

According to the badge pinned to her jacket, the tall brunette, Cindy, opened her mouth to say no to Jennifer's request. She must have thought it through and decided that Jennifer's logic made sense, because she snatched up three bottles of white wine. Cindy shoved them at Jennifer, who just managed to grab them before they fell to the floor.

'Would you like ice?' Cindy's tone indicated that she'd probably swallowed every cube on the plane to perfect her customer service demeanour.

'Nah, I'm good. Thanks a million.'

Jennifer went back to her seat with her haul of goodies clutched in her arms. She drank the water and devoured the sandwich first. Then she opened the wine and took a couple of sips. Powering up her e-reader, she enjoyed a couple of chapters of the book she was reading. It was *Reliance* by Paul McMurrough, and it was about the power going off after a solar flare hit the earth. It wasn't just an ordinary power failure, though. It was worldwide and probably permanent, affecting everything, from pacemakers failing to planes falling. It was good but not an ideal book to read on a plane hurtling through the sky.

She drank the first bottle of wine and read two more chapters, then closed her eyes. But sleep escaped her, so she picked up her device again and switched to another book. One she had started reading a week ago. This was a heartbreaking read about a young woman named Magdalena who was dying of cancer and was telling her life story to her palliative carer, Dora. Mags was a former prostitute, and Dora was very strait-laced, so the two women's dynamic was gripping.

Jennifer spent an hour with Mags and Dora until her eyes grew heavy again. She closed the e-reader, finished her second little bottle of wine and settled down again along the row of three seats.

Only thirteen hours to go, and then I can start again.

Jennifer yawned, closed her eyes and was asleep before thinking about anything else.

On his journey to the airport, Ilan opened his phone and scrolled through his contacts until he found the number of an ex-colleague who worked at airport security. It was a good friend who would be willing to help him. He dialled the number and, after exchanging pleasantries, he explained that he was looking for someone trying to skip the country. He asked for the use of their facial recognition setup.

'Ken. Of course,' his friend said.

Thirty minutes later, at Tel Aviv's Ben Gurion airport, he went to the front desk where his friend and former colleague waited for him.

The men shook hands, and after a few minutes of small talk, Ilan was taken upstairs to the area that was closed to the public. It was the epicentre of airport control where all security matters were managed.

'I'm looking for this woman,' Ilan said as he showed him a photograph of Jennifer from his wallet. It was a spare passport photo she hadn't needed, and he'd kept it. 'I believe she may be trying to leave the country if she hasn't already. I need to find her, if she's still here, or find out which flight she left on and her ultimate destination.'

'That I can do,' his friend, Oren, said. 'If her passport is biometric, once it has been scanned, it will be in the system, and it will take only a few minutes to pull up her details and find out where she is going.'

Jennifer didn't have a biometric passport, so they couldn't check to see if it had been read when she checked in or went through the departure gate. Ilan was reluctant to give his friend her name as it might raise suspicion about why he was looking for her. It was better to let him assume she was wanted by the Mossad. Ilan didn't tell Oren that he no longer worked for them.

'It isn't biometric,' Ilan said.

'Okay. We can use CCTV instead. The surveillance cameras monitor every area of the airport. It will take longer, but we'll find her. Let me scan the photo into the facial recognition system and see what we have.'

This took longer, and Ilan drummed his fingers against the tabletop while he waited.

One at a time, they began to track five women with short, blonde hair. No exact match came up, but they had five possibilities. The first one visited the bookstore and returned to the seating area with a book for herself and magazines for her husband and two children. The second one joined her friends at the bar.

Ilan narrowed his eyes as he studied the third until she pulled out a pack of cigarettes and went to one of the smoking booths.

The next one was Jennifer. He recognised her top, and the bag was a simple shoulder bag made from tan leather that she'd picked up at the Tel Aviv market a few months ago. Ilan remembered it because she took ages to decide if she wanted it. She bought it because it was big enough to hold everything she needed, but it wasn't cumbersome.

Aside from the clothes and bag, Ilan knew his wife by her mannerisms and walk. She seemed nervous and tried to keep her head down and out of the cameras.

'That's her,' Ilan said. His voice was husky with emotion as he watched his wife prepare to leave him. 'Please, can you follow her and see which departure gate she goes to?'

Ilan watched as the camera followed Jennifer through the airport. Like a seasoned professional, she avoided the obvious cameras. He was quietly proud of the way she walked behind tall, bulky people and kept her head down. He watched her turn to the bar, hesitate and then turn away. He wondered if she'd decided to forego a drink because she was afraid of being caught.

I taught you well, neshama. Maybe too well.

Jennifer found a seat, and she opened her e-reader and passed the time in the fictional world she was escaping to as she waited for her flight to be called. Her phone was switched off and she glanced at her watch every few minutes, and then at the departure board.

'A dozen flights left from departure gates in this area from the time stamped on the image. The one of her reading her book, and over the next couple of hours. If you give me her name, I can check the passenger manifests to see which flight she boarded.'

Ilan mulled it over.

'Or we can sit here, watching her, until she boards,' Oren said. 'That could take a couple more hours. It is your decision, Ilan.'

Ilan felt his eyes burning from staring at the monitor screen for so long. But it was the image of Jennifer all alone at the airport that hurt him the most. The pain he felt, while not physical, was as real as if he'd been punched in the gut.

He had a choice to make. He could wait and let her slip farther away from him or give Oren her name and suffer the embarrassment of using government technology to locate his runaway wife. It was a no-brainer.

'She's my wife, Oren. Her first name is Jennifer.'

To his credit and Ilan's gratitude, Oren didn't even blink. Maybe this was a common request.

Jennifer stirred in her seat. She opened her eyes, looked at the time and groaned. Right on cue, her stomach rumbled with anticipation. She had another hour to go before the first stopover when she would have time to freshen up and get something decent to eat.

Ilan will be home by now. He'll be devastated and hate me for doing this, but it's for the best.

Was it? A niggling doubt entered her mind, and Jennifer wondered if running away was her only option. But then she remembered the look Saul had given her when they'd heard about Qahtani's death, and that hungry expression told her all she needed to know. It was that look that had prompted her to run.

Oren checked Jennifer's passport and discovered which flight she was on. Her destination made sense to Ilan. The idea of visiting Australia, spending time with her mother and stepfather and seeing the sights appealed to her. It was something they'd talked about a few times recently. But they never got around to doing anything other than talking about it.

He was tempted to book the next flight, but he needed to go home, get his passport and organise his diplomatic visa, which would only take a day—two at most. And he had to tell Nurit what was going on. Whatever was going on in Jennifer's head would maybe resolve itself in the company of her mother and a few days relaxing by the beach.

That's what he told himself.

Exhausted and hung-over, Jennifer was apprehensive as she approached the immigration and customs area. The queue was long, and it moved at a snail's pace. She held her passport, visa and passenger card and mentally went over her reason for visiting Australia.

I'm here to see my mum. She lives up north, and I haven't seen her for ages. Not since well before the pandemic. Yes, I live in Israel. I'm an Israeli citizen. Though I'm British by birth, I married an Israeli. No, I'm travelling alone. My husband couldn't get off work. He'll join me next week. Shit. I've watched too many episodes of the programme on border security.

The queue moved forward a couple of steps. She maintained an outward appearance of confidence, but she was a bundle of nerves inside. Her main concern was that the authorities, Saul in particular, already knew she'd skipped the country. They would inform Australian immigration that she must be returned to Israel as a person of interest. It was unlikely, but Jennifer couldn't shake the notion.

An hour later, she was out of the airport and climbing into the back of a taxi. Nobody gave her a second glance as she produced her documents and told them she was visiting her mum for a couple of weeks and had nothing to declare.

It was a breeze.

Chapter 43

Ilan lifted the unopened bottle of water nestled between his legs, unscrewed the cap with his teeth and took a mouthful. It was lukewarm but had been icy cold when he bought it. The blazing heat had warmed it despite the SUV's excellent air-conditioning.

What would I give for a cold beer right now?

Other than two stops, one for food and water and one to fill up with petrol, he'd been driving since leaving the airport.

He took another drink and grimaced. It would taste much better chilled, but his thirst for something cold wasn't as important as his thirst to have Jennifer back in his arms again. Only then would his journey end.

The fourteen-hour El Al flight from Tel Aviv to Perth in Western Australia was luxurious, thanks to his diplomatic status and the cabin crew, who had known him for many years. As soon as he boarded the Boeing Dreamliner, he was sent to the almost empty business class section. He spent the journey in comfort. The seating space was designed with privacy and relaxation as a priority. Each seat was a half-pod shaped construction with a touch-screen TV, a side table and a retractable workbench that doubled as a dinner table. The food was excellent, and he washed it down with a glass of fine wine. At the touch of a button, his seat turned into a comfortable flat bed where he rested his head on the pillow, closed his eyes, and went to sleep.

Ilan slept for seven of the fourteen hours and woke up refreshed. Shortly before he landed in Perth, he was served a hearty breakfast. It consisted of scrambled eggs, walnut-tomato paste, feta cheese crusted with herbs and eggplant with tahini, washed down with as much fresh-ly-brewed coffee as he wanted.

From Perth to Brisbane, the next leg wasn't so luxuri-ous. He had a long wait at the airport. When he boarded, he was in a cramped window seat in economy class be-side an old man who snored for the duration. Two rows behind was a family with a crying toddler. But it was only a four-and-a-half-hour flight, so he gritted his teeth and ignored the snoring and the noisy child. He read a few chapters from one of the several dozen novels Jennifer had downloaded onto his e-reader. It's amazing how much resentment you can build towards a two-year-old in four-and-a-half hours. He told himself that he didn't really want him to choke on his cornflakes.

The uncomfortable flight was behind him, and he drove at a steady pace, just inside the speed limit. He watched the changing scenery as Brisbane and its sprawl-ing suburbs were a fading image in his rear-view mirror.

He skirted the coast and the national parks as he travelled north to his destination. Rainbow Beach—home of many campsites and a three-hour drive from Brisbane.

Depending on the traffic, he would get there by early evening.

Jennifer opened her eyes to late afternoon sunlight streaming in through a chink in the curtains. Her head was pounding, she felt sick, and her tongue was stuck to the roof of her mouth. She had no idea where she was.

She reached for the glass of water her mother had put beside the bed and took a mouthful. It was lukewarm in the scorching afternoon heat.

As her awareness returned, so did the memory of why she was in Australia and the heart-breaking pain of everything she had lost.

She touched the necklace at her throat. Her fingertip traced the outline of the two gold hearts, with the smaller one encrusted with diamonds. Ilan said they represented their love and how they would always be linked together. She had brought it with her from Israel, and she would cherish it forever.

Stop thinking about him.

She had a new life to be lived, even if it was without Ilan. She would never love anyone again, but that was okay. She had loved and been loved, and the memories were enough to sustain her for the rest of her life. But right now, they were too painful to think about.

Jennifer pushed the memories away and climbed out of bed. She slipped into the small bathroom, brushed her teeth and showered. She wiped the condensation off the mirror and stared at her reflection. The dark circles under her eyes made her look older than her forty-five years.

I can't be forty-five. Where did the years go?

She felt older today, as though her youth and vitality had been stolen overnight.

Or it could be just jet lag.

She knew that was a lie.

She went into the kitchen, hoping no one was there, but stopped when she saw her mother sitting with her arms folded and a stern look.

Jennifer knew that look. She'd seen it many times throughout her childhood, teenage years, and even adulthood. It meant she was in for a bastard of a telling-off from her mother.

Jennifer ignored her and opened the fridge door, took out a bottle of water, and drank half of it.

'What time of the day do you call this?'

'I call it Jimmy. What do you call it?' Jennifer hit back and took another long drink of water.

'Very funny. There's paracetamol in the cupboard to your left.'

'Thanks. I'm fine. I don't need any.'

Her mother gave a snort of derision.

The conversation was heated and fraught as Jennifer explained why she had turned up out of the blue. She used some clever words to colour-in between the lines of the truth, but without telling her mother the real reason for her appearance on the doorstep.

She tried to say that she fancied a trip and it was a spur of the moment thing, but her mother wasn't buying it. Jennifer admitted that she and Ilan had a row, and she was putting some space between them for a while.

'So, you came all the way to Australia? That's a lot of space.'

'It seemed like a good idea at the time.'

Her mum's eyes narrowed as she watched her daughter, and Jennifer squirmed. She was a victim to that witchy-mother sixth sense. The one that could detect a lie from five hundred paces.

'It's nothing serious between Ilan and me. And I did want to visit, honestly. With flights to Australia operating again, I decided this was as good a time as any.'

They sat out on the porch drinking wine and catching up. A second bottle appeared, and they moved back indoors, where they drank and talked until well into the night.

Jennifer didn't remember going to bed.

'Seriously, mum. I don't have a headache or a hangover. I'm suffering from jetlag, and I need some fresh air. I'm going for a walk to your new glamping site to check it out. You said you were looking for decorating and accessory ideas, so I'll take a notepad.'

Her mother's face softened. 'Thank you, pet. Do you want me to come with you? Alannah is shopping, and Dave has gone to see a bloke about timber for the decking. So I'm on my own, and we could talk some more about what you told me when you arrived. If you want the company.'

'If you don't mind, I'll go on my own. I work better when I have nothing to distract me.'

'Okay. If that's how you feel. But have a cuppa first, eh?'

'Yeah. Good idea. But sit there, and I'll make it.'

She threw a teabag into each mug, filled them with boiling water and added milk. Her dad would complain if he saw her making tea this way. As far as he was concerned, it wasn't proper tea if it wasn't brewed for a week. But he watched too many Guy Martin documentaries.

As the women drank tea, her mother talked about plans for the site. There would be an area for the kiddies to play, a bar and probably some evening entertainment—a local singer and a couple of bands she had in mind.

'Maybe we'll have karaoke nights. I love karaoke, don't you?'

Jennifer nodded absentmindedly, wondering what Ilan was doing and how much he hated her for leaving.

'I'd better be off if I'm going to get any sketching done,' Jennifer said.

'Don't forget your sunscreen and take plenty of water. And your phone.'

'I won't. I might stay overnight. Is it okay if I used the cabin that's furnished?'

'No worries. You'll need something to eat. I'll pack some stuff for you.'

Jennifer waited impatiently while her mother gathered a few items together to feed her into the morning.

'Are you really okay, Jenny-wren?'

Jennifer smiled at the childhood nickname.

'I'm good, mum. Itching to try out some new design ideas on your posh tents.' She gathered everything she needed, gave her mother a kiss and a warm hug, and then set off on the long walk to the campsite.

Her mother and Dave had been planning this glamping venture since before they moved down the coast from Cairns. They wanted to keep the hippy beach-bar vibe but realised there wasn't enough money from passing trade. They needed people to stay over, not passing and only popping in for a drink. Her mum's friend and neighbour, Alannah, hit on a campsite. When Dave pointed out that the place was overrun with campsites, Alannah suggested glamping was the way to go.

The three of them went into partnership and put their savings together, sold up and moved south three months ago. Now they were in the finishing stages, and the twelve pods just needed to be decorated and furnished. Jennifer remembered the lengthy email from her mother about it.

As soon as she arrived, Jennifer was roped in to help.

Jennifer thought her mother was nuts to be taking on a new business at her age, but she held her tongue and pretended to be enthusiastic about it.

As he approached a small town, Ilan decided to take a break before getting to his destination. He needed to find a bathroom, top up on water and grab something to eat.

The town had a diner, where he ordered a light meal and coffee and asked to use the bathroom. The waitress indicated the men's room with a nod over her left shoulder as she wrote his order.

He found a table near the window and watched the passing traffic. His thoughts turned to Jennifer, and he wondered if she'd be pleased to see him, or would she chase him off the property? Doubts set in. He should have left her alone to work out whatever was bothering her. She'd have come back of her own accord in time. It looked bad following her all this way. She'd call him a control freak. Maybe he should turn around and go home.

The waitress interrupted his racing, jumbled thoughts with his meal that didn't look so appealing. There was nothing wrong with the food. He'd lost his appetite under the pressure of his concern about his wife and marriage.

Stopping to eat was stalling, putting off the inevitable argument. In his heart, he imagined a teary reunion, he was her protector, come to save her. In his head, he knew it might be a screaming match.

The Australian heat was different from anything he was used to in Israel. It was humid, and he could feel the moisture like a sauna. He didn't dislike it, though.

He was only thirty minutes away, and although apprehensive about his welcome, he was looking forward to seeing Jennifer again.

Jennifer sat on the steps and watched the darkness fall around her. Her sketch pad lay on the decking beside her. She had worked until she lost the evening light, but she was pleased with her work. Picking up her pad and coloured pencils had seemed strange—it had been so many years—but it came back to her like she had only stopped designing last week.

Although she should go inside before the bugs were too annoying, she sat on. She wanted to stay with the night a while longer.

Thoughts of Ilan crept into her mind. They were never far away.

What's he doing right this second? Is he angry? Maybe he doesn't care.

Darkness had fallen by the time Ilan found the house. He didn't realise it was so far off the beaten track or out in the bush. Three wrong turns, and he had to backtrack to the main road to find his bearings. It was a case of fourth time lucky, and he pulled up at the side of the low-lying wood and brick house surrounded by gum trees and large-leafed shrubs.

He switched off the engine and stared at the property. It was more sprawling than it looked at first glance, and close-up, it was in better condition than it seemed on his approach.

A light above the porch came on, the front door opened, and a familiar face stepped out.

Ilan opened the car door. The figure relaxed visibly when the interior light revealed his identity.

Jennifer's mother smiled as Ilan climbed out of the SUV and went to her with his bag slung over his shoulder.

'Oh, Ilan,' Jennifer's mother said as she wrapped him in an embrace. 'I am so glad you're here.'

'Where is Jennifer, Carol?'

'Come inside and get a cuppa? You must be exhausted after your long journey.'

'I need to see her first.'

'Of course. But she's not here at the moment. She's at the glamping site. What happened between you two, Ilan? She was a mess when she arrived and still is. But she won't talk to me about it.'

'Nothing happened between us. It was something else, but I don't know what it was. I must speak to her. Which way is it to the site?'

'She's staying there for the night. I'd rather you brought her back, but if she wants to stay, I want you to stay there with her until you've sorted it out. In fact, even if it takes a week, don't either of you come back until you have. One pod is furnished, and there are blankets and pillows, and the amenities are connected, so use it for as long as you need. But wait until I pack an esky with food for the pair of you. She hasn't eaten all day, and I only gave her a few things to tide her over until tomorrow.'

It wasn't a bad idea.

Chapter 44

Jennifer sat on the step of the pod's porch, surrounded by a circle of white light that came from a powerful, battery-operated LED camping lantern.

She was impressed by her mother's new business. The campsite had eight curved-roof pods, and although they were completed, the soft furnishings were still to come in all but one. This was where she was sleeping tonight. It had a comfortable sofa that converted into a king-sized bed. There was a shower with a toilet, a hand basin and a fully-functional kitchen and living area.

Her sketchpad was on top of the pull-out table, and several pages of sketches filled it with notes and ideas that she hoped would reflect what her mum liked.

Jennifer leaned back against the post. Beyond her small circle of artificial light, Jennifer could see the full moon hanging above the treetops. A few stars twinkled—their light diminished by the moon. In the distance, gentle waves lapped rhythmically against the shoreline.

For the first time since she'd woken up in the Dream Catcher room, she felt at peace, and she closed her eyes and listened to the trees rustling in the breeze.

Then something crashed through the undergrowth, and she opened her eyes. She gasped and stifled a scream as a large dark figure loomed at her in the park, where she had been the only person for half a mile in any direction.

'Shalom.'

'Bloody hell, Ilan. You almost gave me a heart attack. What the hell are you doing here?'

Ilan put the cooler down.

'I've come halfway around the world to see you, and this is the reception I get? I'm sorry. I didn't mean to startle you, neshama.'

Jennifer glared at him. Although startled, she wasn't surprised to see him. Even if he hadn't put two and two together and realised Australia was where she'd run, he had the technology to track her down. It was impossible in today's world to go dark. Especially when you didn't have time to plan properly.

'Well, you did. Why are you here? Are you going to make me go back with you? Because I'm not going. I can't go back.'

'Jennifer.' Ilan stepped forward until he was in front of her and reached for her hand. 'I'm not here to take you back. I'm here because I can't be anywhere without you. I don't know why you left, and I hope you tell me when you're ready. Right now, I just need to be with you.'

'Seriously? You're not here to arrest me?'

'Arrest you? What for?' Ilan snorted with laughter.

'Oh, Ilan. So you don't know what I did? But I did it for you. To protect you. I killed someone. I'm a murderer.'

'Don't be ridiculous. Who are you supposed to have killed?'

'That guy Qahtani.'

Ilan was still smirking and seemed really amused by his quirky wife and her ridiculous notions. She knew that's what he'd be thinking.

'You don't believe I killed him?'

'No, I don't. It's nonsense.'

'I did kill him, Ilan. I found out that he'd identified you as the Israeli spy who infiltrated his cousin's organisation in Syria. He was going to hunt you down and kill you. I was afraid to tell anyone, so I killed him myself.'

'How?'

'I shot him—twice. Sit down, and I'll tell you everything on the record—you can record it if you like.' Jennifer took a seat on the porch step and patted the space beside her.

Jennifer's confession took thirty minutes, between Ilan questioning her and asking for clarification. She told him everything that had occurred in her last two dreams. She'd overheard Qahtani asking about the survivor who had given a detailed description of Ilan before he died. She told her husband how she'd witnessed Qahtani shooting the messenger and deliberately went into his dream, pulled out a gun and shot him.

'Is that why you didn't wake up afterwards?'

'I'm not sure what happened. I reached for the door, and something hit me on the back of the head. I didn't remember anything until I was in a dark room. It felt like an old cell. It was smelly and musty. I couldn't find the door, but I could hear you calling me.'

'You heard me?'

'Yes. You were telling me to open the door. And you told me you loved me. A lot,' Jennifer smiled as she rubbed her fingertips together.

'Because I do.'

In the lamplight, Jennifer looked at her husband. At the grey hair and beard and the gentle wisdom in his brown eyes.

'What?' he asked.

'I was looking at your hair.'

'You still hate it?'

'No. I like it now. It suits you.'

It was true. She didn't hate the grey anymore. But it told her he was getting older. They both were.

Where did the years go?

But they weren't old. Not yet. They had years in front of them. And with those years came wisdom and maturity. Maybe even some sense.

Or maybe not.

'Tell me the rest of it, Jennifer.'

'What's in the cool box?' She deflected his question by pointing to the cooler Ilan set beside him.

'Oh, I forgot about it. Your mother made sandwiches for our supper, and she packed enough unperishable food to last us a few days. It's called an esky in Australia, by the way.'

'Great. I'm starving.'

Ilan hauled the box closer and opened it. Next to the wrapped sandwiches, enough to feed them for a couple of days were six bottles of water and two beers.

Jennifer went in for a plate, and Ilan cracked open a beer while she unwrapped the sandwiches. They ate in silence. They were putting off the inevitable conversation.

Jennifer took the last bite of her sandwich and gathered up the wrapping paper. She took the beer can from Ilan and took a sip. In the circle of light, their eyes met.

'I dreamed about Lucy again. She helped me get out of that room and wake up. But she told me I shouldn't ever do that again. It was dangerous. She said killing Qahtani was a line that should never be crossed.'

'You didn't kill him, Jennifer. According to the reports, he died from a brain aneurysm, not a gunshot to the head.'

'But I killed him in his dream, and if you die in a dream, you die in real life.'

'No one has ever proved that.'

'Maybe I did. Saul thinks so. And that's why I'm not going back to Dream Catcher. I don't want to be Saul Mueller's sleeping assassin. This is why I took off. I panicked and ran away.'

'Then don't go back to Dream Catcher.' Ilan shrugged his shoulders. 'I don't want you to go back. I never wanted you there in the first place.'

'What if he forces me?'

'He won't.'

'But I'll need something to do.'

'We have more than enough money, so you don't need to work, but if you want to, you can do anything. What about a more permanent position in the rescue centre?'

'I was thinking about that. Or maybe getting back into interior design. This has whetted my appetite again.' She pointed to her sketch pad.

'Or you could write your memoirs,' he joked.

'Only if you write yours first.'

'Ah, there's that little matter of the NDA I signed.'

'I signed it too.'

Jennifer waved away a bug. They'd have to go in soon, or they'd be covered in bites. But she didn't move.

'What would be the title of this memoir you aren't going to write?'

'Good question. Something with the word *Dreams* in it. Or maybe *Rapid Eye Movement*.'

Ilan turned her face to his. He smiled and kissed her gently on the forehead. 'I like the sound of that.'

'I love you,' she said.

'I love you, Jennifer.'

'Don't make a decision yet. Take your time and think about your options. There's no rush. Let's spend more time together. We can do some travelling.'

'Yeah, I'd like that. See as much of the world as we can in case another Covid variant imprisons us all on our patios again.'

Ilan put his arms around her, and Jennifer rested her head on his shoulder as the tears fell from her eyes. They sat on the step for ages, and she felt something loosen and break free inside her. It was emotional but physical at the same time, and it left her feeling changed. She let her shoulders relax as the tired ache of tension left her body. And along with it went the fear that had built up and settled in her heart. The guilt was gone, too. It was like it never existed. She felt happier. The weight of the world was gone. She reached for Ilan's hand and squeezed it.

'Do we have to go home yet? Can we stay here for a while?'

'I'm content anywhere,' Ilan said. 'As long as you're in my arms.'

Epilogue

Eight months later

A splash of beer spilled over the lip of the plastic container as Jennifer struggled to get to her seat without tipping it over. Ilan took it from her as she avoided tripping over the feet and the legs of people seated in the row.

She sat next to him.

'What?' she said with a grin.

'No wine?'

'They only serve beer. I can have some of yours if I want some. I couldn't drink a whole pint because I'd have to rush to the loo, and I don't want to miss a second of this.'

Jennifer was happy. They had stayed in Australia for two weeks, and it was like a second honeymoon. They were reluctant to leave but vowed they'd come back soon.

The hot tub beckoned. It had been installed two days after Ilan left for Australia. Nurit had sent a photo of her and Reuben relaxing in it with dozen smiley faces and a message telling Ilan that they lived there now.

Jennifer quit Dream Catcher with no effort or hassle when they got home. Saul didn't even ask her why. He was friendly and polite and wished her the very best, and they said their goodbyes.

As she made the final drive home, it crossed Jennifer's mind that he'd found others like her. He might have a whole stable of lucid dreamers working for him.

If he did, she didn't care.

Jennifer took in everything—every sight and sound. She looked to her right and saw the Olympic-size swimming pool. Beyond that and high on the monolithic hill, she could see the royal palace in the hazy sunshine. She wondered if the occupants were on one of the balconies watching her from their lofty pedestal. A few clouds in the sky made her think it might rain. Ilan nudged her with his elbow to get her attention and handed her the camera. She put it to her eyes and studied the rich people on board the luxury yachts in the harbour across from their grandstand. He told her to look at one particular boat. She laughed when she saw the table set with expensive silverware and china with a bottle of ketchup perched in the centre of it.

She glanced up at the massive screen. The Monaco Grand Prix was about to start. In anticipation, the cars roared their engines from the start line behind the grandstand. The second hand on the famous gold and white clock edged towards the top of the hour.

Note from the Author

I didn't expect to meet a bunch of wonderful, amazing people when I began this journey. They are all indie authors like myself, who have written great novels but struggle to get their books out.

It is difficult to convince the public that your book is worth reading. We don't have agents to promote our books and get us featured in newspapers or local bookstores, so we have to struggle with promos, seek out craft fairs and use social media just for a few sales.

Reviews are a great help. The higher our ratings, the more Amazon will promote our books.

4 or 5 stars is awesome, and authors rely on reviews more than anything.

As a tribute to the authors I call friends, I've included some of their books throughout this novel because they are what Jennifer and Ilan would read. Ilan likes the murders, thrillers, and spy stories I've mentioned. Jennifer does too, but she also enjoys erotic novels.

As a tribute to these lovely people, I have included a list of great indie authors. Browse through it and check them out.

This is the end of Jennifer and Ilan's story. They've been there and done it, but they want to take it easy now, get on with their lives and maybe travel the world. It's time to leave them.

Perhaps they'll come out of retirement one day for a swan song. If they do, I'll be sure to write it.

Amanda Sheridan

June 2022

Just a few of the amazing indie authors I've got to know—

Onia Fox. Greta Harvey. Laura Lyndhurst.

Ali Fischer. Katherine Black. JJ Grafton.

Adam Gaffen. Pamdiana Jones. Carole Kravetz.

Vicky Peplow. Luce Wood. Nigel Stubley.

R T Breach. Matthew Slater. Lauren Rigby.

Peter Merrigan. Brigitte Starkenberg. Jane Gundogan.

Paul McMurrough. R T Breach. Arlene Lomazoff-Marron.

Donna Lynch. Marcia Clayton. Deborah Roe. Max Speed.

And many, many more.

Acknowledgements

First and foremost, I have to thank the staff at Best Book Editors for their hard work and dedication. They are an amazing bunch of people who put their all into making a book the very best it can be. They edited and polished my book, made an awesome cover and a brilliant book trailer, and I love them.

I want to say thank you to all the indie authors I've met over the last couple of years. Always on hand with friendship and funnies, encouragement and support.

My readers—thank you for taking a chance on an unknown author.

And Hugh, my lovely husband, who Ilan may or may not be based on. I'm not saying.